Jack Zulu
and the Waylander's Key

Other Books by S. D. Smith

S. D. SMITH
J. C. SMITH

Story Warren Books
www.storywarren.com

Jack Zulu and the Waylander's Key

Copyright © 2022 by S. D. Smith and J. C. Smith

Trade Paperback edition ISBN: 978-1-951305-14-7
Signed First edition ISBN: 978-1-951305-15-4
Also available in eBook and Audiobook.

Cover illustration by Cory Godbey.
www.corygodbey.com

Cover design by J. C. Smith.

Map created by Shen Leidigh.

Waylander logo design by Kelsey Kirkendall.
www.kelseykirkendall.com

Printed in the United States of America.
First Edition.

Story Warren Books
www.storywarren.com

To Anne,

Thanks for being my first fan and first friend.
I have been and always shall be yours.

\- Josiah

To Clair and Myrtle Smith,

With deep love and grateful remembrance.
Rest eternal, and light perpetual.

\- Sam

Contents

Prologue

I do not receive; I take. I am between and above the worlds. I am the greatest being to have ever lived, though I began much like any other—doomed to servitude and humiliation. But I do not receive; I take. And I have taken and taken and shall never stop until I have more than anyone has ever had. In my youth I was told that my days were numbered and commanded to be grateful, but, like a thousand other limits I was given, I was not satisfied to abide by these tyrannical laws. I transcend law and life and so searched for the breaking of this greatest limitation. I went to Thandalia and brought war, finally marching on the golden city itself. I took the fruit, killing their last golden-winged guard, and now I shall never die. I will go on and on, augmenting myself with a thousand enhancements wrenched from the most sacred chambers of the twelve realms. I will be everything, free from the frail shackles of my birth lot. I have strained and grasped and shall hold all, ever striving until I ascend and contend for all. I do not receive; I take.

From *The Holy Book of Rancast Waybreaker*,
recorded by Scribe Gelder.

Chapter One

There's No
Home-Like Place

Myrtle, West Virginia
September 1984

The problem with baseball is that at first you're desperate to leave home. Then, once you're gone, you'll do just about anything to get back. Even steal. But you can't get back the way you came. You have to take another way home.

Jack Zulu stepped into the right side of the batter's box, bat poised as he glanced at the left-field fence. A homer would win it. It was only an after-school pickup game, sure, but to Jack it was another step on the long road to greater things—things far from Myrtle, West Virginia. Jack's father, dead now for many years, had immigrated from South Africa, where the last name of Zulu was as common as Robinson. His father had married a West Virginia girl after college and settled into her small town of Myrtle. Jack's background was complex, but his focus was singular. He was going somewhere. Somewhere else.

Hefty Leftwich smirked from the pitcher's mound, spitting a used-up sunflower seed to emphasize his contempt. Jack smiled, anticipating the portly pitcher's inevitable inside fastball. Jack's best friend, Benny Marino, looked up from his comic book as the game neared its zenith. Pushing his glasses up the

11

bridge of his freckled nose, he stomped twice on the aging bleachers, then clapped, looking around as if surprised no one else joined in. The rusty bleachers at Myrtle Park were empty.

Benny stood, raising his arms as if part of an energetic crowd doing the wave.

Jack laughed, glancing from Benny back to Hefty.

"Don't get cocky, Zulu," Hefty said, digging into the deepening trench in front of the pitcher's mound. Jack looked past Hefty to the runner on second base and, beyond him, to the groundskeeper, Mr. Wheeler, mowing the grass around the not-too-distant playground. The sun sprayed in dappled gaps through the apple trees and glinted off Mr. Wheeler's gold-rimmed glasses. Jack could see a smile standing out on his bearded face. Mr. Wheeler was a good man. He owned the bookshop in town and kept the grounds for the park. He also kept Jack supplied with strange old books—the kind Jack loved, about ancient curses and lost lands, about treasure hidden beyond forgotten canyons, cut off but for a fraying rope bridge. He'd also treated Jack to devastating defeats in a series of chess matches stretching back several years. Jack smiled again, shaking his head at the strange old man in the shimmering distance.

Benny sighed loudly, snapping Jack back to the game. "C'mon, Jack, I'm wasting away. Knock in just one teensy run and end this thing so we can go eat!"

Hefty spat again. "Shut up, Marino! Trying to pitch here."

"Trying," Benny replied quietly, "but not succeeding."

"After I strike Zulu out," Hefty said, "I'll deal with you."

"Okay," Benny replied, "so, never?"

"Why don't you ever play with us, Little Benny Marino?"

Hefty asked, taking a step toward the stands. "Seems like all you're good for is bringing Jack his bat. You're a clown!" Several of Hefty's teammates laughed.

Benny was tall, skinny, and freckle-faced, with curly orange hair tufting out beneath a faded Myrtle Cardinals baseball hat. He smirked and sat down.

"Just pitch," Jack said, switching to the left side of the batter's box. His smile was gone.

Hefty snickered and raised his glove to cover his mouth and spoke in a mock whisper. "Benny's so pale 'cause he lives in Jack's shadow."

"We're all living in your shadow, Hefty," Jack said, pumping his bat in preparation for the pitch.

Hefty snarled and began his windup. Driving off the rubber, Hefty brought his considerable bulk to the service of his fastball. Jack's eyes narrowed and his hands flashed, bringing his bat around to crack against the speeding ball. The ball sprang from the bat, rising to climb high into the Appalachian sky, far over the right-field fence.

Jack was rounding second by the time the ball came to rest deep in the woods. The shortstop, Tommy Eaches, slapped Jack's back. "You coming to the cookout? Coach Spatz says the whole middle school team needs to be there, or we'll pay for it in the spring with extra running. Please come, Jack. Hefty will die if we have to run more than a few feet."

"Shut up, Eaches," Hefty moaned.

"I'll think about it," Jack said, heading for third.

Tommy went on. "I heard Coach Furman—the high school coach!—is coming to our cookout to scout. He's coming just to watch you play, man. Some people say you could start, Jack—as a *freshman*, when we get there." Tommy called, "No one's done that in years. Just come!"

Jack stepped on third base and headed for the gate.

"You're not going home?" Tommy asked.

"Gotta get outta here, Tommy," Jack said. "Things to do."

"Nerd books to read," Hefty muttered from his spot, plopped down and sulking on the pitcher's mound.

Jack didn't look back, just snagged his backpack and walked on. Benny was there, already on his bike and holding up Jack's. "Your noble steed, m'lord."

"Thank you, assistant butler," Jack replied, hopping on and strapping on his backpack.

"Assistant butler?" Benny feigned shock. "I was sure that promotion was secured by how well I ironed your trousers yesterweek."

"Alas, no," Jack said, smiling. "Hey, sorry about Hefty. He's a big loser."

"He's big," Benny replied, "and he did just lose, so . . . you have a point. Can we go eat now?"

"Free pizza for a poor half-African kid at your dad's place?"

"Appalachianos awaits!" Benny's braces glinted in the sunlight.

"I can't believe you're not sick of the food at your family's restaurant."

"Mama mia, Jack," Benny replied, mimicking his dad's strong Italian accent. "You've eaten at Appalachianos almost as much as I have. Are you sick of it?"

Jack shook his head. "Negatoriano."

"So, let's go."

"I need to go see Mom," Jack said.

"You visited her before the game, Jack," Benny replied. He spoke softly now, with no hint of humor. Jack's mom, a widow for many years now, was in the hospital, and things were looking bad. Benny punched Jack's arm softly. "Didn't she say you had to stay away until tomorrow after school or you're grounded?"

"She did say that." Jack laughed. "I guess I can go enjoy Myrtle's finest cuisine with you." Jack paused, glancing at the maintenance shed past the outfield fence, where some of Hefty's teammates were searching for Jack's home run ball. Mr. Wheeler was pushing his mower into the shed, beyond which lay the woods. The deep woods held some of the oldest trees for miles, great historical curiosities for their age and enormity. People called that section of the woods the Ancient Glade. Jack kind of loved it.

Benny snapped a few times and waved his hands in front of Jack's face. "Earth to Jack."

"What?"

"I feel like you're going to tell me that you're not coming directly to my—"

"I'll meet you there," Jack said as their bikes rolled down the park toward the bridge.

"And, there it is." Benny frowned at his friend. "I can't emphasize to you how much hunger is happening in my inner person. The troll inside me must eat. Troll hungry, Jack."

"I need to swing by Mr. Wheeler's."

"Run out of weird old books?"

"Of course not," Jack said, feigning shock. "I'm getting video games and video movies."

"Video movies?" Benny rolled his eyes.

15

"They're making movies with video these days, Benny Boy. It's the eighties! Try to keep up."

"So, weird old books?"

Jack nodded. "Yes, of course it's weird old books."

"Mr. Wheeler's always got a stash ready for you, doesn't he?"

"He does. Man, the last one had a story of an ancient diver who could hold his breath for half an hour. He explored the coves of Liff-Haffensdire for years, until he found a silver dagger—"

Benny snored loudly and pretended to almost wreck.

"Very mature," Jack said.

"Mature?" Benny asked, feigning a wound. "Was this treasure diver an elf?"

"He might have been. Okay, yes, he was. Sobrin Diver was a true son of Elleflofflen."

Benny smirked. "How are you so cool and so nerdy at the same time?" Jack shrugged. Benny went on. "I see Mr. Wheeler out there mowing. So you're just gonna break into his shop and steal books?"

"He leaves a stack for me, and I'm free to come and go as I please. Don't worry, I'll get to Appalachianos as fast as I can, Benny Bro."

"Okay. Hurry up! If you're not there very, very soon after I arrive, I won't be held responsible for your half of the pie."

"You always eat half of my half anyway!" Jack began to pedal.

"It's the troll, man. He's outta control." Benny shrugged and pedaled on, acting casual. Then, all at once, he tensed up. "Race you to the bridge!"

Jack smiled. Benny always pulled this stunt, ever since they were little kids. So Jack was already pedaling hard before Benny finished speaking. Speeding down the little hill, Jack easily beat Benny to the old stone bridge for the thousandth time.

The bridge was a local curiosity, fashioned from stacked stone, ornately fitted and bonded with a strange mortar that was a bit of a historical oddity. According to town history buffs, the bridge was older than the town itself. The oldest Indian sources claimed the elders had never known a time when it wasn't there. The stonework was fantastic, both beautiful and sturdy. The old stone bridge—its four parapets, like chess rooks, marking its corners—was featured on the town's crest and splashed across what passed for its tourism industry. One of Benny's favorite T-shirts featured the bridge and said, "Myrtle, West Virginia—a good town with a nice old bridge."

Leaving the bridge behind, the boys pedaled on, through tree-lined roads, up and down a few small hills and dips till they passed Gander's Gas on the left and rode on into the small downtown of Myrtle. Woods gave way to small shops connected on each side of Sequoyah Street.

Benny pedaled ahead with an exaggerated gesture of tapping his wristwatch. "Huuuuurry uuuuup!" he moaned in a Halloween ghost voice. Jack waved him away and veered off the road, stopping at the shop nestled between Mabe's General Store and Myrtle's Diner. Down the road there was an arcade and ice cream shop. According to the sign, Wheeler's Good Books was "Open today: 11:00 a.m. to 8:43 p.m. probably." Jack stashed his bike and walked to the door. Even though he had just seen Mr. Wheeler at the park, he knew the door would be unlocked. It *always* was. Jack had been coming here for years and had never once found it locked. Smiling, Jack reached for the handle.

"Hey!" a harsh voice came from behind. Jack spun to see a policeman leaning out of his cruiser window, his face set hard with suspicion. It softened quickly. "Oh, it's you, Jack. Sorry, kid." It was Officer Hawkins, one of Jack's dad's former coworkers on the force. Ruben Zulu had been the first immigrant to become police chief in the county's history. He was also one of only two blacks to have ever served on the force.

"No problem," Jack said, smiling stiffly and not meaning it.

Officer Hawkins looked embarrassed. "Can't wait to see you hit some dingers in the spring, Jack. Your old man would'a been proud."

Jack nodded, then turned back to the door, twisting the handle and hurrying inside. For a minute, he just stood inside the doorway of the dimly lit shop, breathing that familiar scent of old books and missing his father terribly. Soon, unless something miraculous happened, he'd have no mother either. Sadness welled up within him. He fought it down again with his rock-solid resolution to break free of this small, sad, backward town. What was his future? Fatherless. Soon to be motherless. Homeless. Hopeless. He had to do something to change his destiny.

"Hello, Jack."

Jack looked up to see Mr. Wheeler in his favorite chair, a book open in one hand and a pipe in the other, gray smoke spiraling away, settled and serene as if he'd been there all day.

Chapter Two

The Box
and the Tree

H ow'd you get here so fast, Mr. Wheeler?" Jack asked.
"Ah," he replied, setting his book on an end table,
"have you come for fresh books, my lad?"

Jack nodded, noting once again how Mr. Wheeler had managed to politely dodge a direct question. Laying his backpack on the counter near the ancient cash register—the register Jack had never seen in operation—Jack fished inside and produced three books. They were worn, their once diversely colored covers faded to a gray-brown sameness. They matched the other such volumes in the packed aisles, bindings sometimes still bright with gold or silver words or symbols. Every book in the shop seemed as ancient as the old stone bridge. There were new books, but Jack loved the large section of old ones. These modest-looking volumes held endless adventures inside and fascinating imagined histories of far-flung, enchanted worlds.

"I have three more set aside for you, so I do," Mr. Wheeler said in his unusual accent. It was a mix of Appalachian and Irish with odd old expressions thrown in. He would often add "so

I do" or "to be sure" and things like that to his sentences. Mr. Wheeler pointed to the books on the counter. "Did anything stand out about those last three volumes?"

"Yes!" Jack said, carefully reshelving his three returns on the staging case. "Sobrin Diver was fascinating. A hero in an era of villains. It was cool to get to him and to see his story come right at the end."

"Ah, yes," Mr. Wheeler said, standing slowly. "Sobrin was one of the noblest elves of that age. And a good f—" he paused, eyes twinkling in the lamplight, "a good fable to read, so it was."

Jack's eyebrow arched. "Is there more to the story?"

Mr. Wheeler smiled wryly, tapping his pipe out in a used teacup. "There always is."

Despite him being the closest thing to a scholar Jack had ever known, Mr. Wheeler's hands were a laborer's hands, with long fingers extending to neat nails rimmed with dirt. The last digit on his right hand was half as long as the one on his left hand, a calloused nub ending at the knuckle. "Sir, in the story of his last dive, Sobrin lost a finger. I hope you don't mind me asking," Jack said, "but what happened to your little finger?"

"I never told you about this downsized digit?"

"I never asked."

"Well, Jack," he said, frowning at the finger, "it was, I am sorry to say, caught in a door."

"What kind of door?"

Mr. Wheeler chuckled to himself and closed his eyes a moment. "A very old one, to be sure."

"Gotta watch out for doors," Jack said.

Mr. Wheeler nodded. "You never know where they might

take you."

"Or," Jack replied, "what they might take from you."

Mr. Wheeler smiled wide, opening his bright eyes. "Point, Jonathan Jack Zulu."

Jack bowed neatly, waving his hand in a modest flourish.

"Tell me, Jack," Mr. Wheeler said, his face changing to show concern, "how is your mother?"

Jack winced, inhaling deeply. "She's—sir, she's not doing well."

"I'm so sorry."

"Thanks." Jack bit his lip and toed the aged hardwood floor. "I'm not sure they're telling me everything. I think they're afraid I'm too young to hear—to hear the worst."

"That she is dying, poor dear," Mr. Wheeler said, almost in a whisper.

Jack nodded. "I'm so close to losing everyone—my whole family."

"We never know how much time we have left with those we love," Mr. Wheeler said. His face was knowing and sad, telling Jack these weren't just words.

"What should I do?"

"What does Mrs. Zulu say?"

Jack swallowed. "She told me today that they need to keep her overnight again but that I should stay home and come and see her again tomorrow after school."

"I am sorry, Jack," Mr. Wheeler said. "You are a good son to her. And she knows you love her."

"What would you do?"

"I would do as she says tonight, then tomorrow I would find out the truth. I would go there and show that, despite being just shy of my thirteenth birthday, I am capable of handling what is really happening."

"I'm not sure I am."

"I am sure, Jack," Mr. Wheeler said. "That is the kind of young man you are. The kind of man you are becoming. There is no other way but to face the truth and act nobly in love. That is the only way."

Jack nodded again. "I will."

"Have you eaten yet?" Mr. Wheeler asked.

"Headed to Appalachianos to meet Benny."

"Benito Marino," Mr. Wheeler said, smiling. "Now, he's a character."

"He's basically my brother."

Mr. Wheeler looked out the window. "And you are his."

"I guess so," Jack said.

"So, you are not losing quite everyone. Not just yet."

"I guess not."

"Well, please know I am praying for your mother, and for you. And I hope you know I am here to help in any way I can."

"Thank you," Jack said, walking to the counter where the new books waited. He flipped open the top book of the stack, a pale plum-colored tome with gold leaf edging and a warrior icon on the spine. "*A History of Geldensplat After the Fourth Dawn Charge War?*" he asked, casting a skeptical glance at the older man.

Mr. Wheeler's brow furrowed. "Problem?"

"The problem is . . . why have you been holding out on me?" Jack said, laughing. "I've been dying to pick up the histories after *Dawn Charge Four*. Thanks!" He closed the book and carefully placed it, along with the other two, in his backpack.

"You are most welcome," Mr. Wheeler replied, shaking his head. "There is a love story about a warrior named Cohvaire and a princess named Kreyne in the second book that will get your young heart beating fast."

Jack nodded and smiled awkwardly. "Super," he said flatly. Michelle Robinson's face appeared in his mind, and he inhaled deeply.

Mr. Wheeler squinted at the window, which showed a wide sky above the early autumn hills of West Virginia, and his wry smile vanished in a moment of intense concern. It was a brief flash of panic, but Jack had rarely seen anything approaching worry on the older man's face. Jack usually felt cool and calm himself and thought of himself as being much like Mr. Wheeler. But when it came to Michelle, Jack was anything but cool and calm. The beautiful and enigmatic girl made him sweat and stutter and stammer and grow suddenly clumsy. He hated how hard it could be to even talk to her. A clear memory of their last conversation surfaced. It had involved a profoundly awkward pause that seemed eternal.

Jack's attention jumped back to the present. Mr. Wheeler had been talking. "I'm sorry, sir. I missed that."

"I said," Mr. Wheeler repeated, "have you made your move yet?"

Jack winced, and Michelle's image came to mind again. "My move?" He smiled nervously.

"I am eager to crush you on the field of battle, so I am," Mr. Wheeler said, "but I cannot do that if you do not move."

Jack exhaled with relief, finally realizing that the shop-keeper was referring to their ongoing game of chess. "Of...of course. I'm on it!" Jack hurried down the hallway, past three closed doors, and glanced back at Mr. Wheeler, who gazed out the large window. Jack entered the musty room with the small wooden table and two handmade wooden chairs. A chessboard sat on the table beside one unlit candle. Jack surveyed his position, sizing up the situation quickly. Mr. Wheeler's last move had complicated the game further, and the only way ahead for Jack was a frontal attack with heavy casualties. And inevitable—likely swift—defeat. He moved his black queen ahead. "Check," he said to no one.

Returning to the main part of the bookshop, Jack found Mr. Wheeler hovering over an ornate wooden box on the counter. "Did you lose something—your keys?" Jack asked.

Mr. Wheeler looked back at Jack, his eyes wider than usual. "What did you ask?"

"I asked if you lost your keys. I'd be glad to help you find them."

"Oh, my keys," Mr. Wheeler replied. "Yes. Yes, Jack. I have lost something."

"Okay," Jack said. Mr. Wheeler was flustered. *There's a first time for everything.* "I'll help!" Jack peered at the floor.

"No, thank you," Mr. Wheeler said, squinting. "I will find it, so I will. I think I just need to retrace my steps. I must go back to the park. Did you see a large bird—a crow, perhaps—on your way here?"

"No," Jack replied.

"Ah," Mr. Wheeler said. "Jack, I wonder if I could ask you to look after this while I am gone?" He held up the box, his concerned eyes flitting between it and Jack. Then he looked out the window again, his eyes thinning to slits. Looking back at Jack, he frowned. "Just keep it with you at all times,

Jack. It's very dear to me. And if I am unable to—no, Jack, you have enough on your—well, just please keep an eye on it and . . . I . . . I should be back soon. If I am not back soon and you need to go on to join Benny, please do take it with you and keep it close, will you now?"

"I'd be glad to," Jack replied, feeling some of Mr. Wheeler's nervous energy. "It's safe with me."

Mr. Wheeler slowly handed the box to Jack, then spun and hurried to the door. He hovered by the handle a moment while Jack glanced at the box. Then, with a flurry, Mr. Wheeler dashed through the doorway.

Jack shook his head. There were always odd things about Mr. Wheeler, but it had never before involved panic or haste. Sometimes he would disappear for long weeks at a time. Once, he was gone for over a year. Shrugging, Jack crossed over to the counter and, under the lamplight, examined the wooden box. It bore ancient runes surrounding a spreading tree burned black on the pale grain. There were twelve branches on the tree, and its roots extended down and spread in a near-mirror image of the branches above. Jack flipped it around and saw a latch that no doubt triggered the top to release. He was sorely tempted to open it and see what was inside that so concerned Mr. Wheeler.

Mr. Wheeler had not forbidden him to open the box. *No, he trusts me. I should wait for him to come back.* Still, his hand played over the catch while his mind mulled over possibilities for what could be inside this box. Or was it the box itself that needed watching? *I can slide open the catch and then just reseal it. I don't have to open it.* His fingers found the switch, and he began pressing on it.

The phone rang. Jack spun, breathless and heart pounding. Laying the box on the counter, he hurried to the wall-mounted receiver to answer the phone. "Wheeler's Good Books, Jack speaking."

"Jack!" Benny's voice boomed in the handset. "Get down here, pronto!"

"I'm coming, Benny. I won't be long. You gotta get that hunger troll under control."

"Oh, I already ate," Benny said, "but I've got bigger news. Michelle is here!"

"Michelle?" Jack wiped his suddenly sweating palms on his jeans.

"Yeah," Benny groaned, "you know, the prettiest girl in middle school?"

Jack wasn't sure if that was a reason to avoid Appalachianos or to go. "Right. Dag, man. I'm kinda stuck here at Wheeler's for a bit."

"Jack, you've got to get down here. The jukebox is booming and this is the place to be. You never know how much time you have to make your move, man!"

"I guess I could pop down there," Jack said, thinking that he could follow Mr. Wheeler's instructions to keep an eye on the box and slip down to the pizzeria for a little while. *He knows where to find me.* "Did she order anything?"

"Yeah," Benny said. "Her usual pie. Mushrooms and olives, easy on the cheesy. Her whole family is here."

"Can you get your dad to, um—you know—delay the order a little?"

"I'd have to let him in on the conspiracy," Benny said, and Jack could tell he was smiling by the sound of his voice. "Of course! He's a pizza man, but he also hails from a long line of Italiano romantics."

"Thanks, man," Jack said. "Bye!" He replaced the receiver and grabbed the notepad beside the rusted cash register. He wrote, *I'm just going down to the pizza place. Don't worry, I'll keep an eye on the box. I'll be either there or home.* He signed it "J" and took off toward the door, tripping as he went. He balanced and gripped the door handle, opening it and hurrying outside. The door slammed behind him, and he stopped.

The box! He had, after promising to watch it, immediately left the box inside, along with his backpack. He turned around, muttering insults to himself as he did. *Why do I always lose my cool when it comes to Michelle? Always!* He reached for the door handle.

It was locked.

Chapter Three

Pizza
and Problems

J ack's heart was pounding. Too many things were converging at once. He inhaled deeply, breathing in and out slowly to calm down and refocus.

It didn't work.

He hurried to the large window facing the street and tried to see if he could find a way through. Pressing his palms against the glass, he shoved up. The window rose easily, and Jack hooked his hand into the opening and pulled. He glanced back at the street, suddenly afraid of how it might look to passersby. *Policemen?* Seeing nothing to slow him down, he leapt up and through the window and into the shop. He closed the window behind him and jogged to the counter.

Grabbing the wooden tree box, he carefully placed it into his backpack, surrounding it with his sweatshirt for protection, and tucked it in beside his three new books. *There. I'll keep it with me at all times, until I bring it back here.*

He left quickly, climbed onto his bike, and made quick work of the short distance to Appalachianos Family Pizzeria. Jack leaned his bike against the wall nearest the dumpster and noticed red spray paint on its side. "Stupid vandals," he said, thinking twice about leaving his bike out there. The graffiti was an upside-down red star with a circle sprayed around it. Jack shook his head. *Creeps.* He left his bike and headed for the door.

The jukebox in the crowded restaurant was playing "Cool It Now" by New Edition. Diners—mostly teens, but some families—were scattered across tables, eating slices and drinking pop. Jack glanced around at the small collection of arcade games, two that worked and one that didn't, in the corner. He gazed around, fingers tapping his leg.

"Boo!" Benny shouted from behind him. Jack jumped, then spun around, fist cocked. Seeing Benny's grinning brace-laced teeth, he relaxed his arm but reached out and pretended to strangle his friend. "You gotta stop doing that, man. I'm gonna clock you one day."

"You've never hit anything but a ball," Benny said, slinging his arm around Jack's shoulder and ushering him to the counter, where both boys sat down on the spinnable red stools.

"I knew you'd rush over."

"I didn't rush. I'm just hungry."

"Yeah, right."

"Out of curiosity, where is she?" Jack whispered.

"Why are you whispering?" Benny asked, talking louder and louder. "The music is so loud, no one can hear anything in here."

It was true. The jukebox was still blaring, and the excited chatter in the popular establishment drowned out anything the two twelve-year-old boys were saying.

"She's in the Ladianos Room," Benny said, nodding to the

restaurant's bathrooms beyond the small arcade. "Don't worry, I've been keeping a close eye on her." Jack raised an eyebrow. "Not too close an eye," Benny continued. "Just the appropriate amount of eye for her and . . . c'mon, man, I'm helping you out. Stop giving me the Jack Eye."

"The Jack Eye?" Jack said, eyebrow arching even further as his head shot back and cocked to one side as he side-eyed Benny. "What's the Jack Eye?"

"It's what you're doing right now," Benny said. "You're literally doing it."

Jack shook his head, glancing back past the arcade. "How long has she been back there, Captain Eye-Spy?" Jack asked.

"Who knows?" Benny said, laughing in an awkward attempt at casual. "Probably," he went on, glancing at his new digital watch, "four minutes and thirty-seven seconds."

The two boys were both staring at the bathroom door, Benny with two fingers poised to pinch the buttons on his digital watch, when Michelle emerged and looked straight at them.

They swiveled back to the countertop, Jack somewhat smoothly, but Benny's whiplash twist sent him spinning off his chair. He slapped the countertop and held on, pulling himself up slowly to resume his seat.

Both boys pretended to talk casually, motioning over-dramatically with their hands. Benny had the knack, a little, but Jack looked like a robot. "Did she notice?" Jack asked, resuming his conspiratorial whisper.

"No way," Benny said quickly. "We covered it pretty well."

"Hey, nerds!" a female voice came from behind them. Jack spun around slowly on his stool—in sync with Benny—to see Michelle, hands on hips. "What is up, fellas?"

"Bathroom," Benny said, then let out a weak giggle, before turning back around slowly on his chair to face the counter again.

"That was weird," Michelle said.

"Agreed," Jack answered.

Slowly, Benny spun back around, sipping his pop. "Michelle," he said, wiping his mouth on his sleeve, "forgot to ask. How is dance karate going?"

Michelle's eyebrows rose, and her eyes thinned to skeptical slits. "Thanks for asking, B. I am in karate, which is going really well, and dance, which is also going well. My back's been hurting some, but that's normal for what I do. I'm probably going to take a little time off from both karate and dancing to recover."

"They have a lot in common," Benny replied. He seemed to be ready to continue the thought, but his pause was too long and the other two were staring at him. He finally went on. "Kicking—that's just one of the skills these two activities have in common—"

Jack elbowed Benny covertly, smiling with his head tilted sideways as he did. Michelle was famous for her combination of grace and strength both in karate, where she was a regional champion, and dance, where she was considered a prodigy. Benny opened his mouth to go on, but Jack reached out and spun him back around to the counter.

"He's, um . . ." Jack began.

"He's Benny," Michelle said, smiling. She was beautiful, dark-skinned, and enchanting. She had black eyes with abundant golden flecks. Her hair was parted in the middle and sprang out to frame her beautiful face in big, bouncing curls.

Their dads, the only two black officers in the county, had worked together for many years. The two families grew close and had spent a lot of time together, but they drifted apart when Jack's dad died. Police Chief Ruben Zulu and Officer Steven Robinson had gone missing for weeks on a case. When Officer Robinson returned, he brought back a blood-covered police badge to an endless supply of unanswered questions. There had been an awkwardness between the two families ever since.

"How's Mrs. Zulu?" Michelle asked, hands smoothing the springing curls around her ears, her face showing real concern.

"She's so good," Jack said, still nervous and not thinking straight. "Really, really good."

"Seriously?" Michelle asked. "I thought things were bad. I'm so relieved."

"Wait, no," Jack said, shaking his head. "My bad, Michelle. Sorry. Um, Mom is doing kinda terrible."

"Oh," Michelle said, face scrunched in confusion. "Well, I'm very sorry to hear that. She was always so nice to me when we were little."

"Yeah, she loved you. *Loves* you. We all..." Jack stuttered, "were . . . little, at one time. In the past. In our youth, if you will." Jack could feel sweat forming on his brow.

Someone called for Michelle, and she glanced across and waved. Jack saw her father and entire family sitting together. "Welp, our pizza is here," she said, *"finally.* Service is slow tonight. I'll see you later, Jack," she said, touching his arm. "I'm praying for your mom."

"Thank you," he said. She smiled and hurried over to her table to join her family, playfully messing with her brother's hair as she sat down. Officer Robinson stared at Jack. His expression confused Jack, and he quickly looked away. *Was that hostility? Sadness? Guilt?*

Benny spun slowly back around in staggered stages on the circular chair, sucking on the straw in his super-large pop. When he had returned fully to match Jack's position, he smacked his lips. "Well, that went . . . terrible."

"So bad," Jack agreed, and they both spun back to the counter as Benny's dad appeared and slung a sixteen-inch pepperoni pizza in front of the boys. After college, Alfredo Marino had married a local girl and moved to Myrtle along-side his best friend, Ruben Zulu. To Jack, he was Uncle Freddie.

"Mama mia, Jackie, you look like you just blew it," Uncle Freddie said. "Pizza helps! Eat, Jackie my boy." He pinched Jack's cheek, then hurried back into the kitchen.

"How long do you think your dad will be pinching my cheeks?"

"Oh, it will never ever, ever end," Benny said. "At least he doesn't kiss you in front of everyone all the time."

"Yeah," Jack said, "I guess I'm not going to complain about the cheek pinches."

"Speaking of not getting kissed," Benny said, "I just want to go back to the fact that—back there with Michelle—that went horribly."

"So, so bad," Jack agreed again.

"Mama mia, eat something," Benny said in his best Italian accent, reaching for Jack's cheek.

"Nope," Jack said, slapping the outstretched hand down. He dug into the pizza and guzzled down some water while Benny refilled his pop. Benny drank more pop than Jack thought possible and also ate twice as much as Jack did. Jack had no idea where it all went, because Benny was as skinny as a baseball bat.

Pizza was followed by a pepperoni roll and, for Benny, a hot dog. When Jack had eaten his fill, the boys spun back to scan the crowd. Benny burped stealthily. "The songs these people choose," he said, pointing vaguely toward the kids gathered around the jukebox. "It's disheartening. When I'm a DJ, I'm going to play the perfect songs for every occasion."

"I thought you were gonna be a sports broadcaster?"

Benny nodded. "I can do both. I'm multitalented. You'll be playing for the Reds, and I'll be on the radio calling the games. Afterwards, we'll get pizza and listen to tunes—that I pick."

"I can't wait, man," Jack said, patting his stomach.

"So, what took you so long to get down here?" Benny asked.

"Oh, dang," Jack said, reaching into his backpack. "I gotta show you this thing." He pulled out the wooden tree box.

Benny studied it closely. "What's inside?"

"I don't know. Mr. Wheeler asked me to keep an eye on it, so I'm not sure I should open it up."

"Can't figure out the mechanism?" Benny asked.

"No, I can," Jack replied. "But I'm not sure I should."

"I bet you a dollar—which I will steal from my dad's tip jar with his full knowledge—that you can't open it and I can."

"I could use a buck," Jack said, and he tripped the switch, smiling smugly as he did.

Nothing happened.

"Nope," Benny said, and he swiped the box, spinning it in his hands and examining the casing closely.

"Hey, be careful with that," Jack said, reaching to snag the box back.

Benny smiled as the box top came off with a click, and he laughed, keeping it out of Jack's reach. "Victory!"

"How on earth . . ." Jack began, then grabbed the box out of Benny's hand. Benny resisted. The box tipped sideways, and something silver glinted as it fell out.

"What is that?" Benny pointed down on the floor where a silver-handled something—*a knife?*—lay on the carpet.

Jack bent to pick it up while Benny carefully laid the wooden box and its top on the counter. "It's something Mr. Wheeler was worried about, I know that. And I can see why. It looks ancient and valuable."

"Maybe it's a collector's item, like a Renaissance-era tool."

Jack raised it slowly, carefully. "A tool for what?"

"I have no idea." Benny frowned down at the handle, turning his head as Jack rotated the item.

"Is it a knife?" Jack asked.

"I don't think so," Benny replied, eyebrows knit in concentration. "This inscription, it's Italian . . . no, Latin."

Jack held the tool up close to read the inscription. He squinted and read them aloud. "*Clavis Ignum*—"

"Hey, Jack!" Michelle appeared again, pulling on her jacket.

Jack stuffed the tool—which he thought for a moment might have flashed bright—into his left pocket. "Michelle, hi," he said, standing quickly and almost tripping. "Hi, Michelle . . . Hi."

"I'm heading out," Michelle said, a tight smile on her face as she twisted a finger in curls over her ear.

Jack felt painfully awkward, and he didn't know why. He was almost always calm around everyone, adults or kids his age, but being around Michelle short-circuited his usual cool. In fact, he felt like he was burning. *What is the deal with me?* "Michelle, thanks for leaving," he said stupidly, leaning against the seat and sliding back as it rotated around. He caught himself on the counter, then turned around quickly again. *What is burning?*

"Okay," she said, blinking. "Listen, Jack, I'm starting a book club at lunch on Tuesdays and Thursdays. You still like to read?"

Jack felt a searing pain. He looked down at his pants pocket and saw smoke rising in little rings. It was real. The tool in his pocket was *burning* him. He turned sideways so Michelle couldn't see the smoke coming from his pocket. "Books, I like," he hissed.

Benny groaned, uttered a faint "Mama mia," and slowly spun away on his seat once again, loudly slurping the last of his pop.

"Good. Maybe you can come to my book club?"

Jack smiled at her, teeth showing as he gritted them in agony. He glanced down at his pants again, and his eyes widened as he saw actual fire. His pants were literally on fire.

"Michelle, I gotta go!" he shouted, overly loud, a second after the song stopped playing on the jukebox. He dashed into a startled crowd that was lined up around the counter to pay for their meals. "Excuse me!" Jack cried, dodging around them and making for the bathroom. As he ran, he heard Benny's voice trailing away behind him.

"The Gentlemenianos calls for all of us at times . . ."

Rushing into the bathroom, Jack pulled free the tool, which was glowing hot. "Ah!" he barked, passing the strangely cool handle back and forth before rushing into a stall and tossing it into the toilet. It hissed, and steam filled the stall, just as Jack heard the bathroom door swish open. *Benny*. Jack sighed loud and long with relief, then ended with a barbarian groan.

"Thank goodness you're here," Jack called from inside the stall. "Lock the door! I made it just in time, but now we've got a real problem to deal with."

When there was no answer, Jack poked his head out of the stall and saw Michelle's dad washing his hands. They made eye contact; then Jack sank back into the stall with a groan.

A few minutes later Benny did come into the bathroom. Jack watched through the crack in the stall door but stayed put.

"Welp," Benny said with a sigh. "I hate to be the one to speak of financial matters, but I am owed the sum of one dollar from you."

Jack fished free his wallet, wadded up a single bill, and tossed it over the stall door. He could hear Benny fumble to catch the dollar before the bill dropped to the ground underneath the stall door. "I feel like that was mostly your fault—what happened just then."

"There are," Benny reasoned as he bent to pick up the dollar, "different ways we could look at tonight's events. Blame could be passed around. Or, we could just get you out of town on the next bus. You could change your name and join the circus. I think we both know that returning to school is off the table."

"It was pretty bad." Jack sighed and rubbed his face.

"It started bad," Benny said, "then got much, much worse."

Jack emerged from the stall, pants bearing a blackened hole around the pocket, and Benny held up the box. Jack dried off the tool. They replaced it in its box, and Benny fastened the lid again. Jack returned the box to his backpack. When Benny had assured him the coast was clear of Michelle and her family, they returned to their seats at the counter. Benny got some vitamin E and aloe and gave it to Jack, who rubbed it into his leg burn. Jack winced and Benny said, "Don't be a baby." Then they sat in gloomy silence for several minutes.

The phone rang, and Benny's dad grabbed it. "Hello, Appalachianos!" He listened with order pad ready, then glanced over at the boys. "Yes, he's here. Jack, it's Joe Wheeler on the phone for you."

"Thanks, Uncle Freddie," Jack said. "Please just tell him I'm coming right there."

Uncle Freddie shot Jack a thumbs-up. "Hey Joe, he says he's headed back right now." Uncle Freddie frowned. "Okay." He turned to Jack again. "Joe wants to talk to you. He sounds worried, Jackie."

Jack nodded and reached for the receiver. "Hi, Mr. Wheeler."

"Jack, lad, do you still have it?" Mr. Wheeler's voice was tense and urgent.

"Yes, sir," Jack replied. "I have it. I'm bringing it back now."

"No, Jack," Mr. Wheeler said, breathing hard. "Do not bring it back to the shop. Just take it home and I'll—"

Jack waited, then said, "Mr. Wheeler, are you there?"

Silence.

Dial tone.

Chapter Four

The Witching Hour

J ack arrived home after a nervous ride through Myrtle. Leaving Benny at Appalachianos, he had passed the bookshop and the park and pedaled on up the high hill where his neighborhood lay on the edge of a forest. He entered his house slowly, unsettled by Mr. Wheeler's call. He sat down in the heavy silence of the family room.

No one was there—only the cold fireplace and the pictures placed above the mantle showing beloved faces that had gone from his life or soon would. Ruben and Sarah Zulu. This unusual couple, black and white, African and Appalachian, and deeply in love. Smiling. In happier times.

Jack was afraid. He wanted his dad, a brave policeman with Zulu warrior blood. He wanted his mother's wise words of comfort. Jack glanced at the phone. He longed to call his mother. He needed to hear her voice, to hear her pray for him as she always did when he was troubled in any way, but he knew letting her rest was crucial. He was alone.

Jack took off his backpack and lay down, suddenly exhausted. He reached into the bag and, pushing aside his three new books and his science textbook and homework, grabbed the wooden box and hugged it tightly to his chest. He dipped back into the pack and grabbed his Walkman. Arranging his earphones, he lay back on the armrest and hit play on the tape his mother made for him featuring his dad's favorite American music. The first song began, and he was asleep before Neil Young's voice warbled, "Everybody knows this is nowhere."

Jack jerked awake. Confused, he looked around quickly, then blinked away his alarm. He still clutched the odd box to his chest. His tape had stopped in his Walkman, and his earphones hung askew on his face. He scanned the room, catching sight of the time, 2:37 a.m. *Dang. I was out cold.*

That's when he saw the flashing red light on the counter. A message! He had slept right through a call. *Maybe it was from Mom. Oh, no. Please don't be the worst.* Jack sprang up and hurried to the answering machine. Finger poised over the device, he gazed at the blinking red light. *I can't lose you, Mom. Please, God.* He hit the button.

The beep sounded, and he heard Mr. Wheeler's steady voice. "I hope you get this soon, Jack, lad. I am mortified to ask this, but please bring the box to me at the park as soon as you can. It's 10:13 now, and I can be here till—well, till the witching hour, I suppose. Forgive me, Jack. I must go. Bring it, please. And do be careful."

Jack frowned. Then, he dialed Benny, who had promised to sleep on the couch by the phone. He picked up on the second ring. "Hello?"

"Hey, Benny. Sorry to wake you, man."

"Jack, is everything okay? It's not your mom, is it?"

"No, it's Mr. Wheeler. He asked me to bring the box to the park and meet him there."

"Now?"

"He left me a message. I must have slept right through the ringing."

"Not surprised," Benny said. "You could have an elephant play a saxophone in your ear and you wouldn't wake up."

"I guess so," Jack replied, "but I did have earphones on when I went to sleep. I need your help on something."

"I thought you'd never ask, man. You're going about this thing with Michelle all wrong. See, you want her to actually like you, so you can't act like you act. You have to—"

"No," Jack interrupted, "I need your help on something you actually know something about."

"Okay, what's that?"

"Mr. Wheeler said he'd be at the park till the 'witching hour.' What the heck is that?"

"It's 3 a.m., dude," Benny said, mouth full. Jack could hear him chewing over the phone.

Jack glanced at the clock. "If it's 3 a.m., then I may still have time to meet him."

"You're not going there in the middle of the night!" Benny said, voice rising to a high pitch. "It's the witching hour, dude. That's bad news."

"I don't believe all that, man," Jack replied. "Your old babysitter just filled your head with nutty stuff."

"Man, it's not smart to get mixed up with that stuff. Trust me."

"I'm going, Benny," Jack said. "Mr. Wheeler's counting on me. I'll tell you about it tomorrow at school—I mean, today at school."

"I'll tell myself about it, Jack," Benny said. "I'll be at the old stone bridge in ten minutes. See you there!"

"No, Benny—" The dial tone sounded. Benny had hung up. Jack replaced the receiver on the wall and rubbed at his eyes again. He slapped his face as he crossed to the kitchen to fill a glass with water from the faucet. He drained it in one long drink. He took a deep breath. "Okay."

Jack went to the closet and pulled out his favorite bat. He snagged his Cincinnati Reds hat and pulled it on. Mr. Wheeler's three books came out of the backpack, along with the sweatshirt. Jack set the books on the counter. He left his science textbook and his homework folder in the bag in case he had to go straight to school afterward. He pulled on the gray sweatshirt, then found a dishtowel to wrap the wooden box in. He groaned when he saw the time. Five minutes till 3 a.m. *The witching hour.* He flew out of the house and jumped on his bike.

A full moon shone through a spectacular gap between stationary gray clouds. The cool night was quiet, and Jack rode cautiously past several houses, a few with yard signs featuring *Reagan for President* or *Mondale for President.* Finally he saw a flashlight waving at the bottom of the hill, by the old stone bridge's nearside parapets. Jack squeezed the brakes as he approached and hissed in a whisper, "Turn off your flashlight!"

"Sorry, dude," Benny said, switching it off. "It's super dark out here, ya know?"

Though Jack could see pretty well in the moonlight, he

nodded as he rolled up close to Benny. "What are you doing here, man?"

"Backing up my best friend," Benny said. "I wasn't about to let you face the witches or whatever alone. Oh, and I brought a little firepower," he added, reaching back to retrieve a slingshot from his pocket. "I think we both remember my prowess with Slingy here."

"I remember that you put out that cat's eye in third grade," Jack said.

"That was an accident, and it wasn't Slingy's fault," Benny replied. "Plus, if we're about to face off with witches at this hour, then having some history snapping some blasts at cats ain't a problem. Cats and witches go together like pods in a pea. People think it's crazy, but it's true. My old babysitter has like ten cats. We're better off with Slingy along."

"I feel so much safer, now," Jack said, reaching for his bat. "Remember what your dad said when you shot Mr. Twiggles?"

"Mama mia?" Benny winced.

"After that."

"He said we were both in big trouble, and you started crying."

"Oh, never mind," Jack said. "You joke about your cheek-pinching papa, but you say *Mama mia* when you get nervous."

"I do not!"

"Yep. You said it that day while we were waiting for your dad to get home and lecture us."

"I received more than a lecture from *Papa mia* that day," Benny said.

Jack smiled. "So, did you sneak out tonight?"

"You know me," Benny replied. "Of course not."

"What did you tell your parents?"

"That I was coming to meet you at the park to fight the forces of darkness, 'If necessary,' I said—don't want to worry them—and all about Mr. Wheeler's odd box and phone message."

"You are so weird," Jack said. "No one is honest with their parents like that, you know. It's unusual."

"What can I say? We have a relationship of trust, and I ain't breaking it. They offered to drive down here with me, but I could tell my dad was proud of me for wanting to go on the bike. I'm not leaving you to meet Mr. Wheeler and whatever creeps are lurking out here alone. I've got your back, Jack."

"Thanks, Benny," Jack said, smiling. "It does feel better with you here."

"And Slingy?"

"And Slingy." Jack inhaled and stepped off his bike, setting it down beside the road leading up to the old stone bridge. Benny followed his lead, and the two friends silently walked toward the bridge.

The Cornstalk River rushed below them, swollen from a few days of rain earlier in the week. Jack clenched his bat tightly, twisting the grip as he gazed around.

The night was still. The park across the river, with its fields and playgrounds, trails and caves, was dead quiet. By moonlight they could see each other and the silvered outline of familiar distant shapes. But as they stepped onto the bridge and between the two castle parapets on either side of its entrance, the moonlight vanished behind suddenly swirling clouds, their ghostly gray forms swarming over the faint paling orb.

Real darkness.

They walked on. Benny's hand found Jack's sweatshirt and held on. Jack was glad for it, though he almost swung his bat when he felt the touch. Jack may have been nervous, but one thing he knew was how to swing a bat. That was in the plus column. He tried not to think about the minus column. Jack's ears popped as he crossed the park-side parapets, and the boys crept toward the groundskeeper's shed. Jack didn't know where Mr. Wheeler wanted to meet, but the old shed seemed likely. It was the closest thing to Mr. Wheeler's property in the park.

"What was that?" Benny asked in a tense whisper.

"I didn't hear anything."

"Uh oh," Benny said.

"What is it?" Jack hissed back.

"Nothing," Benny said, as if he were trying to calm Jack down. "It's just bad if these sounds are so silent that we can't even hear them. Let's just find Mr. Wheeler and get outta here."

Jack nodded his head. "Agreed."

They hurried on, eyes adjusting to the deeper dark. Jack scanned the empty outfield of the baseball diamond as they walked past, half-certain a cackling monster would form in right field and tear after them. No monster appeared, and they finally reached the old shed. They opened the door and jumped inside, inhaling the all-pervasive scent of fuel and grass clippings.

"Grody," Benny said, gagging. "Smells like grassoline in here."

Jack sighed. "Breathe through your mouth."

"Flashlight?" Benny asked.

"Yeah," Jack answered. "Let's have a look."

Benny's beam of light arced around the room, illuminating rakes and shovels, boxes of nuts and bolts, and the old mowers.

Then, on Mr. Wheeler's desk, a note.

> *Jack,*
> *Meet me in the A.G. Do not call out. Be wary!*
> *—W*

The boys exchanged a look. They both knew what the A.G. meant. The Ancient Glade, a collection of old trees big enough, in some places, for you to walk inside their hollowed middles with your friends. Jack loved that section of the woods in daytime but was not excited by the prospect of going there at the witching hour. Not at all.

"Welp," Jack said.

"Welp," Benny added.

Jack opened the door, and Benny switched off his flashlight. With a deep breath, Jack walked toward the Ancient Glade. Benny's footsteps followed, and Jack found his sweatshirt gripped again.

The boys entered the woods. The scattered leaves crunched underfoot. Every falling pinecone, every skittering squirrel, made Jack's heart race more. Their eyes adjusted to the thicker darkness, and distant shadows appeared to shift. Each tree branch seemed like an ogre's arm. A small white shape shot in front of them, and the boys gasped and jumped back, stifling cries.

"I kicked it!" Benny hissed, his voice trembling. "Whatever it is, I kicked it!"

"Easy," Jack said, his right arm out in a protective gesture while his left gripped his bat. "Where'd it go?"

After scanning the ground and the surrounding trees

for a few tense moments, the boys walked forward again. Jack kept glancing from the ground to the way ahead, then occasionally up, fearful of a leaping attack from high in the branches. The wind picked up, and they saw the white shape ahead. Jack approached it carefully. He bent down, squinting at the half-covered thing.

"No, Jack," Benny whispered. "Don't ..."

"I think I've seen this before," Jack said, his voice calm again. He lifted up the object and turned to Benny. "I hit it here."

Benny took the baseball from Jack and swallowed hard. "Well, that could have been worse."

They laughed, walking on with momentarily lighter hearts, till they came to the boundary of the Ancient Glade. The trees were so thick here they couldn't see far ahead, even if it had been a sunny afternoon. The boys skirted an enormous oak and fell silent. Passing through a thick band of old trees, they soon came to a small clearing. A heaviness of presence—a certain uncanny gravity—filled the brooding old glen.

They hadn't gone far when they heard footsteps behind them. Jack smiled, grateful that Mr. Wheeler had come. But when he turned, he didn't see the old man.

A giant creature, swollen and grotesque with wide arced wings and armed with a spike-backed war hammer, stepped into the clearing. His ribs stood out like plates of armor against sinewy mesh between.

"Deliver the key to Wayland's gate," he growled in a guttural rasp, hefting his war hammer high, "or I shall pound you deep like a seed in this soil."

Chapter Five

Out of
This World

Jack stepped back, warding Benny away with his right arm while his bat moved forward in a protective motion. The moon broke free of the swirling clouds and beamed into the clearing, illuminating the menacing monster that loomed over the boys.

"I shan't ask again, acolyte," the beast snarled, huge red eyes blazing against the gray-green angles of his impatient face. His wings spread wide as he stepped forward, left hand stretched toward them, fist uncurling to an open palm while his right hand hefted his deadly weapon.

"We—we don't know what you mean," Jack choked out, stepping backward with Benny behind him.

"I sense it, human." He pointed to Jack's bag. "Deliver it or die."

"Give it to him, Jack," Benny whispered.

The creature's head cocked sideways, a satisfied smile touching the corner of its slimy mouth. "Heed your frail page . . . Jack."

Jack planted his feet. He turned his head and whispered

to Benny, "Be ready to run." Then he faced the creature and shook his head. "No."

Benny's high-pitched groan was cut off by the grating cackle of the monster. "Jack," he spat, smile widening in sickly contempt, "it is your deathday."

Jack shouted "Run!" and shoved Benny back, then whirled to deliver his home run swing in a battering attack on the monster. The bat sped ahead, met the surprised creature's defending arm, and shattered into splinters. With an angry curse, the beast coiled and swung his war hammer at Jack, who leapt back in a panic, but not out of the weapon's range. Just before contact, Jack glimpsed a flash of color—like a dart of multicolored firecrackers blurring by—and the monster's weapon was struck from his hands. Jack rose, wide-eyed, and saw Benny scrambling backward on the ground and a man—Mr. Wheeler!—striding into the clearing, his bright blade extended against the monster.

"Benny!" Jack called, rushing to his friend. He helped Benny to his feet, and both boys spun to see Mr. Wheeler's blade clash with the retrieved war hammer, bright sparks flying into the acrid air. Mr. Wheeler blocked a surprising thrust, then whirled and struck at the monster's head with the sword. The creature ducked and fell down. Mr. Wheeler turned, running toward the boys.

"Follow me!" he shouted, and the boys found their feet and sped after the dashing man.

Jack ducked under a low limb, half-dragging Benny through a tangled patch of thorns, as he hurried after Mr. Wheeler. They came to a great tree with a hollowed middle big enough for even that giant monster to get inside.

"The key, Jack!" Mr. Wheeler cried, sliding to a stop and turning around to stand between the boys and the pursuing enemy. Thrashing sounded through the brush behind them and the sick beating of huge wings, as Mr. Wheeler raised his blade. "Set it firmly in the keyhole knot!"

Jack fumbled with his pack, finally dragging out the wooden box with the tree emblem burned on the outside. He shattered the box over his knee and clenched the key. He focused on Mr. Wheeler's commands, shutting out every pressing question rising in his mind. He extended the key toward the keyhole-shaped knot by the opening. "Nothing's happening!"

Benny charged up and shouted, *"Clavis Ignum!"*

The burning key of light extended from the handle in Jack's hand, and he jabbed it into the keyhole knot. After a rising whine and a loud, swishing click, the tree hollow glowed bright and filled with thick, drifting fog. Jack called back. "Got it, sir!"

"Through, lads! Through!" Mr. Wheeler shouted, and then more bright fireworks burst behind them. A screech and a cry, followed by a thud. Jack turned back. The hulking monster had knocked Mr. Wheeler down and was speeding past him toward the boys. Jack grabbed Benny and shoved him through the tree's glowing, foggy gate. Benny disappeared with a wail, and Jack spun back to see Mr. Wheeler's outstretched hand just trip the monster. Mr. Wheeler leapt up, dashed over the enemy, and dove through the door. Mr. Wheeler's voice came through the gate. "Through, Jack, and then pull free the key!"

Jack stepped inside the foggy door and reached back through for the key, pulling it loose just as the monster lurched for the doorway. The rising whine reached its height, then the loud, swishing click sounded. The monster's enraged wail faded as Jack crashed into Mr. Wheeler's arms.

Jack gasped and staggered over the soft grass. All three were breathing hard, and Benny seemed to be trying to say something but wasn't able to make the words come out. Slowly, Jack looked around and noticed that the fog surrounding them hovered close to a stone wall stretching around a place that seemed pulled from some strange fable. Ancient streetlamps illuminated a cobblestone avenue twisting into a small town ranged over a modest slope toward what seemed in the distant darkness to be a steeper ascent. There, lights shone, hazy in the distance. The small town stood only a few hundred yards away. White brick buildings with broad dark beams of wood and roofs of thatch—which Jack assumed were cottages and shops—lined the avenue, many tucked behind dry-stacked stone walls.

"Did we go back in time?" Jack asked, straining to comprehend what had happened. What *was* happening. "Or is this another world?"

Mr. Wheeler laughed, blowing out a relieved breath. "You are in a place between worlds, boys," he said, gesturing to the town and its surrounding countryside edged with the thickest band of fog imaginable. "Welcome to the Wayland."

"The Wayland?" Jack blinked and tried to find words. "The tree," he said, pointing at the tree that rose wide between the stone wall on either side, "is a gate. And it goes both ways?"

"Yes. This is the gate to Myrtle," Mr. Wheeler replied. "And there, it is the gate into the Wayland."

Jack rubbed his eyes. "The creature—that thing you fought—"

"*We* fought, Jack," Mr. Wheeler said, smiling at him. "I

saw you stand your ground and fight back. He is a shardhark, a particularly bad one, too, so he is. His name is Mordok, by the way, and it is a serious problem that he is in Myrtle."

Benny coughed. "He looked like Mothman." Jack nodded. He did look like the frightening images the tabloids would print of the monster that supposedly first showed up in West Virginia in the 1960s.

Mr. Wheeler nodded. "He *is* the Mothman, Benny. We've had some trouble before with his kind slipping into our world."

"Is that why you were so worried and had to leave the bookshop?" Jack asked.

"Yes, Jack. There were troubling signs, and I had to act swiftly indeed. I did not know it would be him. But I knew it was bad. The crows. I saw the crows."

"What's odd about crows?"

"These were crows from Kaalgrad, larger and more deadly by far than the crows of our world. They serve their dark master and can more easily slip through the boundaries between worlds. They are the reason so many stories from earth have crows or ravens as a sign of evil."

Jack frowned. "The sharkhawk knew—"

"Shardhark," Mr. Wheeler corrected.

"The shardhark, he knew," Jack continued, "Mordok knew I had the key."

"Yes," Mr. Wheeler replied, "but you kept it out of his hands, which is more important than you know. He would dearly love to get into the Wayland."

"This magic key doesn't belong to me now, does it?" Jack asked, uneasy. "I don't have to fulfill some prophecy or end a blood feud between monsters and men?"

"No," Mr. Wheeler replied, reaching out his hand. "In fact, I shall take it back now, Jack."

Jack handed the key, which was no longer glowing, to Mr. Wheeler. "That's a relief."

"I am impressed you tried to battle him, Jack," Mr. Wheeler said, "though it was a terrible risk. Shardharks do keep blood grudges if they're hurt badly in battle. If your bat were a flaming blade and it had taken off his ear instead of shattering against his arm, he'd have tracked you down all your days to settle the score."

"Who was he?" Jack asked.

"Mordok is a denizen of darkness and an enemy of all free races."

"He hates blacks *and* whites?" Benny asked.

"Ah," Mr. Wheeler replied, "yes, he does. But I mean races in a different way. He hates the human race—with all its varying sizes, colors, and shapes—but he hates other races as well. Non-humans. He is in league with . . . well . . . suffice it to say he is most dangerous and deadly."

"Should we call the cops?" Benny asked, his face frozen in a horrified disbelief, "or get some grub? Mama mia, I don't know what's going on; help me."

"I am sorry, Benny," Mr. Wheeler said, patting the boy's shoulder. "I never intended for you to be involved. I had hoped not even to involve Jack at this time."

"Involve us in what?" Jack asked.

"In my troubles," Mr. Wheeler said. "In an old war that seems suddenly—and very sadly, indeed—unwon."

"We're in a war?" Jack asked. Something inside him sparked to life at this prospect.

"No, no," Mr. Wheeler said. "The war is not your bother. I had hoped—I yet hope—to keep the people of Myrtle and beyond out of this . . . this . . . disruption."

Jack frowned. "Good," he said, unconvincingly.

Mr. Wheeler gazed at him, eyebrows raised. He smiled and went on. "Yes, yes, my friends, this is not your concern. You shall see a bit of the Wayland and then go home, not to be bothered by the troubles of other realms. You, Jack Zulu," he said, smiling over at Jack with a fanciful expression, "are not tied up in this adventure. You have troubles of your own at present in your own world, and I would not add to them."

"Uh, guys?" Benny said.

They turned to see Benny, who had wandered back toward the tree lodged in the stone wall and its arched opening through which they had entered the Wayland. Benny bent and reached into the mist lying low around the gate. His face was worried.

"What is it?" Mr. Wheeler asked.

Benny lifted a clawed hand from the fog, attached to a dark gray-green forearm. It was the severed end of Mordok's limb, cut off below the monster's elbow when Jack had closed the gate.

Mr. Wheeler winced, then muttered quietly with widening eyes, "Mama mia."

Chapter Six

At the Wayfarers' Inn

What?" Jack asked, spinning to Mr. Wheeler, whose face showed grave concern.

"Jack," Mr. Wheeler said, taking the huge forearm and hand from Benny, "I am sorry to say that this is very bad."

Jack nodded, eyebrow rising.

"The Jack Eye," Benny whispered.

"May I have your backpack, Benny?" Mr. Wheeler asked.

Benny nodded and handed it over.

"Is there anything in here that is precious?"

Benny shook his head as Jack stripped off his sweatshirt and handed it to Mr. Wheeler. He had lost his Reds hat. Mr. Wheeler wrapped the monster's sliced off limb end in the sweatshirt and stuck it inside the backpack.

Benny gagged. "This is the grodiest thing I have ever witnessed."

"Come along, now," Mr. Wheeler said, helping Benny put the backpack on again. "Let us get into town before the dawn. I need to consult with a friend."

"Is Jack in danger?" Benny asked as they followed Mr. Wheeler away from the misty wall, over a bridge very similar to the one in Myrtle, and onto the cobblestone road.

Mr. Wheeler frowned, then looked over at Jack. "Yes."

Jack nodded. "Mr. Wheeler, I can't stay in here. I have to get back to see my mom. I want to see everything here, and I'll do what you ask, sir. But I have to get back as soon as I can."

"Of course, Jack," the older man replied. "I just want to give you the best chance possible to get through the park. Once you are beyond the old stone bridge, you are safe."

"That bridge we just crossed?" Benny asked.

"No, the one in Myrtle. Your bridge."

Jack glanced from Mr. Wheeler to the street, then up at the town, which was coming into focus. "Can't Mordok cross the bridge?"

"Something about monsters and bridges?" Benny asked.

"Not exactly," Mr. Wheeler said, his hand touching the first stones of a dry stack wall that lined the road into town. "The gate in the tree has an area around it where inter-realm travelers can explore. All the gates out of the Wayland have this feature. Think of it like the narthex at church."

"Narthex?" Jack asked, eyes darting from Mr. Wheeler to Benny. "That sounds made up."

Benny patted Jack's back. "Like a lobby or foyer?"

"Exactly. And Mordok can travel inside this sphere—and it is a sphere, a full orb around the gate—but he cannot go beyond it. Your homes are beyond the radius and therefore safe. Your school, churches, and Appalachianos are all safe."

"The hospital?" Jack asked.

"Safe," Mr. Wheeler replied, smiling back sympathetically.

He turned to the road and hurried past the first lamppost and the first few dwellings lining the street. On both sides, the pale white buildings glowed faintly in the moonlight. The first few seemed to be homes, with yards that were mostly gardens. Benny gasped and stepped closer to a fence. There a patch of luminescent flowers bloomed on vines that twined around the fence, stretched over the rock wall, and climbed up and around a nearby lamppost.

They walked on past several such small wonders till they reached a tall, many-storied brown-sided building with a swinging wooden sign over the door. Jack saw several different types of runes but recognized the name of the place in English. *The Wayfarers' Inn.* Above the sign, high on a pole extending from the roof, hung a flag. It bore the same tree emblem as the key's wooden box had.

A rhythmic clopping sounded from the avenue outside the inn, and Mr. Wheeler led the boys into the small alcove by the door. A man on horseback passed by, his attention ahead. The rider had a sword at his side, and—was Jack seeing things?—the huge horse was six-legged. He glanced at Benny, whose face was stuck in an astonished expression.

When the rider was out of sight and the clip-clopping sound faded into the distance, Jack whispered toward Mr. Wheeler. "Are you afraid of being seen?"

Mr. Wheeler shook his head. "Not afraid of *me* being seen, no. And it is likely no matter at all. I simply need to find out a few things from my friend inside." Benny groaned, his eyes darting around nervously. Mr. Wheeler knocked and then turned to gaze fully into Benny's face. "Benito Marino," he whispered, "I have guarded ambassadors of realms of such high and bright splendor it would make you weep to see them. I have walked dark roads as protector for the remnant of a fallen world and seen the last blinking stars vanish from their skies while wild beasts pursued my wards. I will see that no harm is done to you this night."

"Um, okay," Benny whispered back. Goosebumps rose on Jack's arms. Mr. Wheeler seemed like a being out of legend just then, and Jack was in awe. Mr. Wheeler's sheathed sword reminded him of the battle with the Mothman. Jack swallowed hard.

"Now," Mr. Wheeler said, turning back to the door and knocking again. "We can battle mothmen and use a magic key to get through enchanted tree portals, but I do not have a way into this blasted inn I've been coming to for ages. I need my crowbar, so I do."

Benny and Jack exchanged a wide-eyed look.

Mr. Wheeler knocked harder. "Hello, the house!" he called, louder than Jack expected. He looked down the street where the rider had gone.

The door opened, and a tall, hooded man stood with a lantern. "Wheeler?"

"Aye, Edwin," Mr. Wheeler replied, "and a pair of young friends."

"Come in," Edwin said, eyebrows high as he stepped aside.

They passed the threshold and entered a large common room edged on one side by a counter bar with stools up against it. Tables dotted the open area and stretched into several adjoining spaces—more rooms with overlapping thresholds throughout. The room was probably twenty times as large as Appalachianos but had a few things in common with the pizzeria, like the arrangement of tables and the counter design. No jukebox, though. A flag like the one outside hung from the rafters. The field was divided in two, the top blue and the bottom a golden-brown. The tree and roots emblem that had been on the wooden box adorned the center.

Jack's eyes lowered, and he looked around. He'd supposed the inn was empty, till he spotted a muttering cluster of men—wait, were they men?—in a corner of the main hall, sitting around a table with a single candle. Jack blinked and looked closer. The beings were small, half the size of an average man, with furry cheeks and arms and odd hawk-like faces. Jack blinked and did a double take. Benny's hand caught Jack's arm.

Edwin walked beside Mr. Wheeler, and they exchanged a knowing glance. Mr. Wheeler smiled tightly. "A table?"

"Of course," Edwin said, and he nodded to a corner booth on the opposite side of the common room from the other guests.

Mr. Wheeler led the boys to the booth and chose the side where he could see the room and door well. The boys sat down across from him. They would have to crane their necks to see the other guests, and this Benny did at once, squinting into the dimness.

"Benny," Mr. Wheeler said, "do not gawk at the mouterslaabs, if you please. They are prejudiced enough against the human race and need no further provocation."

"Mouterslaabs?" Jack asked. "Like from *The Folk of Reshur Falls?*"

"Exactly like them," Mr. Wheeler replied, smiling. "That band is out of Jutt's Hollow, just outside of Fallston."

Jack's breath caught. He swallowed hard. He had dreamed of seeing these creatures, and many more besides them, for years. "Is it all real, sir?"

"Everything you read in my books?"

Jack nodded.

Mr. Wheeler's eyes were bright, and his gold-rimmed glasses reflected the lantern at the bar and the distant candle. "Yes, Jack. The stories are too good to not be true, the legends are as real as reality, and the tales are far more faithful than fables."

Jack closed his eyes and put his head down on the table. Benny patted his back and Mr. Wheeler went on. "I am sorry, Jack. It must be quite a shock to hear. I did not mean to deceive you. I wanted to see . . . I wanted only to give you a gift. Do please forgive an old man?"

Jack raised his head and looked into Mr. Wheeler's face through welling eyes. "I could never regret reading those books, sir, and I'm not at all sorry to hear that they're real. I always almost knew it to be true. Thank you, Mr. Wheeler," he said, extending his hand across the table. Mr. Wheeler took it, and they shook.

Warmth flowed through their clasped hands.

"Thank you, Jack," Mr. Wheeler said. "I always believed you were that sort of soul. Now I have no doubt."

Benny exhaled heavily, and Jack glanced over at his best friend. Benny smirked. "Well, it's super-duper weird to me. So anytime you want to catch ol' B up on what in the Sam Hill is happening right about now, I'd love to hear it!"

"Yes, Benny," Mr. Wheeler said, "I shall do my best. First, I must speak privately to Edwin. I will see that you get some food and drink, and I shall return as soon as I am able."

The boys looked at each other, then back at Mr. Wheeler. Jack inhaled deeply, then replied, "We'll be here, sir. Do what you need to do."

Mr. Wheeler smiled, then turned to head toward the bar. A growling sounded from the far corner of the room, and Mr. Wheeler paused, then spun back. "Oh, and lads, don't go near the mouterslaabs."

Benny saluted, sneaking another nervous glance across the hall.

When Mr. Wheeler had gone into a backroom with the innkeeper, Edwin, Jack turned to Benny. "This is jamming my brain, B."

"Your brain? What about my brain? You're obviously in the know about mountyblabbers and monsters and wizard warriors who mow the park in their spare time, but for me, this is all new."

"I didn't know," Jack said. "I mean, it was a dream to me, a place I'd escape to."

"Here? The Wayland?"

"No," Jack replied. "I've never heard of the Wayland. It's not in any of the books I read. I read of legendary places, with elves and mouterslaabs and dwarves and verins and Garthians and dagliths and Thandals and Thaons—"

"I feel like you're just making up names now," Benny interrupted.

Jack smiled. "You ever hear of those—those races?"

Benny frowned. "I heard of elves and dwarves and trolls, but not varminz or doglicks or mountainslobs," he said, then held up a finger. "I take that back; I have met *several* mountain slobs."

"Mouterslaabs, dummy," Jack whispered. "I don't think we should risk getting their names wrong, given the apparently touchy relations."

Benny nodded. "Is my voice carrying?"

"A little."

"I'll be quieter. I don't want any trouble with trolls or elfies or dwarfies or pixies or . . ." He paused.

Jack enunciated, "Mou-ter-slaabs."

"Mouterslaabs," Benny repeated quietly.

They were aware of a presence beside them. They turned to see one of the strange beings. "You speak of us, Vandals?"

The boys lurched at the sudden appearance. Benny clung to Jack, his eyes wide. Jack gently shoved Benny away and smiled.

"By the Silver Falls and Every Crag of Hez," Jack said calmly, "greetings, friend."

The mouterslaab seemed to curl its beaklike mouth back in an expression Jack took for skeptical consideration. Finally, he nodded. "By the bottom to the top of Silver Falls and Every Sacred Crag of Hez, greetings."

Benny coughed, then rubbed his hands together. "Um. By Sliver's Craggy Bottom—"

Jack elbowed him, and he slowly leaned back in the booth, grimacing.

"You walk with a gray sage, so we won't provoke you. But be warned," the mouterslaab said, eyes narrowing to slits, "and be wary. The wars of our world are caused by your kind. And we will never misremember."

Jack blinked, unsure what he meant or what to say. "I'm sorry," he said at last, as the odd being turned and walked back to his table.

Benny smiled nervously at Jack. "I think that went pretty well."

Jack scowled. "By Sliver's Craggy Bottom?"

"Mama mia, Jack," Benny said, "I'm nervous as heck, and I can't think straight when I'm nervous and hungry."

"It was not a high point in human-mouterslaab relations, I think."

A door behind the bar opened, and another cloaked figure, hood over his head, emerged. He was tall and bore a wide tray. Jack's nose caught the scent at once. It smelled of coming home from a long journey, of a refreshing meal after a hard-fought victory.

"Mmmm," Benny said, rubbing his hands together as the food neared, "pancakes!"

The hooded figure slung plates of—yes, Benny's nose hadn't failed him—pancakes on the table, with a butter dish and two ceramic cups, and turned to go.

"I think you forgot the syrup, my good man," Benny said.

The server turned, and his pale face was clear in the flickering light. A fire was kindled in his eyes, his gaze angry. "I am no man, Vandal scum," he spat, then threw back his hood to reveal pointed ears extending into a golden mane, pulled back in an ornate binding.

Benny coughed, then looked nervously from the server to Jack, then back at the server. "Um, you forgot the syrup, my good . . . elf?"

The golden-haired elf snarled, turned, and walked back to the kitchen.

After exchanging bewildered looks, the boys shrugged

and dug in. Soon Mr. Wheeler returned. "No fight with the mouterslaabs?" he asked. "That is surprising and encouraging."

Benny swallowed and took another bite, managing to say as he chewed, "Jack hit 'em with a Sliver of the Ol' Craggy Bottom small talk and they seemed impressed and then came back at us with something about everything being our fault and then skedaddled."

Mr. Wheeled closed his eyes and sighed. "We have bigger problems than them."

"The elf waiter was also a leeetle bit testy, too," Benny said.

Jack frowned. "What did the mouterslaab mean when he said the wars of his world are caused by our kind?"

Mr. Wheeler's face fell. "'Tis true. Humans caused the wars on his, and most other, worlds. Specific humans. I was there. I was one of them."

Chapter Seven

The Wayland's Refugees

J ack dropped his fork. "What do you mean?"

Mr. Wheeler inhaled deeply and smiled at the boys. "It is a long story, but I shall do my best. First, I must eat something. That bout with Mordok was draining. I am not as young as I used to be, for all love."

Benny nodded and tucked into some more pancakes. Mouth full, he murmured, "Our pointy-eared waiter didn't supply any syrup, Mr. Wheeler. You'd think the pancakes would be super dry, but they aren't. It's so good."

"It is rightly called geffbred," Mr. Wheeler said, "something of a specialty here. I see the resemblance to pancakes, but they are quite different. Personally, I prefer Myrtle flapjacks loaded with syrup and enough bacon to feed a tolerable-sized army."

Jack was feeling less hungry. "Was that angry waiter really an elf?"

Mr. Wheeler cocked his head as he swallowed. "Some would say that, yes. Back in Myrtle, yes, they would call him an elf. But here, he is more rightly called a Thandalian—a kind of elf."

"Thandalia is real, too?" Jack said, his eyes wide. He had read about that land with the keenest interest.

"Jack," Mr. Wheeler replied, wiping his mouth with a long cloth napkin, "it's all real. It's all true."

Jack whistled. "The wild lands of Brune are real? The Destronn Plain and the Valley of Stars? I could, with my eyes, see the sun rise over Fantell Mountain? Thandalia! *The* Thandalia?"

"The very place, Jack," Mr. Wheeler said. "Though you have indeed only read of a long-ago age of Thandalia. Much has changed. So very much."

Jack frowned. "Can you tell us what's going on? And what the Wayland is?"

Mr. Wheeler nodded, set down his fork, folded his napkin across his plate, and stood. "I shall show you. Come on, lads."

They followed him out, Benny taking a last pancake—or geffbred—in hand as they headed for the door. Leaving the Wayfarers' Inn, they walked up the street, the tree gate further behind them. They passed several still-closed shops. One had a wide window in front and featured a swinging sign reading "Apothecary Shoppe" in English and the name painted again and again, in at least ten other languages, all strange to Jack. The proprietress, a lovely plump woman, worked inside by candlelight. She was mixing in a pot that was set on a counter with neat lines of bottles laid out beside. Jack felt a tug of wild hope inside him. He had so many questions about everything, but especially about her cures. If he could only speak to her. "Can we go in here, sir?"

"No, Jack," Mr. Wheeler replied. "Mrs. Hoff is up early to prepare for her day. She isn't yet open. It would be rude to bother her now, so it would."

Jack lingered a moment in front of the shop, while Benny followed Mr. Wheeler. Soon Jack hurried to catch up. "Sorry."

"Not a problem," Mr. Wheeler said. "Now, lads, this street is one of the oldest in the Wayland. These cobblestones were laid long ago, and most of the shoppes have been around for centuries. But we shall take a left up here at this break in the lane." He led them past a large white cottage on the left and opened a gate that fenced a rising green. Stepping through, he closed the gate behind them and began walking up the grassy hill. It was an ordinary slope, and there were structures ahead. Ramshackle huts, battered canvas tents, and other signs of a hasty encampment lay all around. This area stood out in contrast against the neat buildings surrounding the vast green, buildings with a strong sense of centuries on them. These huts were shabby and made in haste. "This is usually a common green, kept clear and used for pleasure." They neared the hovels on the edge of the knoll. Topping the hillside, they stared out at the encampment stretching into the distant darkness. Jack winced. Mr. Wheeler sighed. "'Tis the war in Thandalia that has brought them here. We have almost never taken refugees inside the Wayland, but the need was urgent and there was nowhere else to send them. The other open realms have already taken in all the Thandalian refugees they say they can hold."

"Realms?" Jack asked.

"Ah, yes," Mr. Wheeler replied. "The gate we came through in the Ancient Glade from Myrtle is one of twelve gates into twelve realms that surround this city. There." Mr. Wheeler pointed toward another foggy gate tree on the edge of the green, across another small bridge. "That is another doorway.

The Wayland is a city on the edge of many lands. It is a thin place between many worlds."

"And earth is one of them?" Jack asked.

"Yes, earth is one of them. But folk here usually call it Myrtle or, more commonly, Vandalia, because of a mix up with where this gate led into earth."

Benny smiled, shooting up a confident index finger. "Vandalia was once a name for West Virginia—or at least our region. It was considered as a possible official name when President Lincoln made us a state."

Mr. Wheeler smiled. "That is quite true, to be sure. It appears someone has been paying attention in West Virginia history class."

"Oh yeah," Benny said, "I crushed fourth grade. John Henry, John Brown, Chuck Yeager, Jerry West—I know my West Virginia history."

Mr. Wheeler's eyebrows arched. "That could come in handy—especially the John Henry part. But the point is that to folks in the Wayland and to those in the other realms, humans are most often known as Vandals."

"Vandals? That's a name for villains, people who vandalize," Jack said. "Doesn't seem fair."

"To be sure, the name did not originally mean that here, as Benny pointed out," Mr. Wheeler replied, "but it has come to have much the same meaning. See, a human has brought war to many of the twelve realms. He was once a leader among us, and I have known him a very long time." Mr. Wheeler glanced at the gate below. "He has already destroyed one world entirely—it is a forsaken place—and he wreaks havoc now on Thandalia."

"Can't you stop him?" Benny asked.

"We have stopped him, in a sense," Mr. Wheeler said, shaking his head as the camp of Thandalians stirred awake, with several of the elven folk emerging from their rickety homes to wash and prepare for the day. "Yet in another sense, we have not stopped him very much at all. He is in custody now in our jail here in the Wayland. But his forces still flock to his banner and fight, inspired by his tyrannical cause. His influence reaches deep, even here. This war has displaced so many, and the Wayland is vexed with quarrels over what to do."

Jack frowned. A near tent flap bulged, and out punched a small dark-skinned child with black eyes and wild hair tucked behind his elven ears. The child's nightshirt blew in the wind, and he hurried to fill a pitcher of water from a rain barrel shared by several folk at their morning chores. Jack eyed the child as he balanced the pitcher carefully and walked quickly back into the tent. Since all this talk of the troubles in Thandalia, Jack had one question bubbling up. "Does the Golden City stand, Mr. Wheeler?"

Mr. Wheeler sagged and had started to speak when he was hailed by an elderly elf, a female with wrinkled pale skin and cascading silver hair. She wore a bronze choker around her neck and a long purple dress. She hobbled along in sandaled feet, aided by an ornate cane carved in elaborate patterns and glowing white in the predawn. Mr. Wheeler turned away from the boys and bowed to her. The boys imitated Mr. Wheeler, Jack with elegant ease and Benny awkwardly. "Matron Elder Swane, greetings," Mr. Wheeler said.

"Greetings, Sage Wheeler," the elf matron said. "Light and hope to you."

"Light and hope, Matron," Mr. Wheeler said. "May the stars meet over you again."

Her placid face bent in a temporary grimace at his last words, but she resumed her formal civility. "May I speak with you, privately?"

"Of course," Mr. Wheeler replied. "Excuse me, lads." He walked apart with her, and Jack gazed after them, wincing. He felt the constraint between them, the sadness in the old Thandalian's face. Some deep wound, no doubt. Was it personal? Was it the war?

Benny's fist popped his arm. "Earth to Jack. What's going on? I was picking up some vibes there—some *vi-bi-zuz*, my brother. You look like you were reading that loud and clear. What's the deal?"

Jack swatted away Benny's fist, then gazed at Mr. Wheeler and the elf again. "I don't know, B. But I don't like it. Something's really wrong."

"War. Refugees. Yeah, not great, Jack. A lot is wrong."

"There's more. I loved reading about them. In the stories—er, histories, I guess—they are the most beautiful people. These people are not nomadic, as the other elven cultures I've read about are. The Thandalians are a stable, noble people. They are artists, poets, and musicians. They are gardeners and architects, cooks and historians. They live in a dry part of a small planet, using barely any of the planet's land. They've been slowly growing their habitable territory for thousands of years, making each acre they settle work for them in every kind of way. There are only a few provinces, and they are all near one another. They all surround the Valley of Stars."

"I guess maybe the provinces are fighting for control of

the valley?" Benny ventured.

Jack shook his head. "It's sacred, that valley. They were always unified around it. Every year they all meet and camp out and have a festival for seven days. On the eighth day, the Thaons come."

"The what?"

"Thaons," Jack said, his eyes alight. "They are winged creatures, a second race of magnificent beings on their planet. They are only seen once a year in the skies, flying over the valley as a reminder to the Thandalians of the long-ago victory over the dragons of Skeev in that same place. Their appearance means hope. It means light. It means life. Most of the art depicts this yearly event or the war of thousands of years that the celebration commemorates. The songs are about the Thaons, and the Thandalians all make fire lanterns—you've seen those, right?—and send them into the sky once the Thaons fly back to Andos, their golden city. The lanterns glow and rise and mingle with the stars."

Benny touched Jack's shoulder. "Jack, buddy, that's amazing. The Thaons sound like angels."

"That's how I've always thought of them too. Golden angels from the golden city of Andos."

The elderly elf and Mr. Wheeler still looked grave but seemed to be wrapping up their conversation. Jack watched, his heart heavy with a grief he couldn't name. After a few minutes, the two came back, and Mr. Wheeler introduced the boys. "Honored Matron Swane, may I name my young friends? This is Jonathan Zulu and Benito Marino. Boys, this is Matron Elder Swane."

"Light and hope to you," she said.

They bowed, and Jack said, "Very pleased to meet you, Matron Swane. We are honored."

Matron Swane looked at Benny. "You are very pale for a sailor, young sir."

"A sailor?" Benny asked, coughing. "No ma'am. My brother is a—was, um—was a sailor. But I am landlocked, personally."

"Your names are ceremonial?" she asked.

"Oh," Benny said, clapping his hands together, then pointing at the Thandalian elder. "I get it. Marino, as in 'mariner.' I gotcha. No, our family is in the pizza business now. I freckle very easily in the sun, as you can see. Mom's people descended from the Scots-Irish, so I think her maiden name means 'Get Ye In Yon Shade' because, wow, we are very pale and ginger. But Dad, on the other hand. He's Italian through and through. Mama mia, he is very physically affectionate—"

"Thank you, Benny," Mr. Wheeler said, cutting him off.

Matron Swane raised an eyebrow and pushed her silver hair behind her ear. "Are these your novice acolytes, Sage Wheeler?"

Mr. Wheeler glanced at Jack, then back at her. "No, honored matron, only my friends. They are new to the Wayland."

"As am I," she said, head dropping. She smiled a sad smile, said, "I was pleased to greet you," and walked back toward a sagging tent.

"I'm sorry I got blabby, Mr. Wheeler," Benny said when she was gone. "I was very nervous."

"It is all right, son."

"Can't anything be done for them?" Benny asked, wincing as the first light of dawn edged over the horizon, revealing more plainly the ragged conditions of the refugee camp.

"They are a noble race," Mr. Wheeler said, "and perhaps

too proud. It is a tricky thing to help them, with their idea of honor. They are in a sad state, to be sure."

Jack watched more and more beautiful, pointy-eared children of a wide variety of skin tones and sizes emerge alongside haggard parents. As the sun rose, they waited. Most had their backs to the boys and Mr. Wheeler, but when one would turn, Jack saw forlorn faces. As the full disk of the sun emerged, the Thandalians knelt and bowed, touching their heads to each knee in turn.

Mr. Wheeler knelt, and so the boys did too, but Jack saw that he did not touch his head to his knees. He seemed to kneel to honor their ways but did not mimic them. When they rose, Jack drew close to Mr. Wheeler. "Do the Thaons still fly above the Valley of Stars?"

Mr. Wheeler winced. "The Thaons have fallen, and the Valley of Stars is a desolate waste."

Chapter Eight

The Tower
and the Tree

J ack hung his head at hearing Thandalia's fate. He had only just learned it was real. Now, fast on the heels of that knowledge, he learned this magical land was a desolate wreck, ravaged by war.

"Come, lads," Mr. Wheeler said, hurrying from the green and toward the cozy town center. "There is more to see here than sad sights and more to know than woeful tidings."

They followed, eager to leave the scene of displaced families and the helpless sorrow they felt in their presence. Now that the town was illuminated by the rising sun, they could see a high tower, like something from a fairy tale, and several domed buildings around its base. Near the tower, a spectacular tree spread its wide limbs in an arc across the sky. The tree's leaves were golden-brown, and sparkling fruit glinted from its swollen boughs.

They approached the tree, and Jack felt an awe fall over him as the light from the rising sun shot through its thick limbs. The fruit was golden, and he had a keen desire to eat it.

A low stone wall encircled the area surrounding the tree's

base. A troop of soldiers guarded the entrance. Seeing Mr. Wheeler, the captain of the guard saluted and let them pass. Benny stepped toward the archway leading to the tree.

"Can we eat the fruit?" Benny asked.

Mr. Wheeler smiled. "Yes. It is magical, so be careful."

"What does it do?" Jack asked, cautious.

"It takes away hunger," Mr. Wheeler said, stretching to snag a low dangling piece.

"Forever?" Benny asked, hesitating.

"No," Mr. Wheeler replied, smiling. "Just for a while. It is an apple, like ours in Myrtle."

"But you said it was magical," Benny said, biting into a golden piece.

Mr. Wheeler chewed his bite and swallowed. "It is."

Jack ate as they walked around the tree. "This tree is like the gate tree," he said, squinting as he ran a hand over its bark.

Mr. Wheeler nodded. "Very good, Jack. Yes, it is indeed like the gate tree. It is like all twelve gate trees. It is the central tree, linking all the gate trees together. This is the mother tree. Their roots connect deep beneath the Wayland. This is the center of the Wayland, at least spiritually."

Benny picked another golden apple. "So, what would happen if it got chopped down?"

"I do not know, Benny," Mr. Wheeler replied, "but I believe it would mean the gates would no longer work."

Jack eyed the guards. "Would any enemies do that? Chop it down?"

"I do not believe so," Mr. Wheeler replied. "He should rather want to control it. He wants to rule the twelve realms."

"Who?" Jack asked, his heart feeling a sudden pang.

"I shall explain," Mr. Wheeler replied, heading toward the gate. "Follow me."

They followed Mr. Wheeler toward the tower, which was dark blue. A line of uniformed students, most elven-eared but some very strange looking, with fur all over, passed them, bowing to Mr. Wheeler as they hurried on. The streets were more modern here, but there were no cars or other such conveyances. Horses, huge and six-legged like the one they'd seen dashing past the Wayfarers' Inn, trotted along, sometimes carrying two or three riders. Occasionally they pulled carriages or carts. The blue-and-gold tree flag flew from various buildings, with a huge banner blowing at the base of the tower. Other flags appeared, but Jack could not see them clearly enough to distinguish them. Mr. Wheeler was leading them away from the tower now, on a little tour of the area surrounding the tower and the tree. They walked past more shops and homes, some regal estates with wide, walled gardens and grand, pillar-lined manors. There were grave offices and jolly parks, more inns and some scattered cafés, and a few centers of industry where a dull chorus of clatter accompanied glimpses of intense labor. They walked quickly through it all, Mr. Wheeler pointing out various details, and then turned back toward the blue tower.

The elven guard at the entrance saluted Mr. Wheeler, scowled at the boys, and stood aside. The boys followed their guide beneath the gilded archway, emblazoned with twelve stars, and entered the tower. A sparse entryway tunnel with spear-wielding guards led into a large open space where tapestries and elegant ancient paintings set off the oddly wide TV screens with scrolling words. Jack squinted to try to read the message ... *comminatio erectus in finibus* ... but lost the thread when he bumped into a speed-walking student. She had been distractedly reading a note on top of her stack of books. The collision sent the girl pitching sideways, and Jack shuffled quickly to catch her, while her books sprayed out and slid across the marble floor.

"Excuse me!" Jack said, as Benny bent to help gather up the scattered books.

"*Ignosce quaeso*," she said, before receiving the books and hurrying off again. She was short, with large purple eyes and long black hair. Her ears weren't pointed, her skin was brown, and she wore a uniform he now noticed on several other young people scattered among the adults: a golden-brown skirt—the males wore pants—and a white button-up shirt, with a blue jacket. Their arms bore white bands, which all seemed to vary in design.

"This way," Mr. Wheeler said, "and though I know it's difficult, please avoid accidentally running into the female acolytes, Jack."

Jack protested. "But, sir, I was trying to read—"

"Yeah, Jack," Benny said, smirking dramatically, "let's try to stay focused here, my friend. Where are we headed, Mr. Wheeler, and what's an acolyte, and why are people calling you Sage Wheeler? We use a lot of sage in our pizza. Are you, like, a famous cook here? That reminds me...anyone else kinda hungry? That magic apple isn't sticking to my ordinary ribs."

"The answers await you at the top," Mr. Wheeler said. "The answers to good questions, I mean." They passed under another archway and reached an iron stairwell that wound up and up. The older man, hand instinctively settling the sword at his side as he moved, led the way with long strides up the steps.

The Tower and the Tree

Up and up they went, Jack's heart rising as they climbed. Occasionally, they passed a descending official, and each bowed to Mr. Wheeler as they continued. Finally, just as Jack began to sweat with the effort, Mr. Wheeler pushed open the last door in the stairwell and led the boys onto a rounded balcony surrounding the top of the tower.

"Wow," Jack said, squinting against the brightness to scan the scene below. A beautiful view of the town lay below them, nestled nicely around a huge green hillside, partially marred by the refugee shelters. The great tree rose high and lovely, surrounded by its little wall and garden. Roads wound through and around the town and surrounding woods, extending into variously developed boroughs, but everything he could see was bound at its outside limit by a high wall and a dense ocean of fog beyond. The sky was the color of earth's sky, but Jack's jaw dropped when he saw a second sun, paler and far distant, rising beyond the first.

"The Wayland is an island with two suns," Mr. Wheeler said, motioning to the wall and its misty edge. "There is the one great tree, and then twelve gate trees in the ancient walls, each leading to another realm. It is a land of ways: the wayland. It was sometimes called 'the Between' and other times 'the Haven,' but for a long time now it has simply been the Wayland."

"What's out there?" Benny asked, pointing at the mist.

"Beyond the fog? No one knows. No one goes. It is forbidden, for good reason. But that is another story for another time. Is it not enough that there are gates to other worlds, and the one leading to your world goes, of all places, to Myrtle, West Virginia?"

Jack laughed. "If there's anywhere on earth that needs an escape hatch, it's gotta be Myrtle."

Mr. Wheeler frowned. "I like Myrtle. It is my home and has been for a very long time."

"It is?" Benny asked. "How? What even are you? I mean, you're clearly more than a groundskeeper. I haven't ever seen a groundskeeper flash out a rainbow-edged sword and battle a mothman."

Mr. Wheeler smiled. "I am like you, a man. Older, yes. Originally from across the Atlantic, to be sure. But I am from your world. Our world. I am human. A Vandal, if you will."

"Why do they call you a sage, sir?" Jack asked. "Is it because you're wise?"

"That makes a part of it, yes," Mr. Wheeler replied. "I am a leader here. I sit on the council of twelve sages who decide things for this place. We represent each world and are tasked with protecting them and the Wayland herself, to be sure."

"And you protect earth by weed-eating the park and keeping an old bookstore nobody but Jack ever visits?" Benny asked. "No offense, sir. It just seems odd."

"It is odd, indeed," Mr. Wheeler said, smiling, "but what would you expect a sage from an interworld society who protects an ancient gate with a sword of legend to do? Run a bowling alley?"

"You love to bowl," Jack said, grinning.

"I do love to bowl, to be sure," Mr. Wheeler agreed. "The sound of those suddenly struck and tumbling pins is like poetry to my ear bones."

"I'd love a bowl of cereal about right now," Benny said. "What's an acolyte?"

"An acolyte, Benito, is a student at the academy here. Most anyone you see here in the Wayland who is of an age with you will be an acolyte, unless they are from a family who lives in town. A small population of true natives are here, and they are always considered in the sages' council. But even most of their children are acolytes, together with the children of the twelve realms. Well, of most of the realms."

"Why not all?" Jack asked. "Are the Thandalians excluded because of the war?"

"No, there are many Thandalians in the academy. More now, because of the refugee crisis. But there have been troubles in several worlds. One called Kaalgrad," here Mr. Wheeler pointed to a gate, not so far from earth's, and near the Thandalian refugee camp, "is uninhabited. It was ruined by the same Vandal whose army is threatening to destroy Thandalia."

"Who is he?" Jack asked.

"His name is Rancast," Mr. Wheeler said, a pained expression on his face. "He is human, like us. That is, he *was* like us, long ago. He has changed in many ways—enhanced himself by many dark spells and pride-hearted techniques. We used to be on the council together and were very close, even before that. In fact, he is the nominal sage of Kaalgrad to this day. His statue is alongside those of other sages ringing the fountain near the academy common. However, he ruined Kaalgrad with his wicked machinations and endless lust for supremacy. After the fall of Kaalgrad, he made incursions into other realms, sometimes with the help of wayward allies among the powerful—even some sages, though I can scarcely believe it, even now. His adventures ended when he was captured. He is in prison here in the Wayland. His crimes are abominable and his cause a blight on all that is good. He is the enemy of us all and allied with our oldest enemy."

Jack felt sick. "Is he the reason for the end of the rite of hope at the Valley of Stars—for the end of the flight of the Thaons?"

Mr. Wheeler nodded. "And several similar atrocities in other worlds, though to me the slaughter of the Thaons was as gross a violation of all that is good as all the rest together."

"Why?" Jack asked.

"As with many such men throughout history, he was looking for the fountain of youth, to lay hold by force the fruit of eternal life."

"Did he find it?" Benny asked quietly.

"He did. He will never die of old age or disease. He will die only if he is killed."

"Why don't the sages have him executed?" Benny asked.

"We have to have unanimous agreement for such a dire penalty," Mr. Wheeler answered, "and we have nothing like agreement on that. Many believe it immoral. And even discounting his own seat and his open allies, there are a few sages who do not share my view of his crimes. To my great regret, we are at an impasse on the matter."

Jack threw up his hands. "So nothing happens? The war in Thandalia goes on, with his minions terrorizing the people, and nobody does anything?"

"I share your frustration, Jack," Mr. Wheeler said. "It has been my life for many years. What you can't feel is my guilt."

"I'm sorry, sir," Jack said. "I don't know anything. It's not my place to judge you. I'm sure it has been hard for you and the other sages."

"You feel the injustice of it, Jack," Mr. Wheeler said. "I am glad of that. I gave you those books so that maybe you could one day join the academy here. I had hoped to invite you. I would have sooner, but your dear mother's illness caused me to delay. I am sorry for that, of course, but I am glad you are here."

"Thanks, Mr. Wheeler. I'm glad to be here too. I've wanted to escape Myrtle for so long. I feel so trapped there, with Mom, school, and—"

"School!" Benny said, eyes widening as he gazed at his watch. "School!"

"Oh, man," Jack said, looking at Benny's watch, "we're late for first period!"

Chapter Nine

Dealing With a Bad Hand

As soon as Jack left the Wayland, he wanted to return. His mind was alive with a desire to escape Myrtle and explore the twelve realms through every gate in that fantastical place. But Jack thanked Mr. Wheeler for the escort as they crossed the old stone bridge, and the boys mounted their bikes and pedaled off toward Myrtle Middle School.

"Bad news about your backpack," Benny said. Jack's pack had been left in the park when they escaped through the gate into Wayland, and, though they searched around the Ancient Glade when they came back through, they weren't able to find it. His Reds hat was another casualty.

"That's all you've got to say?" Jack asked as they passed Gander's gas station and gained momentum. "We are finally on our own again after *that*—all that, Benny—and you're talking about my crummy old backpack?"

"Dude, that was a solid backpack," Benny said, "the way you'd two-strap that thing and just haul all your books and baseball trophies around. I'm considering lighting a candle for it tonight at church."

"If we miss that history test," Jack said, "you may have to light a candle for both of us."

Benny nodded. "Do you think you'll join the Wayland school?"

Jack thought about it. "I wonder if they have a baseball team."

"Whatever sport they have, I'm sure you'll be irritatingly great at it."

"What about you, B?"

"What do you mean?" Benny asked, with a faint hint of surliness.

"Will you join up and become an acolyte too?"

"I wasn't really invited, Jack."

"Yes, you were! Mr. Wheeler just invited us both to come back after school."

Benny shook his head, adjusted his grip on the handlebars, and grimaced. "That was an Anjoocan invite, Jack."

"What are you even talking about, B? You trying to speak Wayland-ese?"

"I think English is the dominant language in the Wayland, dude."

"What do you mean by . . . Angelican?"

"Anjoocan, Jack. It's an Anjoocan invite, man," Benny replied. "I know one when I see one, my dude. I get them all the time. 'We want you Jack; come on, Jack; come, come and be cool with us, Jack Zulu, please! . . . ummmm, *and you can* bring Benny.'"

"Anjoocan?" Jack asked, frowning.

Benny nodded. "Anjoocan bring Benny, as long as he stays in your shadow."

Jack frowned but said nothing for a while. They rode on, past Wheeler's Good Books, then Appalachianos, and finally neared the schools. As they pedaled past the decaying sign—Myrtle High Cardinals: AA Baseball State Champs 1978—and continued to Myrtle Middle School, Jack spoke again.

"I'm sorry about that, Benny. You're my best friend—my brother. I know you had a brother—and it's horrible that you lost him—but I've never had one. There's only you. I'm sorry if it felt like Mr. Wheeler's invite was an Anjoocan. That's lousy. But the truth is, I want to do it, and I want you with me."

Benny smiled as they stopped and stood over their bikes. "I'm with you, Jack. That's what I do. I'm in."

After an elaborate fist-bump and high-five combo that was nearly a decade in the works, they tossed down their bikes and rushed inside.

A few hours later, the bell rang for science to begin. Jack was basking in post-history-exam euphoria. "How'd you do?" he asked, as Benny slid into the desk beside him.

"I am alive," Benny replied, covering a belch.

"Did you pass, B?"

"Uncertain about the passing part, Jack. Very certain it wasn't a B."

"Well, I'm relieved we made it. Missing that would have killed our semester, and Mrs. Wayne isn't about to let anybody retake a test."

"I know. My brother used to tell me stories about her," Benny said. "She's been here forever. A kid in his class didn't get to graduate because he missed a test when his dog died."

"Yikes," Jack replied. "That's cold."

"She said, 'Next time get a healthier dog.'"

Their science teacher, Miss Dyer, came in and walked to the chalkboard. "Okay, quiet down, you maniacs. It's like a zoo in here! Settle down, or I'll call the pound, er, the, uh, zookeeper," she said, eyes wide, mouth open, expectant.

The class quieted down amid groans and giggles. Jack gave her a sympathetic smile. "Good one, Miss Dyer."

Someone coughed and said, "Miss Dyer? More like Misfire!"

Miss Dyer reddened. Jack glanced across and saw Michelle glaring at the bullies. She was remarkable. Dark hair bounced around her lovely face, framing huge eyes like pools of deep meaning. Jack wasn't a girl-crazy guy, but there was something about Michelle that he could not explain or even understand.

A loud cough brought his attention back to the teacher, who was smiling at him and glancing back and forth to Michelle, who seemed embarrassed.

"Earth to Jack," Benny whispered, following up with another cough.

Was I staring at Michelle? Oh, no. I was. He put his head down.

Miss Dyer laughed into her hand. "At least some students are finding this class mesmerizing." Jack looked up and smiled as she went on. He kept his eyes ahead and did not let them wander toward Michelle. Miss Dyer gestured toward the board, where an elaborately drawn arm with all the parts labeled was displayed. She pointed. "Today we come to the hand, so it's time to *hand* in your homework."

She stepped toward Jack, and that's when he remembered that he'd lost his bag and, with it, his textbook and the homework he had already done. Jack almost never made excuses, and he never lied to teachers. What could he say? A monster ate my homework? It might be true or close to it, but it wouldn't fly. Miss Dyer, never the most confident of teachers, would think he was making fun of her. He shrugged, glanced nervously around, and caught Michelle's inquisitive expression. *Oh, great.* He turned back to the teacher. "I'm sorry. I lost it, Miss Dyer," and, feeling this wasn't enough and disliking her injured expression, went on. "I lost it in the woods. In the park. In the park woods. I am so sorry. I will make it up. I mean, I will make up the homework, not the story." He smiled awkwardly. "The story is not made up. It's true . . . true as true is or can be."

Miss Dyer's eyebrows raised, her expression saying, *Are you finished?*

He looked down, and she turned to Benny.

Benny was smiling at Miss Dyer and nodding as his hand dropped down to unzip his bag. He grinned. "I'm excited for today's lesson on the hand. I have to *hand* it to you, Miss Dyer. That was a good one—ahh AHHHH!" he screamed, his face changing from smug confidence to terror. Miss Dyer, who moments before was ready to burst into a giggling fit, now leapt back in alarm. Benny had taken hold of the monster's hand, which he must have forgotten had been stowed in his backpack. Jack reached down to hide the grotesque appendage wrapped in his sweatshirt, zipped the bag back up, and jumped to his feet.

"Miss Dyer," he said, grabbing Benny by the shoulders and pushing him toward the door, "it's just a small injury to a hand—to Benny's hand, not Mothman's—I mean, Benny had a hand in the injury, and I need to handle this by taking Benny down to see the Mothman—I mean, the school nurse. May we be excused?"

Miss Dyer, breathing hard with her hand over her heart, nodded.

Benny's face was frozen in a disgusted mask and his hand was set in an upturned claw. Jack shoved him toward the door, while Hefty Leftwich jeered, "The weirdness of Benny Moron-o is rubbing off on Jack pretty bad now."

"Shut up, Hefty," Michelle snapped.

"Now Jack's got his little girlfriend fighting his battles for him," Hefty retorted. That was the last Jack heard as he and Benny hurried from the classroom.

Alone in the hallway, Benny unclenched his hand slowly, his face still set.

"Benny, snap out of it!"

Benny blinked, then pointed at the bag. "Jack, we have that hand with us. It's the Mothman's hand. It's a hand of a legit monster. I'm going to barf."

Jack peeked in the classroom door's small window. He saw Michelle, head down, taking notes on whatever Miss Dyer was talking about. His heart felt heavy, and he turned slowly back to Benny. "Let's get out of here. I want to go see Mom."

"Ditching?" Benny asked, surprised. Jack was a reliable student, and Benny always followed his lead. "We're ditching?"

"Yeah, we're ditching."

"Let's at least go to my house," Benny replied, "grab some food and maybe a catnap—starting to feel that whole middle-of-the-night marauding-through-enchanted-worlds catching up with me."

Jack headed for the wide double doors. "You can catch a catnap. I'm going to the hospital."

"If you show up there now, then Mrs. Z is gonna worry. Come over to the Marino casa. Eat something, Jackie Boy!" Benny said, reaching for Jack's cheek as they reached the door.

Jack slapped away Benny's hand and smiled at his friend. "Okay. But once it's time for school to be out, I'm going to the hospital."

"And I'm with you, brother," Benny replied.

"I've been thinking, Benny," Jack said as they jogged to their bikes. "You've been including me in your family's life: food, sleepovers, holidays—basically everything—for as long as I can remember, and especially since Mom got sick. You've made me feel like a member of the family. That's the biggest Anjoocan thing ever."

Chapter Ten

Sickness and the Other Side

While Benny grabbed a snack, Jack fell asleep on the couch with "Our House" by Madness playing on Benny's radio. So later that afternoon, Jack felt rested, though apprehensive, as he walked into room 213, Lively Memorial Hospital, and saw his mother lying still on her bed. His heart sank, and he stood rooted in place, prepared to drop the bouquet of wildflowers he'd carefully picked and arranged on his way. Then she stirred, and he felt his heart beating again. He hurried to her as her eyes opened and a big smile broke out on her face. "Jack!" she said, reaching for him. "I'm so glad you came, my boy. Oh, son," she said, squeezing him weakly.

"I love you, Mom," he replied, his voice catching. "I've been worried about you."

She took his face in her hands. "When you feel worried, just pray."

"I'd be praying all the time, then," Jack replied, clearing his throat.

"That wouldn't be the worst thing."

"I guess not."

"Sit down, my dear Jack." He sat on the chair beside the bed, hands linked with hers. "How was school?"

"School was same as always. I survived my history test, and Benny made me laugh."

"Thank God for Benny," Mom said, "and the Marinos. I don't know what we'd have done without them. Is Benny with you?"

"Down the hall, reading a comic. He'll come and see you before I leave."

She smiled. "Ah, good ol' Benny. His mom and I had so many adventures when we were girls. She would come to the farm and stay for days. I'm sure I've told you."

"Go on," he said. "I like to hear it."

She smiled. "We would play and pretend and go all over, skipping rocks and singing to the cows. We had so much fun. I remember one day we had done everything we could possibly do and hadn't stopped all day. Before we knew it, it was evening. We were in the pasture, making daisy chains. We looked up. The sky was like a painting, and we just stopped what we were doing and stared. For once, neither of us spoke. We just watched the sunset in silence. Then a dusting of snow started falling slowly, and the world was silent except for the touch of a thousand drifting snowflakes. I'll never forget that night."

"It sounds wonderful," Jack said.

"It was, son. I hope you and Benny have big adventures planned for today," she said. She let go of Jack and coughed into her hand. Jack scrambled for the glass of water on her bedside table and brought it close. She drank and smiled at him. "I'm fine. Just a tickle."

"Are you?" he asked and took the water from her, replacing it on the table, then gripped her hands again. She was so thin and pale. Sarah Zulu was fair-skinned, with strawberry blonde hair fading to gray in places. She was always pale, but she looked ashen now. Worse and worse. "Please, tell me the truth. People ask me all the time, and I never know what to say. Because I don't know. But I can take it, Mom. I just need to know what's really happening."

She let go of one of his hands and gently smoothed the worried lines on his face. "I hear you, son. And I'll be honest with you. The truth is that if the treatment they are trying doesn't work, then, my dear Jack," she paused, tears filling her eyes, "I'm going to die."

He nodded, his chin and lower lip trembling. "What are they saying about our chances?" he struggled to say.

"*Our* chances, indeed," she said, wiping her eyes. "We are in this together, son. And I feel terrible about the prospect of leaving you without either parent. It feels so wrong."

"Don't worry about me, Mom," Jack said hoarsely. "I just want you to be okay. I want you with me."

"I want to be with you, son," Mom replied, "I really do. I feel so guilty about being sick. I just always meant to be here for you. You're too young for all this hurt. I keep asking why it has to be like this."

"Me too." Jack fell into his mother's frail embrace.

"But the story isn't over yet," she whispered, shushing him as she had when he was much younger. "You asked about our chances? Well, I know the doctors are sometimes pessimistic and they're trying some hard things now, but I know that one thing is true. I'm not the one who controls things, and the one who does knows better than you and me. Death would be a sad separation, but son, there are worse things than death. And, until I'm buried beside Ruben's grave, the story isn't over. And I'll keep fighting until it is."

"Me too, Mom," Jack said.

"If we both keep fighting and praying, then who knows?" she said, grinning and wiping at her eyes, "maybe there's a surprise ahead."

"Excuse me."

Jack turned to see Dr. Singh in the doorway. He waved.

"I'm sorry to disturb you," he said. His Indian accent had always pleased Jack, hinting at far-off places he could escape to. "I could come back in a few."

"Come in, Doc," Mom said, motioning him in. "We're just in here talking things over."

"Hello, Jack," Dr. Singh said, extending a hand. "How are you?"

"I'm pretty well, sir," Jack said, shaking hands.

"I'm excited to see you back on the diamond this spring," Dr. Singh said. "My Robby said you just keep getting better and better, says you have—how did he put it? Oh, yes—killer bat speed."

"Thanks," Jack said, head dipping in modesty. "Robby's a good player who I look up to a lot. I hope I get to play with him again."

"He says you'll probably start for the high school when you get to ninth grade, when he's a senior. That would be something. Some people say you might make the big leagues someday. Imagine that!"

"I just want to help my team win," Jack said.

Dr. Singh looked at Jack's mom. "See," he said, "already answering like a pro. I hope you can see—that is, I hope . . ."

"Hope I can see Jack slamming homers out there in the spring? Me too," she said. Jack had noticed his tone, and his stomach lurched. *He's sure she's going to die.*

The doctor tried to sound casual. "My uncle was a pretty good cricketer, but it would be fun to know a professional baseball player. Maybe you'll play for the Pirates."

Mom shook her head. "It's gotta be the Reds for Jack, Dr. Singh."

"Okay," he said, glancing at his clipboard, "I suppose I could cheer for the Reds, if Jack was playing for them."

Mom smiled at Jack, then turned her head back to Dr. Singh. "Have you gotten the bloodwork back, Doc?"

Dr. Singh turned to Jack. "Jack, if you'll just excuse us a few minutes, I'll come and let you know when we're finished."

Jack frowned and had started to speak when his mother spoke up. "Doc, I think he's ready to be included more in this. He's had to grow up quick in lots of ways, and he and I have decided to face this thing together."

Dr. Singh tilted his head, a concerned look on his face. "That's your call, Sarah." He looked down at her chart, glanced at Jack, then looked at Mom with a pained expression. "Sarah, the tumor is growing again. The treatment isn't working."

An hour later, Jack and Benny were pedaling over the old stone bridge, headed to meet Mr. Wheeler at the gate. Headed to the Wayland. A daytime attack from Mothman was unlikely, according to Mr. Wheeler, but they were still alert. They had said little on the ride from the hospital. "I'm sorry, Jack," Benny said.

"Me too, B. Thanks."

"Maybe they'll figure it out. Dad says Dr. Singh is a great doctor and that we're lucky he's in Myrtle at all. He should be far away in some big city."

"I wish we all were," Jack said. "I don't know what to think, B. It's almost like it isn't really happening. But then, sometimes it is. And I hate it. But I'm going to try to follow what Mom said, and that's to do as much living as I can. I've always hoped to get out of Myrtle, and maybe I won't have to wait till I'm a pro athlete, or I join the military, or I inherit a million bucks from an uncle I never met. I'm leaving now, and every day! If Mr. Wheeler makes us his acolytes, then we can be in the Wayland all the time, and then who knows what kind of medicines they have in there?"

"I guess so," Benny said, his face showing concern.

"Are you afraid of Mordok?" Jack asked, glancing around as they pedaled past the baseball field.

"Yeah, I guess so," Benny said, not looking around, just studying Jack.

"Mr. Wheeler said that creep isn't likely to do anything in daytime. We're safe, I think, except at night. And only then if we cross into the radius of the gate—basically past the bridge."

"Jack, are you sure you're okay to go on today?" Benny asked. "Want to come over and have dinner with my family tonight? We could play video games and eat too much candy."

Jack shook his head. "I've never been so sure of anything, Benny. I want to become an acolyte in the Wayland. I want to be the best one they've ever had, and then maybe I can make a life there and bring Mom with me."

They rode up to the maintenance shed and leaned their bikes against a nearby tree. Mr. Wheeler emerged from the shed and waved. "Greetings, gentlemen."

"Hi, Mr. Wheeler," Benny said.

"Hello," Mr. Wheeler replied. "Tell me now, have you seen any crows at all?"

The boys exchanged a glance. "I don't know, sir," Jack said. "Maybe. Like, bigger crows, right?"

"Yes, they are bigger," Mr. Wheeler said. "They are often five times the size of an earth crow, sometimes more. They have a strong purple sheen on their feathers and teeth in their beaks."

Benny made a gagging sound. "Grody. I hope we don't run into them."

"Nor I," Mr. Wheeler agreed. "If you do see them—or Mordok in daytime or somehow out beyond the bridge—come and find me. Come to the Ancient Glade and strike the tree three times in the keyhole knot."

"Will that summon you?" Benny asked.

Mr. Wheeler smiled. "I'll be alerted that you need me."

"Like the bat signal?" Benny asked.

"Something like that."

Benny raised his eyebrows. "Maybe he sees a wheel in the sky," he whispered.

Mr. Wheeler smiled and shook his head. "You lads ready to return to the Wayland?"

"Yes," both boys replied in unison.

He smiled, wiping his hands on his coveralls. "Are you ready to train as acolytes?"

"Ready," Jack said, eyes thinned to slits and head nodding, "willing, and able."

Mr. Wheeler smiled. "We shall see about that."

Chapter Eleven

Cue the Waterworks

Mr. Wheeler popped back into the shed and strapped on his sword. Glancing around, he led the boys into the forest, eventually coming to the Ancient Glade. At the gate tree, he drew out the key, stuck it in the keyhole knot, and whispered, "*Clavis Ignum.*" The tree's middle glowed, then opened, and thin fog glided through. The Wayland was visible, even from the Myrtle side of the gate. Jack smiled as they walked through.

Jack inhaled deeply as he entered the town at the nexus of twelve worlds. "This place is amazing," he said.

"I suppose so," Mr. Wheeler replied, pocketing the key. "It is a lovely day, to be sure."

Benny swept up a handful of grass and breathed it in till he coughed, staggered, sneezed, and then held up a hand. "I'm okay. Just sniffed a wee little bit too much Waylandgrass. Won't happen again."

They crossed the stone bridge, remarkably like the one back in Myrtle. "The bridges, Mr. Wheeler? Are they all the same?" Jack asked.

Mr. Wheeler nodded. "Similar, yes. Most were built long ago. They mark the border of the radius gate, where the limits of inter-realm travel lie."

"How come we can pass them with no problem?" Benny asked.

"Anyone can pass them, usually, coming into the Wayland. But we can pass them going the other way, into Myrtle, because we are from earth. We do not need any special dispensation to travel in our own world."

"How do you get a dispensation?" Jack asked.

"They can be achieved through skill and, in some cases, from an endowment. But that is a long story, and we may come to it later. You have more elementary challenges ahead of you."

"It sounds like leveling up," Benny said, "like, in a video game."

"There are levels," Mr. Wheeler replied, "and for now, you are novices."

"Newbies," Benny said.

"Indeed," Mr. Wheeler agreed as they hit the cobblestone street and strode past the Wayfarers' Inn.

Benny's hand half-extended toward the ancient inn. "So, we're not stopping to grab some geffbred?" Mr. Wheeler grinned but kept going. "Okay," Benny said, nodding as he followed along. "We'll hit it after. Not a problem. Novices need to be patient, I assume? And maybe know karate? Fortunately for you, Mr. Wheeler—and all of us, really—I've been working on my crane technique, and it is pretty much impossible to defend."

Mr. Wheeler raised his eyebrows. "You may try it on me and my sword today."

Benny gritted his teeth nervously. "Yeah, okay, of course. Right, I'll just try to fight you, I guess?"

Mr. Wheeler, garbed in his faded blue groundskeeper coveralls and bearing a sword at his side, led them onto the common green. "Fighting is not the entirety of an acolyte's training." Benny looked relieved. "Nor," Mr. Wheeler continued, "is it minor or unimportant. You will learn to fight. You will learn to defend yourself and others. You will learn battle strategies not gleaned from movies."

Benny muttered. "It's all I've had so far. Not many rad karate dojos in Myrtle, double-yoo vee."

"Michelle Robinson competes in karate, does she not?" Wheeler asked.

"She has lessons in the next county over," Jack said, "has to drive an hour and a half both ways."

As they crested the hill and the refugee camp came in sight, Jack's gaze turned to a tree gate below and to the left. The tree seemed dead and charred in places. "Where does that lead?" Jack asked, pointing.

"Nowhere," Mr. Wheeler replied. "Nowhere good, anyway. It is the Kaalgrad gate. The world Rancast ruled and ruined. He will do the same to others if he is not stopped."

Jack looked from the gate to the refugee camp. *Rancast's ruins are all over.*

"Where do we begin?" Benny asked.

"There," Mr. Wheeler said, and he pointed to a stack of clay tiles shaped in a U alongside framing poles and lumber. A small team of students nearby was laying out supplies.

"Is this shop class?" Benny asked.

"In a way, Benito. We are partnering with some senior

Thandalian acolytes in order to bring fresh water from a nearby reservoir through an aqueduct into the camp. Please report to the matric—or, senior—officer below, and I shall come again for you in one hour."

"Only an hour?" Jack asked. "Sir, it seems like this project will need more than an hour."

Mr. Wheeler nodded, glancing over at a gathering of elf-eared chiefs on the hill's peak, watching the students with grave faces. "The Thandalian elders have tasked their students to lead this temporary construction and allowed outsider students to participate for a maximum of one hour. So, you will work one hour and then you will stop. See you soon, lads." Mr. Wheeler bowed to Matron Swane, staying beside the boys a moment as the other chiefs turned and saw them together. Then he left.

"Welp, let's get down to it, B," Jack said.

"Can't wait to get a-buildin'," Benny replied, fretful.

They walked down to the field base and waited as the clear student leader, an olive-skinned elf with black braids and a patch over his left eye, gave commands and pointed at a schematic showing the aqueduct path. "Our aim today is to shape the receiving end of the aqueduct, here, and then work our way back up to the stream. Does everyone understand their role? I should very much like to leave you to it and be free to lead the other team. Any questions?"

"Sir," Jack said, raising his hand slightly, "my friend and I are new. We may need some instructions before you go."

Jack heard a few students mumble "Vandals" with anger and exasperation.

The leader glowered at the new boys, a scar standing

out beneath his eyepatch. "Who assigned you to my detail, Vandals?"

"Sage Wheeler, sir," Jack replied.

The leader's eye widened a fraction. He barked at the rest, "You know your tasks. Get at it." Then he swaggered up to Benny and Jack. "You are novice acolytes?"

Jack nodded. "We aim to be, sir. It's our first day."

"And they send you to work with me," he snarled. "Well, Vandals, you'll get no special treatment from me because you know a gray sage. I will treat you as you deserve."

Benny scowled. "So, we deserve to be treated like scum?"

"Yes," he replied, hand absently playing at the scar down his cheek, "until you prove otherwise." Jack stepped forward, and the Thandalian student squared up to him. "Have you had battle training yet, novice?"

Jack shook his head. "Not yet, but I'm ready to get started any time."

Another Thandalian student appeared over the leader's shoulder, a female. "They don't know the rules here, Tytrus. Give them a chance."

Tytrus smirked and glanced back at the tall stack of clay tiles. "You will move these tiles, from here," he pointed to the stack, "to there," and he pointed to a place ten feet across the green. It was neither closer to the work nor farther.

"Yes, sir," Jack said, and he hurried to the stack and began lifting them in stacks of five each and transporting them to the designated place. Benny fell in, imitating Jack.

"Well done, Tytrus," the elven girl said, "you're really helping to heal the rift."

"Remember, So-addan," Tytrus retorted as he stomped

away, "that they made the rift. I simply live in the world they made."

Jack hustled. He knew how to do that, how to dig in at a demanding task. It's what made him a great athlete. He worked hard, charged with an inner fire to overcome whatever challenge lay before him and escape his fate in Myrtle. Now that he was outside Myrtle and had a chance at a new life for him and, he hoped, for his mom, he wasn't going to shirk the work, no matter how trivial or petty.

"I return in an hour," Tytrus, the patch-eyed student leader, called to the whole group. "I instruct that no one speak to the Vandals. They must learn child's work before they can be trusted with more serious tasks. We all know what happens when Vandals are allowed to command." He glared at Jack, then glanced toward the Kaalgrad gate. "When the decisive moment comes, they will always choose themselves. That's what they do." Heads nodded and angry faces turned toward the boys. Jack didn't stop; he only worked harder. Benny tried to keep up.

So-addan shook her head, seemed about to speak to the boys, but instead went back to the group working to stage the aqueduct supports.

"Shew," Benny said, straining to lift two tiles, "I'm starting to think Captain Elf-Pirate there doesn't love us."

Jack laughed, grunting as he placed more tiles at the assigned location. Glancing at the work being done to prep the supports, he worked out a way to stack the tiles that would make that work easier once the other students were ready for them. "He's prejudiced," Jack said, hurrying back to get a new stack. "I've had a little bit of experience in this department."

Benny nodded. "It all feels so different here. Nobody seems to care about skin color. They just seem to all be united in hating us—humans."

"Then we've got to do our part to show them the truth," Jack said, pointing out how he wanted Benny to lay out the tiles.

"What's the truth?" Benny asked, nodding at the tile setup.

"That we won't slither away and cry," Jack said. "We are here, and we won't be bullied into quitting."

"Is that what Mr. Wheeler wants us to learn?" Benny asked.

"I don't know, B. I just know that when Tytrus the Kindhearted comes back, we're going to have finished moving this stack."

"Jack," Benny replied with a whine, "that's not possible. This stack is huge."

"We're doing it, Benny. And we're going to do it with a smile."

Benny shrugged. "Okay. I've got your back, Jack."

The boys worked hard, straining to haul and shape the presentation of the tiles in a more user-friendly way. Sweating and thirsty, they worked, with Jack occasionally encouraging a faltering Benny to battle on.

In less than an hour, the stack was nearly done. Jack signaled Benny to keep carrying the rest, while he began staging the new stack in relation to the framed supports that the other students, including So-addan, had built. The line of supports stretched into the distance, and the Thandalian refugees had gathered along the edge of their camp to see the construction coming into focus.

When Tytrus returned, he smiled at the well-built supports and congratulated the team. Then his gaze fell on the neatly stacked tiles and his eyes narrowed. Everyone could see that not only had the two Vandals done the worthless labor he commanded, but they had reoriented the tiles in a way that would shorten everyone else's work. He met So-addan's eyes, and she smiled with eyebrows raised. He smirked. "Let's get this last stage completed," he said. "Vandal novices, you are dismissed."

Jack stepped forward, sweating and breathing hard. "I am Jack Zulu, and this is Benny Marino. It was an honor to work for you this day. Thank you for including us. Light and hope to all of you and yours. May the stars meet over you again." With that, he dropped to his knees and bowed low, touching his forehead to each of his knees. Benny imitated him, gasping as the sweat rolled down his face.

"Light and hope," Benny added, gasping.

Chapter Twelve

Swords
and Sages

Jack and Benny followed Mr. Wheeler away from the refugee camp. The two boys ached with exhaustion. "Are you thirsty?" Mr. Wheeler asked.

"We're fine," Jack said at the same time as Benny said, "I've never been so parched in all my life."

Mr. Wheeler nodded. "It is all right now, Jack. You are with a friend. You do not have to act a superhuman with me."

Jack smiled. "Okay then, I'm dying of thirst."

"Come along." Mr. Wheeler led them toward the Wayfarers' Inn. Soon they entered the bustling establishment. Far from the scenes of the night before, the inn was crowded with elves, mouterslaabs, and several other races Jack wasn't sure of. They found a table, and Mr. Wheeler ordered. "We shall have three tall jaybrews, if you please."

"And some geffbred?" Benny said, eyebrows high.

"And some geffbred, thank you," Mr. Wheeler continued. The waiter nodded and hurried off.

Benny threw up his hands. "Sorry, Mr. Wheeler. Not sure about the money sitch here, but I can trade you some geffbred

113

for some pizza anytime."

"Deal," Mr. Wheeler replied. "I love a pie with all the vegetables it can hold."

Benny shot out a hand, and they shook on it. "Weird, but cool."

Mr. Wheeler smiled. "So now, lads, one hour into your novice acolyteship. How do you fare?"

"I love it," Jack said.

Mr. Wheeler cocked his head at Jack, then turned to Benny. "Benito?"

"Super good," he replied, rolling his eyes.

"You certainly made an impression," Mr. Wheeler said.

"We're starting at the bottom," Jack said. "I don't mind that. As long as we know where we stand, we can do this."

Their drinks came, and the boys drank gratefully. Jaybrew was a sweet citrus drink, and it went down cool.

"This is a Thandalian drink," Mr. Wheeler said. "It is from the jaybonn tree, native to the Valley of Stars. There is a small grove of the trees here in the Wayland that Edwin, the proprietor, owns—brought here long ago. They are nearby his barley field out back. Access to jaybrew is one reason why you will find so many Thandalians taking meals here."

"Is geffbred Thandalian too?" Benny asked, though he wasn't attending closely. He was intent on his food and was chewing as he spoke.

"No, it is in fact a Wayland original. Edwin's great-grandmother created it from the germ of a barley grain grown only here."

Benny nodded absently, tucking into his new favorite snack. "Germans can be very inventive. Look at their cars, for instance."

Eyebrow arched, Mr. Wheeler stood. "Now, gentlemen. Hurry and finish your drinks—and food, Benito. We have two meetings with faculty dons to get to. In fact, I am afraid we shall be late if we do not hurry off. Come now, fellows. Bred in hand, Benito; bred in hand. And follow me."

They drank a last gulp and hurried behind the sword-bearing, coverall-wearing man. As they exited, Jack felt the eyes on them. He read scorn, doubt, fury, confusion, even fear in the expressions of Wayland's population as they left the Wayfarers' Inn.

Walking up the street, Jack again turned his eyes to the Apothecary Shoppe on their right. "Mr. Wheeler, do we have time to stop in?"

"I fear not, Jack. We shall be late if we do not hurry. And I cannot abide lateness."

"Neither doth I abide it," Benny said, stuffing the last of his geffbred into his pocket for later.

They hurried along, passing carts with vegetables fresh from the fields, a jaybrew stand, some ragged Thandalian families with sad eyes, and countless students. Occasionally they would pass an older person wearing a robe. Jack asked about them.

"Those are dons, or professors. They tutor the students in various subjects in the academy."

"Like teachers?" Benny asked.

"Yes," Mr. Wheeler replied. "But you will find some differences. Here, you are tutored in a subject by a don, and he or she leads you through the study with a small group of fellow scholars."

"I had to get tutored one year in math," Benny said.

Mr. Wheeler smiled. "This is different than that sort of tutoring. Every student is tutored. That is the approach here. You are learning, and they are guiding you. You are reading Twelve Realm Greats, and Mistress Sprool is tutoring you as you do. You meet to discuss the poetry of Vin Vinzer or Shakespeare, and you write papers occasionally. Every scholar must read a language each term, so you may be reading Verino with Master Golensed or Heentu with Mistress Kun. Other courses include diplomacy, culture, culinary arts, devotion, physical mastery, and many more. The subjects are many, and the tutors vary in skill, as at any institution. We are proud of our academy. She is not in her best years at the moment, but neither is she in her worst. She nurtures a fine band of scholars who, turned out into the worlds, do her credit and their worlds good. At least most of the time."

They had passed the tower and the tree and the bustling center of town, where, in addition to the horse-drawn carts and pedestrians, they saw a kind of electric gliding scooter with a rounded roof and open sides. Most riders were in seated position, and they would weave neatly through traffic and ease into charging stations set up along the roadside. Jack and Benny exchanged an excited glance.

"When do we get to try those?" Benny asked.

"They are quite expensive," Mr. Wheeler said, frowning, "and controversial. Some of the dons believe they are a sneaky subversion of our classicist laws."

"What do you think?" Jack asked.

"I am not opposed to innovation, Mr. Zulu," he replied, "but the academy leadership and the sages' council have insisted on a certain archaic elegance in this place. I sympathize with those who believe these electrogliders do not keep that spirit well, though they break no official statute."

Benny nodded. "I understood some of that."

"Well, sharpen that brain, Benito Marino," Mr. Wheeler said. They turned up a lane leading through a tunnel of faded stone arches. They followed this path till it ended in a courtyard before a series of neatly laid-out dark gray buildings. They were tall and made of stone, beautiful and ancient. Jack could not place them in his mind; they reminded him of castles and churches, but they were neither of those. They were strong but not forbidding, rather warm and inviting. He liked them.

"This ain't Myrtle Middle School," Benny said. "This makes M.M.S. look like a factory."

"Or a prison," Jack added.

"The similarities abound," Mr. Wheeler muttered. "Welcome to the heart of Wayland Academy. This is the Gock."

"Say what now?" Benny asked, nose wrinkled.

"This is the Gock," Mr. Wheeler said. "Welcome."

Jack shrugged. "I was expecting something more fancy, but okay. Hello, Gock. Is that a mouterslaab term?"

"It is English," Mr. Wheeler replied, "an acronym originally that has morphed into a permanent name. G.O.C. It stands for Good Old College. When the founders of the academy built here first many years ago, they called it Good Old College until they should name it properly. But it never was named, so it is still the G.O.C., and the name stuck, and it is now spelled with a *K* on the end. Gentlemen, the Gock."

"What's first, Mr. Wheeler?" Jack asked.

"We've already made a lot of progress in history," Benny quipped.

"If we forget our history," Mr. Wheeler began, "we shall be doomed to repeat the class."

"That's an old joke, Mr. Wheeler," Benny said, "but still pretty good."

Mr. Wheeler smiled. "Follow me, boys. And meet two of your tutors." They followed Mr. Wheeler along a cobblestone walkway lined with hip-high stone walls. They did not enter any of the old building's arched doorways but instead continued through a lane between them and further into a courtyard where a cadre of cadets gathered around two robed elves. They looked to be the same age as Mr. Wheeler. One was dark-skinned and wore his black hair in a cascading tangle of braids down his back. He held a silver sword and was pointing to its hilt. The other elf, short and balding with pale skin and a long scar above his right eye, held a slick flint stone. Mr. Wheeler and the boys drew close enough to hear, finally making their way to the back of the pack of uniformed students. Their armbands varied according to their races. Most of the many elves showed a white band with stars between golden wings. The black elf master was speaking.

". . . why the blademasters of Dower-en and Genhardeth have always preferred a long handling space. Their training and techniques favor this design. If the grip is wet with sweat or blood, this notching will help you hold, as well as the resin applied at times. That was a good question. Anyone else?"

A young elven acolyte bowed, then spoke up. "*Gel-frinden holt due rame celterflon—*"

The short, pale master held up a hand. "We speak Common in all college sessions, Derkuel, as you well know. We are not in the House of Thandal, nor the tower. Common English, if you please. Do you choose to favor us with your input?"

The student, olive-skinned with short black braids, shook his head and grumbled. Jack and Benny exchanged a glance. The younger elf could easily have been Tytrus's little brother. He looked just like him, only a bit smaller and with no eye patch.

"Master Du," another acolyte asked, looking to the dark elf with the sword, "has anyone ever combined the thunderstones with any powered sword hilts and made a hybrid weapon?"

"I have never seen one," Master Du said, glancing past the gathered students and catching sight of Mr. Wheeler. "But we have with us the keeper of one of the Wayland's greatest blades—its greatest, I would argue. Sage Wheeler, would you honor us by answering some acolytes' questions—maybe even some from the masters?"

Mr. Wheeler smiled and slowly walked toward the front. "My dear Masters Du and Ferrin, I would be delighted to join you for a moment. I have new novice acolytes with me, and I hoped only to expose them to your gathering so they might see the kinds of learning we have here in the academy. Two birds with one stone, to use an expression from Myrtle."

"Thank you, Sage Wheeler," Master Ferrin said, laying the thunderstone on a nearby table.

Master Du sheathed his blade. "May we see the Prism Blade?"

A rumble ran through the gathered acolytes, and Jack and Benny exchanged another glance, intrigued. Benny whispered, "Dude, the groundskeeper at our park is some important somebody in another dimension." Jack nodded.

Mr. Wheeler bowed to the tutors, then turned to the gathered acolytes. "Dear scholars, I am honored to say a few words in this joint session. Novice acolytes, like my friends there, will not know that often our disciplines intertwine, and we try to collaborate in instruction and experience so we can multiply our understanding. We live in a universe, and so this academy is a university and must approach all areas of learning with a comprehensive view. We do not merely learn the maths in isolation, or the languages. When we learn anything about something, we learn something about everything. So, Master Ferrin's history and culture course rightly collides with Master Du's physical mastery and battle course on the subject of ancient weaponry and tactics. This blade," he said, drawing his own effortlessly and swiftly, "is called Caladbolg. It has many names, in fact, including the Prism Blade. It is one of the seven enchanted blades of my realm and originates in a part of it called Ireland. It was used in early Irish wars and came to me in battle. It is one of the very few blades that can only be properly used by its proprietor—its champion-owner. To all others it is an ordinary blade. But to be what it is meant to be, it is a conqueror's prize, a won object. Do you know what that means?" He raised an open hand to the gathered scholars.

Jack heard a soft voice speak up and craned his neck to see the same purple-eyed female he had run into in the tower the day before. "You must kill the owner to claim ownership yourself," she said. "You have defeated the former owner of the Prism Blade in combat, and you are its sole master now."

Mr. Wheeler nodded. "Caladbolg, the hard-cutting sword of Ulster, did come to me that way. And it has, as far as I know, nearly always passed from hand to hand this way in its history. But there is another way to transfer ownership of the blade. A surrender ceremony accomplishes the same thing."

"Without honor," an acolyte murmured loudly.

Mr. Wheeler cocked his head to the side and replied softly, "Without bloodshed."

"Is it true," chimed in another young acolyte, this one very short and hairy, "that you cut the tops off hills with the Prism Blade?"

"That was not me," Mr. Wheeler replied, smiling.

"But it was done?"

"The feats of the blade are forever tied to the men who have carried it. Sometimes that has been for evil, other times for good. May I share with you some thoughts on powerful weapons and history?" Mr. Wheeler bowed to the masters. They bowed and showed him their open hands. He nodded thanks and sat on a large stone. "Please, sit," he said to the gathered acolytes. They all sat, and Jack and Benny joined them on the grass. Mr. Wheeler was smiling, but then his face turned cold. Jack followed his gaze to the other side of the gathered class and saw a robed man standing apart, with a retinue of servants behind him. He was tall and powerful, much bigger than Mr. Wheeler. His skin was gray and his head and face were shaved clean. Jack thought he looked like an ancient Egyptian prince, with heavy eyeliner and smooth, glistening skin. Golden earrings dangled from each ear. One of the man's entourage had a huge purple-black bird perched on his shoulder, its beak parting to reveal razor-sharp teeth.

The acolytes began to whisper, and Jack overheard snippets of their murmurings.

"Enemies at council."

"Sage Raftereen sides with the Vandal cause."

"Rancast's ally."

"Surprised they don't fight. Sage Wheeler could cut him down right now."

Master Du raised his hands for silence. The acolytes' chatter died down fast. "We are honored to be visited by two sages in one day. Welcome, Sage Raftereen. Should you choose to address our gathering after Sage Wheeler, we would, of course, welcome your wisdom here."

Sage Raftereen nodded slightly. "We thank you, Master Du," he said, his voice slippery with a strong bite of contempt. "Sage Wheeler is more apt to seek such public opportunities to lecture. I am come only to observe and not interfere. I have acolytes I am watching for potential entrance into our program. Carry on. *I* do not choose to disrupt your class." The giant crow hopped from the other man's shoulder to his, and he stroked its head.

Master Du bowed, then glanced at Mr. Wheeler, perplexed. "Sage Wheeler, uh, please go on."

Mr. Wheeler's icy gaze at Raftereen changed into a smile as he returned his attention to the students. "My dear friends," he said, patting the rock he sat on, "you are becoming what you will always be with every habit you forge for yourself, with every discipline hard-won. You are becoming something solid, like this rock. However," he said, sheathing Caladbolg in a slow, deliberate motion, "you must remember that you are not done yet. You are not done becoming. Think of clay, not rock. It is never," voice rising as his eyes darted at Raftereen, "too late to change a wrong thing. Even stubborn rocks can move over time and make way for the water of life to flow. It is never too late to take the better path. If you have started down the wrong way, turn around. Turn around! Go back. Begin again.

This takes humility. I know, because I have doubled back on my path a hundred times. I have never regretted aiming to get it right. Nor will you."

Raftereen interrupted from the back, his grotesque crow screeching out a rasping caw. "Will you not show these bright young acolytes what they hoped to see? They need not another moralistic lecture from a pious old windbag. They want to see the Prism Blade slice through that fat rock upon which you sit. Will you now show them?"

A rumbling amid the acolytes proved he was right, that they wanted to see such a thing. Jack wanted to see it too, but he felt conflicted by the other sage's obvious disrespect. All eyes fell on Mr. Wheeler. He smiled at the students. "Thank you for letting me speak to you today, dear acolytes. I have the greatest respect for you, and your masters. Please," he said, bowing to the masters, "continue your work."

A collective groan of whispered disappointment sounded from the crowd of students. Raftereen snickered, then pushed out his bottom lip in a mock pout. His retinue, all primly dressed in flowing robes, smirked at one another. The gray sage stepped back, and the swish of his robe revealed a long blade at his side and a powerful build beneath the shimmering robe. Jack knew an athlete when he saw one. Despite his sickly prissiness, Sage Raftereen was a fighter. He was deadly. As they walked away, Jack noticed the blood-red emblem on the back of the group's robes. It was an upside-down star inside a circle, like the one on the Appalachianos dumpster. But here the shape was topped by a three-pronged crown. *What is that?*

Mr. Wheeler walked back to the boys. "Excuse me," he whispered. "Please, continue observing the class. I shall meet

you gentlemen afterward on the green near the new aqueduct."
He looked around and saw that Raftereen was leaving. "You
know the way, do you not?"

"Yes, sir," Jack replied, concern in his tone.

Mr. Wheeler's distracted attention shifted, and he looked
each boy in the eyes. "There is nothing—well, there is not
much—to fear, for you lads."

"I'm not afraid for us, Mr. Wheeler," Jack said.

"Oh, I shall be fine. These scuffles are the stuff of every day.
It rarely escalates beyond words. But I will admit that Raftereen
and his sect are a prickly thorn in the sages' council's side."

"You go deal with the thorn, sir," Benny said, "and we'll
meet you at the green."

Mr. Wheeler smiled and patted Benny's baseball cap.
"There's more to you, young Benito, than it would sometimes
seem." He left, and the boys watched his progress as he followed
the thorny sage.

Chapter Thirteen

A Friend
in the Way

Jack and Benny enjoyed the last of the gathered class, though the excitement seemed to ebb away with the departure of the sages. When it was over, the two masters introduced themselves and invited the boys back for their usual sessions. Jack led Benny through the civilities, and soon they were making their way back toward the green.

The girl Jack had bumped into in the tower met them outside the archway. "Hello again," she said, smiling. "I'm sorry I was so rude at the tower yesterday. I was late for an examination."

Jack smiled and had started to reply when Benny spoke up and slid in front of his friend. "It's no worries. Jack is always running into people. I'm Benny," he said, shooting a hand out for a shake, then thinking better of it and half-bowing with his hand dangling.

The girl took his floppy hand and half-bowed in return. "I haven't met many Vandals," she said. "Lots of students here are really biased. I'm Evayner, or Vayner for short."

"It's great to meet you, Vayner," Benny said. "You look like a Vandal—uh—no offense—like a human, like us. Where are you from?"

"I'm Garthian, from the Gartren Helix, and yes, we do look very alike. We are usually shorter, and none of us have the pale skin like you two. Our shades are much darker. As a race we are known as builders and mathematicians. We are a confederation of several planets, making the Gartren Alliance. I am from Beldore Main, but I've lived on Galden Prime since becoming an acolyte."

Jack nodded, stepping closer. "So, your native tongue is Bellern?"

"It is, Jack," she said, shaking hands with him. "You are a scholar?"

"He reads too much," Benny said, stepping between them again. "I mean, he reads enough. Just enough. Enough to be dangerous, that's what I always sometimes say."

"Do you read, Benny?" she asked as they walked on.

"The classics, yes," he replied, pretending to yawn. "The great works of our people. Captain America. The Incredible Hulk. The Amazing Spider-Man. The giants."

Her eyes widened. "The amazing Spy Derman? The Incredible Halk? This is like the epics of Beldorian and Raffen?"

Jack looked away quickly, hand rubbing at his mouth to hide his smile. Benny nodded. "Yep. So much similar, really. Those dudes were amazing and incredible, I think. I mean, it's my contention that Beldorian was pretty dang amazing."

She smiled. "Do you speak Bellern, Benny?" she asked.

"Not at the moment. Mostly a Pig Latin guy right now. A little Italian, but mostly only with kitchen items. You speak Latin, though, right? Why did you speak in Latin to ol' Clumsy

Jack at the tower?"

She looked puzzled. "You are very new here, I suppose. We speak Common—or, Common English—everywhere in this Wayland. But in the blue tower, they still speak Latin officially. In each realm's house native tongues are spoken, but outside of that it is always Common, or Latin in the blue tower."

"Weird," Benny said.

"Not that weird," Jack replied. "Latin was the language of learning on earth—Vandalia—for most in the West. So, if there were humans involved with the founding of the Wayland, then it makes sense that they would have spoken Latin at the tower. But Vayner, isn't it frustrating to the acolytes, especially from Thandalia, that people speak English here—and that another Vandalian language is spoken in the tower? Are they resentful?"

"Yes," Vayner replied. "It used not to be an issue. My parents were both acolytes, and they say there was never any thought of it. But since Rancast's turning, and the wars he brought, it's been different. Some Thandalians believe it is insulting to speak the Vandal tongue."

Benny coughed. "Speaking of mouths, where is the best place to eat in the Wayland? All this talk of wars and betrayals and resentments is making me very hungry."

Vayner laughed. "Many would say the Court of Ahoy, with its many options. But I favor Roond's. It's a Gartren restaurant, and it's authentic. I have a free hour, if you fellows would like to try it out."

"Let's do it," Benny said, but Jack shook his head.

"We're supposed to meet Mr. Wheeler, Benny."

"Right, oops," he said. "Maybe another time, Vayner. Thanks for the invite. It sounds like a cool place. My family runs a restaurant back in Myrtle."

"What's it called?" she asked.

"Appalachianos. It's good."

"I shall have to visit it one day," Vayner said, "if the ban is ever lifted."

Benny held up his hands. "The health department has apologized. We were only shut down for like, three hours. Anyone is welcome. There was a misunderstanding with some of my pet mice—pet mice, mind you, not rats, as the paper said—but everything is clean and correct."

Jack put his hand on Benny's shoulder. "I think the ban is on the Wayland side, bro."

"You don't know?" Vayner asked. "No one from the Wayland or any of the realms has been allowed inside Vandalia, for a long time. It is forbidden. Ever since Rancast's wars. Ever since the fall of the old alliance. They are afraid of Rancast's allies."

Jack shook his head. "I can't believe Rancast has allies. How is that possible? He's a murdering tyrant, right?"

Vayner nodded. "He is. But some men are drawn to him. Including some on the sages' council."

"That slippery gray guy from class," Benny said. "Rafferty?"

"Sage Raftereen," Vayner said, "yes. He's a fairly open ally of Rancast. Which makes it tricky since the sages' council has Rancast imprisoned here in the Wayland, something Raftereen says is illegal."

"Illegal?" Benny replied. "But he's the dude that's busted up the worlds, right? What does Raftereen want the sages to do, give him a slap on the wrist?"

Vayner frowned. "Sage Raftereen and their other allies on the council want him released, free. But that's not possible to get passed in a vote. So they are working on a compromise. Most of the sages know he's a villain and won't ever allow him to be free. But there are always rumors of his agents working to break him out. Some even say the shardharks are active again."

Benny and Jack exchanged a worried glance. Jack looked back at the Garthian girl. "Vayner, how many on the council are for Rancast and how many against?"

"Rancast has three solid seats in his corner, including his own Kaalgrad seat, now occupied by his minion, Balltron Golend. He has Sage Raftereen in Oland and also Sage Hrenfor of Hulle. Hrenfor is a puppet. She will do whatever Raftereen says, and Raftereen will do as Rancast says. It is a shame. There are six, maybe seven, solid seats that align with Sage Wheeler and my sage, Honorable Frinx of Gartren. I know very well how solid that seat is for justice."

"So many names," Benny said. "My head is spinning."

"The important thing to remember, Benny," Vayner said, patting his arm, "is that there is a majority opposing Rancast, and that alliance has held for many years. But there is always a dark force organized against it. That is why the Myrtle gate is closed, and most other gates are closed as well."

"You're super smart. How do you know so much about all this?" Benny asked.

"Most know what I've said," she replied, "but my family has always cared about such things. The alliance is important to us. We esteem your sage very highly."

"Speaking of him," Jack said, "we'd better go meet him. I don't want to keep him waiting. And I'm a little concerned about him after all you've said."

Vayner nodded. "You're right to be concerned, but Sage

Wheeler has been through the darkest lands of danger with only the Prism Blade as his companion and come back alive. He has fought the shardharks in their lands and even battled Rancast himself. He is the one who captured Rancast, which many said was impossible. He is a great warrior. If he ever fell, we would be truly doomed."

"Thanks for talking to us, Vayner," Benny said. "We'll see you around."

They waved and parted, and the boys continued on, past the tower and the tree and through the old town center, saying little till they came to the open gate of the green's entrance. "She was nice," Jack said as they climbed the hill and came to the edge of the Thandalian refugee camp.

"Yeah," Benny agreed. "It's cool to finally meet someone our age who isn't ready to knock our heads off."

"Speaking of," Jack murmured as Tytrus—the Thandalian acolyte leader with the eye patch and long scar—appeared from one of the hovels in the camp. He saw them, glanced back at the simple tent, and inhaled deeply, anger plain on his face.

"Not so high and mighty now," Benny whispered.

"Don't say anything," Jack replied. "Just be cool. We need to play the long game."

Benny hissed. "So he can be as mean as he likes, but we have to be as nice as old ladies?"

"Read the game, Benny," Jack said, looking ahead, where Mr. Wheeler was speaking with Matron Elder Swane. "We're down, and they've got the bases loaded with no outs. We need to stay calm."

"We need to strike him out," Benny said.

"He's not the enemy," Jack replied.

"Well, he sure acts like it."

The boys stopped a respectful distance from where Mr. Wheeler and the Thandalian elder spoke. She was smiling, and they both looked down on the working aqueduct system, where hundreds of refugees were filling their vessels with water. Jack smiled at Benny. "Not enemies. Same side."

Benny smirked but nodded. "I guess you're right, Jack. But I don't like the way he treats us—especially you. He doesn't understand who you are. That makes me mad."

"Benny bro, you're the best," Jack said, punching him lightly on the arm.

"I've got your back, Jack," Benny replied. "Always."

Mr. Wheeler bowed to Matron Elder Swane and crossed to the boys. "You have done well here, gentlemen. Matron Elder Swane was complimenting me on the behavior of my novice acolytes. It means very much to me that you should respond so well under such challenging conditions, to be sure. It pleases me to know my trust was not misplaced. Well done."

Benny spoke up, "It was all Ja—"

"Thank you, sir," Jack interrupted. "What's next?"

"Dinner?" Benny asked.

Mr. Wheeler smiled. "You lads have had a long day. Maybe we should call it quits."

Jack glanced at Benny, then back at Mr. Wheeler. "Sir, we're ready to do what we need to do. What's next?"

Mr. Wheeler smiled and tapped the hilt of his sword. "Let us fight," he said.

Chapter Fourteen

Fighting
and Fading

In the fog on the edge of the Myrtle gate, Mr. Wheeler stood across from Jack and Benny. All three held wooden swords, and two of them were nervous.

"If you fight with caution for my safety, you will be hurt. You must try to harm me. I assure you that you shall not succeed." Mr. Wheeler held his practice blade in his left hand. With his right, he beckoned the boys. "Come along; bravely now."

Jack leapt ahead, swinging hard in a slice that Mr. Wheeler deftly avoided. Mr. Wheeler's wooden blade shot out and tagged Jack's middle. Benny swung down and cracked Mr. Wheeler's blade. The older man kicked out and connected with Benny's hip, knocking him to the ground.

"I warned you, Benito Marino," Mr. Wheeler called, "not to go easy. You struck at my sword when my body was open to you. Do not fight my sword; fight me."

Jack helped Benny up, and the two boys nodded to one another. They advanced together, striking out with a wild attack. Mr. Wheeler casually stepped between them, deflecting their occasionally accurate strikes with seeming ease.

Jack worked at hitting him. He set a goal to at least graze his coveralls with his practice blade once today. But Mr. Wheeler blocked everything and danced between the two boys, causing them—when he darted aside—to strike one another.

"Ow, Jack!" Benny cried. "That's my arm!"

"And that's my face," Jack replied, using his sleeve to wipe the blood from the cut on his chin.

Mr. Wheeler laughed. "Here, Jack," he said, pulling an old band aid out of his wallet—thankfully still in its original packaging—and applying it to Jack's bleeding chin. "You do not, I believe, need stitches."

"Thanks," Jack replied. "How'd you get so good at this?"

Mr. Wheeler sat down. "I have been at it a long time. I am old, Jack, older even than you think. Sadly, most of my life has been spent bearing the sword."

"How can we get better?" Jack asked.

"Tell me, now. What have you learned so far?"

Benny raised a hand. "Don't get into a fight with you."

Mr. Wheeler smiled. "That is actually quite wise, Benito. Assess your opponent's strength and judge your course based on reality, not just on what you hope. That is, in fact, a good principle. What else, now?"

Jack rubbed his head. "Fight the man, not the blade."

Mr. Wheeler nodded. "Good. What else?"

"Turning two opponents against each other is a good tactic," Jack added.

Mr. Wheeler smiled.

"Don't fight on an empty stomach," Benny said.

Mr. Wheeler inhaled deeply. "Attack is often the best defense, Benny. Your fear is holding you back. You must get in the fight in order to win the fight. You fall back in support of what Jack is doing, and that is well, but you need to learn to complement his moves."

"Great moves, Jack," Benny said.

"Not *compliment*, complement—with an E in the middle," Mr. Wheeler said, "as in something that is different, but fits together. Two puzzle pieces are different, but they fit together. That is what I mean. You do not have to be Jack. In fact, it is good that you are not. Be Benny, but be a better Benny."

Jack grinned. "He's the best Benny I've ever beheld."

"Well, I should very much like to behold him attacking from the side when you are attacking the front. I should like to behold him stepping closer when I step in to divide you. I should furthermore like to see you, when you are divided, using it to your advantage. I am giving you two homework."

"Mr. Wheeler," Benny moaned, "we've already got homework due tomorrow."

"What subject?" Mr. Wheeler asked.

"Math," Benny replied.

"This is more important," he said. "This might keep you alive. Come by the shop on your way to school in the morning, and I shall have a book for you each."

The next morning, after the deepest sleep Jack could remember, the boys stopped by the shop and found two books with sticky notes, one labeled "J" and one "B."

"*Swordplay for Novices*?" Benny read as he opened the book. "Great. What's yours called, *Swordplay for Genius Star Athletes*?"

Jack laughed. "*Great Blades and Their Masters*. It's some history and technique, looks like." He placed it carefully in his new backpack—Benny's parents had given both boys new ones—and they left. They pedaled to school and stowed their bikes. Their fist-bump and high-five combo ended with its customary handclasp, and they headed inside.

Jack turned in his math homework with a sigh, then sat through class with difficulty as he dreamed of the Wayland. *If I do well, I can bring Mom there. Maybe the air there will have healing properties. Maybe I can find a wizard or a potion that can extend her life. Sure, Rancast found the fountain of youth, but maybe there's a small stream of Curing Cancer? I'll find it if it exists. I'll find a way to get us out of Myrtle, West Virginia.*

"Mr. Zulu? Mr. Zulu!"

Jack snapped out of his daydream to see Mr. Hines, the math teacher, staring daggers at him. Jack nodded. "Thirty-two?"

"I'm sorry," Mr. Hines said, "that is not the answer to the question 'Why aren't you paying attention to my lecture?' Mr. Zulu."

"Maybe," Benny said from the desk beside Jack, "he's thinking there are thirty-two things he'd rather be doing." He smiled, then seemed to regret it.

"Both of you," Mr. Hines said, "to the principal's office, right now. You boys are slipping. Slipping, I tell you. You used to be a good student, Jack. I don't know what happened. Get on out of here."

The boys rose and strapped on their backpacks, Jack feeling low. "I'm sorry, sir. I didn't mean any disrespect. I just . . . I'm sorry." He left.

As Benny closed the door behind them, Jack heard

Michelle whispering, "Mr. Hines, Jack has a lot on his mind. His mother . . ." The sound of her voice faded as they walked toward the office.

"I meant it as a joke," Benny said, "to lighten the mood. Once again, I did not read the room at that moment. I think I was daydreaming too."

"About the Wayland?"

"Specifically, geffbred," Benny replied, "but yeah."

"What's geffbred?" Michelle asked, stepping beside them. Jack's heart jumped, alarmed at how easily she had sneaked up beside them.

"It's not an elf thing," Benny blurted out. "Not from another world, no. It's normal."

Jack scowled at him, eyebrow arched.

Michelle smiled. "Jack Eye."

Benny nodded. "Yep, that's the ol' Jack Eye."

"I do not have a Jack Eye," Jack said, stammering. "I mean, I have two Jack eyes, but not a, uh, not a look."

"You have a look," Michelle said.

"Yep, a look," Benny agreed.

"Mr. Hines said you can come back to class," Michelle said. "Or you can just take a walk to clear your heads before next class. He's not going to say anything to the principal."

"Thanks, Michelle," Jack replied.

"How's your mom?"

"We'll go see her after school, but I think things are looking pretty bad." Jack hung his head.

Michelle put her arm around him in a side hug, and Jack's heart raced. Then Benny jumped in, and they had an awkward three-person hug tangle. Unhooking arms, they laughed and began walking again. The halls were quiet as they passed classroom doors left and right. Michelle coughed. "How'd you guys do on the math homework?"

Jack said, "Okay," and Benny said, "Terrible," at the same time.

"It wasn't easy," Michelle said.

"I'm sure you aced it," Jack said, feeling his tongue on the verge of tripping. "You have the smartest girl in class."

"I do?" Michelle asked, covering her grin with her hand.

"I mean," Jack stammered, "you are the prettiest math student in school. I mean smarty-est!"

"So, I'm smarty-est," Michelle asked, barely containing her laughter, "but I'm not pretty? Ha! I'm kidding, Jack. You've got a lot on your mind."

Benny looked around in a dramatic effort to seem not to notice this conversation and Jack's awkward collapse. Jack slapped his forehead. "I'm sorry, Michelle. I meant you're really smart. And you're pretty . . . smart, too, I guess."

Michelle smiled and slapped Jack's arm. "You know in England they say 'smart' as in well-dressed? For our word *smart*, they say 'clever.' Weird, huh?"

"Yeah," Jack replied. "You ever think of going somewhere like England? Like, another place, away from Myrtle?"

Michelle nodded. "Of course. I mean, I love it here. But I'd love to visit Europe—maybe Ireland, for a dance competition? I went to Cincinnati for a karate tournament once."

"Did you win?" Jack asked.

"I placed high," she replied, fingers twining around the bouncing curls over her ears.

"Number one is pretty high," Jack said.

"Jack'll be in Cincinnati one day," Benny put in, "playing for the Reds."

"I bet you're right," Michelle said. "He's the best. Everyone says it."

Jack bit his lip. "I used to think that was my only shot. My one way out of here. But maybe there's another way to escape."

Michelle frowned. "Well, Jack. Don't forget us all when you're gone. You may not love this place, but there's a lot of love for you here. I'm going to head back to class. Please say hi to your mom for me. Tell her we're all praying for her."

"Thanks, Michelle," Jack replied.

A few hours later, Jack told his mom what Michelle said.

"She's always been so kind, that Michelle," Mom said. "A special girl, that one. A star, really." She coughed, and Jack reached for her water. "I'm okay, son." She recovered and leaned back on her pillow.

"Any new info since yesterday on the treatment plan?" Jack asked.

"Nothing new yet, son. Dr. Singh came in this morning just to check on me. He's consulting with some oncologists from his days in Charlotte, and they are going to see if anything else can be done. I'm sorry to say, my dear Jack, that the prospects aren't good."

Jack's head dipped, and he felt the weak squeeze of his mother's frail hand. He looked at her. "I'm not giving up, Mom. I'll never give up. Will you keep fighting?"

She nodded. "I will, Jack. For you, I will. I know where

I'm going. I know the story isn't over for me, even at death. But I'll fight, son."

Benny knocked at the door. "Can I come in?"

Mom brightened. "Benny Boy, yes. Come in, dear." Benny shuffled over and hugged her, then kept holding her hand. Mom held Jack's hand in her right and Benny's in her left as the boys stood on either side of her bed. "My boys. Brothers from best-friend mothers. Your mom—my dear Grace—came to see me this morning. She brought me those," she said, nodding to the colorful flowers on the windowsill. "Beautiful. She's been working hard at the restaurant. She said they've had some real trouble out of that Allegra. Theft. Destruction of property. Threats."

"Your old babysitter?" Jack asked. "You didn't mention it to me."

"Bro, you've got a lot cooking, man," Benny said.

"I'm sorry, Benny," Mom said. "I didn't realize Jack didn't know. I tried to do that—keep secrets from him—with my treatment, and it didn't work. I guess we just have to tell him everything."

"Allegra is pretty messed up, man," Benny said. "She's got a major grudge against Mom and Dad, and she's been threatening them. She's going downhill fast."

"It's true," Mom said. "Grace says she's aged a decade in the last year. She lives who-knows-where on the streets and has been dabbling in some dark stuff."

"Dark stuff?" Jack asked.

"Yeah," Benny replied, "like witchcraft stuff."

"The occult is not a game," Mom said. They talked on then, about mostly pleasant things, keeping her company over the next hour. They ate candy from the vending machine and played rummy. Soon Jack's mom was drifting off again, and she sleepily said, "Go have adventures . . . live, boys . . . and don't come back till tomorrow." It was a drowsy version of her customary command. They kissed her on each cheek, Jack whispering a prayer as Benny crossed himself, and they left.

Jack winced as they walked into the fall sunlight. The forest surrounding the town was changing clothes, and swathes of orange invaded the vast green hillsides, with darts of red and yellow pocketed throughout. He slapped Benny's back. "Let's get out of here."

Chapter Fifteen

A Dangerous Boy and the Way of Life

They met Mr. Wheeler at the Ancient Glade. He extended the key to the tree's keyhole knot and whispered, "*Clavis Ignum*," and the gate swooshed open. Jack didn't look back as they crossed into the Wayland.

"Today, lads," Mr. Wheeler said, "you shall continue sampling from the courses offered to full acolytes. You will not be admitted to any course until you are full acolytes, but as novice acolytes, you may be permitted to observe nearly any lower-level course."

Benny snatched a flower blooming on the path and inhaled its scent. "This won't kill me, will it?" Mr. Wheeler shook his head, and Benny went on. "How do we become full acolytes, Mr. Wheeler?"

"You pass for it," Mr. Wheeler replied. "You sit for an exam and pass, or fail, and are welcomed or rejected. The exam is not merely academic and is certainly not all sitting, but we still say that you sit for the exam. Until then, you are under my protection and my supervision. I decide what courses you will sample and what supplementary texts and activities are required. That will include books, trainings, and field work."

"Field work?" Jack asked. "What's that, Mr. Wheeler?"

"It is real work out in the field. If you are my NAs—novice acolytes—then I might choose to take you along on my work. Maybe meeting a dignitary in another world or attempting to resolve a dispute between two parties in the tower. That kind of thing."

"Thanks, Mr. Wheeler," Benny said, "for including me."

"I am indeed delighted you are with us, Mr. Marino," he replied. "And another thing I have meant to say to you lads. Here you need not call me *Mister* Wheeler. I am simply Wheeler. Or Sage Wheeler, when an honorific is important. I understand and appreciate why you do it, and I have the same custom back home in Myrtle; but here you may simply call me Wheeler with no disrespect at all. I prefer it, on this side of the gate."

"Yes, sir, Wheeler," Jack said.

"I always feel bad when adults ask me to call them by their first name," Benny said. "It's like keeping your hat on during prayer or talking during the national anthem. It's weird."

Wheeler laughed. "It is not my first name, Benito, but I take your meaning. You shall grow used to it."

"What's first?" Jack asked.

Benny crossed his fingers and closed his eyes. "Please be moving a billion tiles ten feet . . . Please be moving a billion tiles ten feet."

Wheeler smirked. "You are in luck."

Benny gasped. "Oh, no."

Wheeler chuckled. "Follow me."

They followed him past the Wayfarers' Inn and the open

way to the common green. Jack smiled to think of the Thandalian refugees and their abundant fresh water. An image of Tytrus came to mind, and his smile faded. There was a look about Tytrus he had seen in other boys over the years. It was a look of inevitable looming conflict. There was a longing to conquer Jack in the Thandalian boy's face. But Jack didn't want to be conquered. Thus, conflict.

Benny hurried up to stride beside Wheeler. "Have you heard of Roond's, Wheeler?"

He nodded. "The food is quite delicious there, especially if you enjoy some heat with your meat."

"It's spicy?" Benny asked.

"Spicier than anything you have ever tasted, Benito."

"Wowzers."

"They have a meat from an animal called a mowett—basically a cow or goat type of creature that runs on all sixes—and they soak its meat in a brine of peppers from a valley so void of water that it is not habitable for any species."

"How do the peppers survive?" Jack asked, catching up.

"They only barely do. The farmers have gliders they take into the valley, and they drop the absolute minimal amount of water they can. It just touches the pepper plants, and they fight to stay alive. These peppers fight like caged monsters to live, and they are picked at a late stage when their venom is most potent. They are ground and mixed with other spices too hot to touch with the naked hand and blended with an ooze of biting sap from a spice tree. This is what the mowett meat soaks in for weeks. It is quite delicious. But also illegal in some realms. Roond's has it in the back. But you have to ask for it."

"No thank you," Jack said.

"I'm intrigued," Benny said.

The great tree loomed ahead on their left as they walked. It was glorious, with light from two suns glittering from its golden leaves. The fruit hung like dewdrops, and Jack marveled at its unseen power. He marveled at the wonder of this ancient tree, its roots spreading all across the Wayland, making gates to other worlds. "Does the tree have a name?"

"It has many names, in many worlds," Wheeler replied. "Even on earth, many peoples have stories of a magical central tree that intersects with mankind's destiny."

"Oh yeah, like Adam and Eve?" Benny asked.

"Beyond that," Wheeler replied. "Humans have always told stories about trees. Many are true myths, like the Eden narrative, but many are distortions or part-histories that have become legends."

"What do you call the tree?"

"It is simply *the* tree," Wheeler replied. "The life of the Wayland is in the tower and the tree. The tree is its heart, and the tower, its head."

They followed Wheeler past the grand tower, through a crowd of hurrying acolytes and dignitaries of varying races, into the busy town. Wheeler hailed a carriage, and a six-legged horse, oversized even for the largest earth horses, trotted up. The boys leapt into the open-topped compartment and sat on a bench facing Wheeler.

"Colony, if you please," Wheeler said to the driver, a short mouterslaab with furry arms and a hawk-like face.

"Aye," he replied with a cold glare at the boys. "Not surprised," he whispered under his breath.

Wheeler ignored the remark and pointed down the road

into the distance. "Old Colony Town used to be the center of Wayland, but it was somewhat abandoned when the new tower was built. It has become a rather seedy section of our island, a place where black market goods are exchanged and the least desirable elements of our society mingle."

"Then why are we going there?" Benny asked.

"To shop," he replied.

Soon they crested a rise on the cobblestone road and began to descend into a small valley crammed with tightly packed shops and surrounded by blighted buildings. Black smoke billowed out half-broken chimneys, and dangerous-looking persons staggered in the streets.

"This is good," Wheeler called, and the driver pulled the reins. Wheeler handed the scowling mouterslaab three coins. The driver nodded, then whipped his horse into a quick gallop away.

The boys turned from the escaping carriage to the shop in front of them. One rusty dangling chain hung from the sign pole, but the sign was long gone. The shop windows were boarded up and broken in places, and where Jack could see through dim glass it looked dark and unkempt.

"Here?" Benny asked. "We're shopping here? What exactly are we getting today at JC Penniless?"

"I know it looks bad on the outside, but on the inside," Wheeler said, smiling, "it is much worse." They followed him in and quickly discovered he was right. The inside of the shop was strewn with clothes and broken-down old furniture. A sign on the top of a stack of disused equipment spelled out a strange word Jack couldn't read, in dots of old lightbulbs, most of which were broken and none of which were working.

Wheeler pointed. "That used to be on a ride at an old carnival. It was down the road from the lake. I loved it."

Benny and Jack exchanged a worried glance. "What are we shopping for," Benny asked, "dank nostalgia?"

"That is a fine name for a shop, if not a product," Wheeler replied. "Ah," he said, as a creaky door opened in the shop's corner. He walked forward, and, after another nervous exchange, the boys followed him through the cracked door and down a tight spiraling stairway. Wheeler proceeded through another cracked doorway, followed by Jack, then Benny. Now they found a neat little shop, with books and clothes and weapons and gadgets all on their own shelves. These all surrounded a central bar where an old woman sat in a rocking chair and smoked a pipe behind the counter. She was reading a newspaper, *The Old Colony Trader*, and scowling. Her chin shot up in greeting to Wheeler, who waved. "This is Sylvia's Curiosities and Arms Shoppe," he whispered. "Sylvia is from earth. She was a *maquis* resistance fighter in France during World War II, and she helped a lot of allied soldiers escape the Nazis. She came to the Wayland with Rancast years ago but soon caught on to his schemes. She had nowhere else to go, so she settled here in Old Colony Town and went back to what she knew best. Underground trading. There are polite customs—sometimes laws—about what from varying realms can be exchanged here in the Wayland. Sylvia usually has inventory that stretches the edges of what is strictly legal."

"You bring two more stinking Vandals into the Wayland, Joseph Wheeler?" Sylvia asked in a thick French accent, her head buried in her newspaper and a smoke cloud swirling above. "Just what we need. That black boy has the look of another Rancast, does he not? The ginger one is of no concern. But why you bring them here, I cannot tell. Always hopeful, this Monsieur Wheeler. A fool, yes, but a hopeful one."

"Thank you for that vote of confidence, Mademoiselle Sylvia," Wheeler said, stepping closer. "I am looking for swords."

"Oh, fantastic," she replied, scowling over her paper, "they will also be trained to kill. *Magnifique.*"

"You have them?" he asked.

"*Oui*, of course," she replied, nodding her head to a door in the corner.

Wheeler turned to the boys. "I shall be right back." He crossed the room and disappeared through the door.

Jack and Benny stood still, glancing nervously from the door back to the woman enveloped in smoke. An awkward minute passed before Sylvia lowered her paper and glared at Jack. "The black one, he is dangerous," she said.

Jack didn't like hearing that. "That's been said before."

She nodded seriously. "It's been true before."

"A lot of people think it's not possible we can be anything else."

Sylvia smirked. "You are not dangerous because you are black. You are dangerous because you are powerful. I served with many blacks in the resistance, and we were all dangerous. But so were the Nazis. Which are you?"

"I'm not a Nazi," Jack said, "I can assure you of that."

Benny nodded. "I can vouch for him on that one. I would know. Plus, I don't think they'd let him in. Me? Open invite, I assume. But I'm not interested. No, I've always steered clear."

"You are the clown," she said. "You need a mask, clown." She pointed to one aisle over. "There," she said.

The boys followed her finger to the shelf and saw three

149

masks. Each was gray and simple, with eye and mouth holes, but no decoration. "Kind of boring," Benny said.

"Try one on," she replied, blowing smoke rings their direction, "unless you are afraid, clown."

Benny's lip curled, and he reached for the first mask. Jack's hand shot out and caught Benny's. "Maybe we should wait for Mr. Wheeler—for Wheeler."

Benny shook his head. "I'm trying it." He grabbed the mask and put it on. His back was to Jack. Jack looked past Benny to the suddenly smiling face of Sylvia. Her dark teeth grinned against painted red lips, and Jack tapped Benny on the shoulder, turning his friend around.

Jack leapt back.

The face looking back at Jack was his own. It was like a distorted mirror, and Benny had disappeared behind it. Jack reached for the mask. "Take it off!"

"What is it, Jack?" Benny asked, blocking Jack's hand.

"*Quoi!* Hey, there!" Sylvia shouted.

The boys stopped. She pointed to a tall mirror on the wall, and the boys walked to it. Gazing in the mirror, Jack saw two of himself, and Benny saw what he looked like.

"Weird," Benny said, touching his face carefully. "I'm you, Jack."

Sylvia set aside her paper and stood from her chair. "What were you thinking right before you put on the mask, clown?"

"I don't remember," Benny said.

"Something about being the jester for your king there—the dangerous black boy?"

"He's my friend," Jack replied, "and I'm no king. I'm just a kid."

"You aren't just a kid, Jacque Zulu," she said, "you are destined to greatness. It is written in the night skies and on every line in your hand. You are dangerous, Jacque. Dangerous, indeed."

Benny pulled off the mask and was clearly relieved to see his own face again in the mirror. He moved to replace the mask on the shelf.

"Tut," Sylvia said, "you break it, you buy it."

"We didn't break it," Benny replied.

"But you did use it," she said, "and it only has five more uses before its enchantment is ended. So, you must pay for it."

"You can't make us pay for that," Jack said. "You told us to try it on!"

She looked at Benny. "Does he always disappear you into a plural? Are you nothing without him? Can you not have a talk with me without your dangerous king interrupting and fighting your battles?"

Benny frowned. "I don't have Wayland money, lady."

"I accept U.S. dollars," she said. "That one is fifty dollars."

Benny pulled out his wallet and drew out two twenty-dollar bills. "That's the best I can do."

"I would have done it for ten," she said, snatching the two bills and placing them in her register. *"Merci beaucoup."*

Jack scowled at her smiling face as Benny crammed the gray-faced mask into his backpack. Wheeler emerged from the back with two long blades in leather sheaths. "Charge my account?" he asked.

"But of course, Wheeler," she replied. "But keep an eye on your little king there. He reminds me of a man I used to know. A man that is more than a man now and sitting in a prison down the road."

"Jack is no Rancast," Wheeler said. "Do not say such things, Sylvia, I beg! I trust him, and he is a good soul."

"You once said the same about Rancast," she replied.

Wheeler shook his head, then headed for the exit.

Soon they were bumping along in a carriage on their way back to the town center, the tower and the tree looming large on the distant skyline. The boys examined their new swords as they rode. Jack loved the blade Wheeler had chosen for him, and he tested its weight. He smiled and expressed his gratitude again and again, but the shopkeeper's words nagged at him. "What did she see in me that reminded her of Rancast?"

"Greatness, perhaps," Wheeler replied. "Rancast isn't good, but he is great. Right now, you are good, but not great. When you become great, you will have a choice about whether you will still be good. You can exalt yourself or humble your heart. You can choose the way of life or the way of death. There are no other paths."

"How do you stay humble?" Jack asked, looking from his new sword to the one at Wheeler's side.

"My life," Wheeler replied, "is a constant invitation to self-sacrifice. I am a sage, yes; a warrior, yes. I am someone with status in the Wayland. I could let that turn me to the way of death, but I try to surrender every day. I try to live my life as an action of surrender."

"Doesn't the sword make it harder?" Benny asked. "It sounds like the Prism Blade is something people would kill for."

"It is that," Wheeler replied. "Rancast has tried to kill me for it many times. But even owning this blade means surrender. If I go the other route, I am doomed. Many think this blade means I can never surrender, but it is not so. It means that every day I must surrender. I must be owner, never owned. I must use this as a servant and must be a servant myself to something greater, or I am lost—lost as Rancast is."

"Do you pray, Mr. Wheeler?" Benny asked.

"Every day, I do," Wheeler replied. "Where else can I go? And I have been praying about Myrtle lately. There are some signs that other pathways may open. Have you heard of thin places, boys?"

Jack nodded. "Where the spiritual and earth planes are close?"

"English?" Benny asked.

"There are places on earth," Wheeler said, "in fact they are in all worlds, where gateways could be built. They are liminal spaces, or thin places. They have usually been seen as places where Faerie, or another dimension, is close to ours. Most humans since our so-called 'Enlightenment' dismiss them as bogus, but they do exist. I am concerned that the thin places in Myrtle may be accessed."

"What happens then?" Benny asked.

"Well," Wheeler said, gazing off toward the tower and the tree, "then anything could get through."

"Through into Myrtle," Jack asked, "beyond the gate radius—to our homes, our school, the hospital?"

Wheeler sighed. "Yes."

Chapter Sixteen

Pavilion
Siege

The carriage let them out on the edge of the common green closest to the Gock.

"Now boys," Wheeler said, reaching for the new swords, "you will earn these blades if you do not disgrace me in the battle today."

"Battle?" Benny asked.

"Yes, a battle."

"Not sure we're quite ready for that after a single very one-sided session with you last night," Benny said.

"You are not ready," Wheeler replied, motioning for them to follow him, "but this will be a good test and a baptism by fire into the martial arts."

"Like a karate tournament?" Benny asked.

"You may use karate, if you like," Wheeler replied. They followed him up an incline to the top of a hill where they gazed down on acolytes assembled in two opposing camps across a long field. Spectators gathered on staggered steps like an old amphitheater stadium on the long edge of the rectangular field. Huge banners flew above two opposing pavilions about a football field's length away from each other. Each pavilion was flanked by four smaller flags on thin poles stuck into the ground. They looked like slightly larger golf hole flags, each a small copy of the huge banner flying above the pavilion. The near army's flags were red with blue trim and a symbol of a stag's head in maize gold. The far side's flags were purple and silver, but Jack couldn't make out the symbol. Wheeler pointed to the stag team's pavilion. "The contest is called Pavilion Siege, or 'Pav,' for short. Report there to the commander and ask to be admitted provisionally to his army. If he rejects you, then cross to the other side and beg for a place in their army. Hopefully one side will accept you."

"What are the rules of…Pav?" Jack asked, his heart racing with a mixture of fear and excitement.

"They are fairly simple," Wheeler answered. "You have a weapon—the wooden sword we fought with yesterday. As for strategy, it is like your game of capture the flag, but your object is to spike their pavilion. The pavilions are tents, and if you can destroy the enemy's pavilion, then you win. Alternately, you may carry off a majority of their flags and plant them in your own pavilion row to win. This happens less frequently these days but once was more common. You will be suited with a vest and headguard, each containing burst-able pockets of a liquid—think of them as small, sturdier water balloons. If you are struck and any of these bloodpockets burst, you are dead and must lie still upon the field until the battle ends."

Benny nodded. "So, run out there and get swatted with wooden swords until we fake bleed to death?"

Wheeler laughed. "Well, I hope you shall do a bit more than that, Benito, but my expectations are not unreasonably high for your first outing. Now, boys, you must be going."

"Yes, sir," Jack said. He patted Benny's back as they began to jog across toward the pavilion. "We've got this, bro."

Benny cocked his head at his friend. "I'm pretty positive we do not have this. I for sure do *not* have this."

Wading through a sea of acolyte soldiers, all geared up with bloodpocket vests and fitted with red armbands, they reached the busy pavilion, which was fixed to the ground by four stout cords. Jack's heart raced, and the nervous energy of the first game of the season coursed through his body. He asked the guard if they could speak to the commander. The guard, frowning contemptuously, held up a finger and stepped inside. Returning a moment later, he said, "The commander is very busy. He will give you twenty seconds to state your business."

Jack nodded and entered through the opened tent flap. Inside, several senior acolytes gathered around a table, discussing battle strategy. They all wore the red armbands, but theirs were decorated with ranks, and each wore a kind of hood with blue and red stripes around their headgear. A series of quick three-horn blasts sounded outside, and the guard ducked his head inside and saluted. "Fifteen minutes, if you please, Commander."

The commander turned, a tall dark Thandalian with an eye patch. It was Tytrus. *Of course*, Jack thought. Tytrus saluted the guard. "Thank you, guard." Then he looked at Jack and Benny, a dismissive expression on his face. "What's your business here?"

"Sir," Jack said, imitating the guard's salute, "we are here to ask permission to join your army provisionally for this battle. May we join, sir?"

"You're imposing upon our Pav, are you? And you want to join my army?" he asked, hands hooked into the neck of his padded battle vest. His helmet—topped with a kind of golden crown—lay on the table where his fellow officers planned their attack.

"If you please, sir," Jack replied, with a quick bow.

"Could be humorous." Tytrus grinned. "All right, then. Scum of the army. Melee attackers. Get suited up and get out of my command tent."

Jack saluted and they left. To the guard, he said, "We're joining the army. Where do we suit up?"

The guard pointed to a row of tables where acolytes of all shapes and sizes were fitting out in vests and headgear. As they approached, Jack studied the gray-white suits. The vests had four large pockets in front and back, and the headguard, like an Olympic boxer's, had one pocket across the forehead and one larger bloodpack on the back of the head. Reaching the table, he and Benny were quickly geared up by the smirking quartermaster, including a battered wooden sword each. "Don't lose any teeth," he said, shoving them toward the pavilion.

"Where do we go?" Jack asked.

"What are your orders?"

"Commander said we're with the melee attackers. Where's that?"

The quartermaster laughed. "Front of the army. That gang of idiots too green for any real participation in the battle. You'll find them gathered at the front like frightened mowetts for the butcher's cart."

"Sounds awesome, thanks," Benny said, and the boys turned back to locate their assigned place. Benny's Myrtle

High baseball hat poked out from under the headguard, and his braces glinted in the sunlight. Jack inhaled deeply. *Not exactly Achilles.*

"Don't be scared," Jack said. "It's like their version of gym class."

"Except with swords. And, like, real violence," Benny replied. "This is not good, Jack. Not good at all. I'm rethinking everything."

"Where's your backpack?" Jack asked.

"Wheeler's got it."

"That mask would've come in handy," Jack said, squinting as he scanned the layout of both armies.

"Yeah," Benny replied. Another horn blast, this time two in quick succession, sounded over the green. "One minute, I think."

Just as they reached the twenty or so soldiers in the melee group—an unimpressive band—Tytrus emerged from his pavilion and raised a hand for silence. He held his gold-crowned helmet at his hip and spoke loud enough for all the gathered army—about a hundred acolytes—to hear. "Remember what they did to us last battle? We will not suffer a third loss in a row. It has never happened that we lose three battles on the trot since I came to command. It cannot happen today. Follow your officers' orders. We have a strategy that will lead us to victory—if we all do our part. Think of the whole, not just yourself," he said, and his eyes fell on Jack. "And fight for our colors!"

The gathered acolytes in red armbands shouted a hearty cheer, then turned to face the enemy. A last, single trumpet blast and another shout echoed across the field as the melee attackers, prodded by shouts and threats of the officers at their back, charged ahead.

Jack ran with them, staying close to Benny. Benny shuffled along, his eyes darting back and forth in panic. The enemy army's melee band clashed with theirs, and a clumsy fight ensued. Jack glanced back and saw amusement on their officers' faces, including Tytrus, who watched with undisguised mirth. "Go on," he shouted, "decorate the field!" Jack assumed this was a traditional start, where the least qualified acolytes would battle it out for the amusement of the crowd and the more senior soldiers—a preliminary to the real battle.

I am no pawn.

The first enemy soldier, purple armband on his raised arm, reached him and swung clumsily at Jack's head. Jack ducked the swipe and kicked the attacker's middle. The clumsy kid's bloodpack burst, and purple fluid soaked his cloak. He fell with a disappointed groan.

Jack swiveled to see Benny dodging attacks from two enemies and he darted over to his friend, striking one enemy on the back with the wooden blade, the attacker's pack bursting at once. Benny tripped backwards to avoid the second soldier's punch, and Jack darted quickly between them. He blocked a telegraphed stab, then spun and swatted his opponent's head. The bloodpack burst and oozed over the dejected kid's face as he fell to his knees, then the ground. The red-clad crowd, laughing only a moment before, oohed and aahed at Jack's fighting. Some pointed and began to cheer.

Jack spun to help Benny up, calling, "Follow me!" Benny fell in behind Jack as he raced away from the sluggish melee and toward the enemy line—about thirty yards away.

"Jack," Benny gasped out, "where the heck are you going—are *we* going?"

"I'm not sure!" Jack said, and it was an honest answer. What was he supposed to do? He knew he didn't like the script he had been delivered: go die like a fool in the pre-match entertainment. He wanted to die more gloriously. "For the pavilion!" he cried and darted for it, leaving Benny gasping behind him.

Jack rushed ahead, and the amused expressions of those around the enemy pavilion turned to anger, then alarm. The pavilion was not well-defended at this moment. Jack swallowed hard. *I guess this mad tactic isn't normally used.* He drew near the soldiers guarding the pavilion amid shouts from the enemy commander. Flummoxed by the surprise move, he ran out himself to face Jack. A much older student, the enemy commander was tall and strong, and his crowned headgear loomed high above Jack.

"What the devil?" he cried as Jack, instead of slowing, increased his speed. The crowd rose in expectation. They would soon come together, and Jack had no idea what he would do. Glancing at the tall commander's legs, he decided.

Ten feet from the clash, Jack tossed his sword high in the air and darted at the enemy. Just before he reached him, Jack slid—baseball style, like stealing a base—between the legs of the leaping commander. A wooden sword whooshed by Jack's head, and the young speedster emerged behind the commander as Jack's own sword arced down. Jack snagged it and brought it down hard in a slash against the shocked leader's back. His bloodpack blew apart and splattered the field.

Dumbfounded, the commander fell to the ground as his stunned officers groaned and a hundredfold gasp sounded from the enemy army. A moment passed. Another. Then a cheer from the red army and their crowd filled the air, and Jack felt the whole of the enemy force approaching. He didn't wait but raced directly at the pavilion.

They were closing fast, but many were attacking from the sides. He left them on the field in front of the pavilion tent as he raced ahead. The first enemies to reach him were easy to dodge around, but the last line of soldiers formed in front of his object—the pavilion—and crouched with swords poised. Jack blocked a swipe by the guard on the far left, then ran for the nearest purple flag. He tore the flagpole free with his left hand. With his sword in his right hand he blocked wild strokes from angry trailing soldiers. He ran for the next flag but stopped suddenly and spun back, causing his chasers to slide past him and collide into one another. His confidence rose. It was plain they hadn't dealt with someone like him before. Those hours of sandlot football imagining he was Cowboys' running back Tony Dorsett hadn't been wasted.

Jack raced for the pavilion and, quickly switching the flagpole to his right hand and his sword to his left, launched the flagpole like a javelin. It struck the side of the command tent, tearing away a section of the pavilion. Papers scattered within, and an angry shout followed from the officers in pursuit. Meanwhile, a side glance told him that Benny had fallen, and the red army across the way was cheering louder than ever and rushing the field to meet the disorganized enemy.

As he ran, Jack raised his sword to the red host, and they shouted an exuberant war cry. The crowd cheered louder and louder. Jack smiled and shaped a dodging course to the pavilion. Enemies multiplied, and they struck at him as his fleet-footed jaunt neared its end. Seeing he could not dance away anymore, he lunged for the tent and swung his blade, snapping free two of the four cords holding the pavilion down.

Hammering blows fell on his back and head as the blood-packs exploded all over his body. He slid to a stop as the enemy pavilion lifted and flew up on one side. For a moment, he held his breath along with every soldier around, but the tent settled and held in place. He lay still, a few feet from enemy headquarters, while the red army poured in and overwhelmed their purple opponents.

Chapter Seventeen

Encounter at the Old Stone Bridge

J ack was wiping the purple liquid from his face with his sweatshirt sleeve when Tytrus found him on the field. "If you were really in my army," Tytrus hissed, "I'd invoke article nine and have you sidelined with a ten-week battle ban."

Jack got to his feet slowly. His back ached from the battering he'd endured, and his head was ringing. "Commander, I'm not sure what I did wrong."

"You disobeyed orders, Vandal!" he snapped.

"I was given no orders, sir," he replied, rubbing his head.

"It doesn't matter," Tytrus said, "you proved what you are today, a self-centered Vandal who is looking for personal glory at the expense of his duty to his companions and community. You are just like Rancast."

The well of Jack's calm coolness was deep, but not endless. "That's not true," he said, raising his voice a fraction.

"Just like him," Tytrus repeated quietly to Jack as the crowd swelled around the victorious commander and the hero of the day.

"What a tactic!" one soldier shouted, clapping Tytrus on the back. "Well done, Commander!"

Others poured in, and they tried to raise Jack on their shoulders. They didn't succeed, but they carried Tytrus off toward a celebration of their triumph and begged Jack to come.

"Thank you," he said, again and again, shaking hands with many happy acolytes with red armbands. When the crowd had thinned, he found Benny waiting at the edge, his face covered in purple ink. "Do I look as bad as you?"

Benny bowed with an elaborate hand flourish. "I think not. If you had turned back from your wild, fantastic gallop, you would have seen a certain Benito Marino charging after you."

"How far did you get?" Jack asked.

"Not far. No, no. Not far at all, my friend," Benny replied, inhaling deeply. "I slipped as they came for me, hit myself in the head with my sword, splattering this grody ooze on my face. But I didn't fall immediately. No such luck. Blinded, I tried to rush away and staggered into a big-bodied soldier so hard that I burst both our bloodvests, or whatever they're called. When I sorted my eyes out and caught my breath, I saw that it was Commander Eyepatch himself I had killed in my moment of glory."

"Not the best stats for opening game," Jack said, hiding his grin with a purple hand.

"Indeed, sir," Benny agreed. "Two killed, both on our side. Not the best numbers. I believe you killed the enemy commander?"

Jack nodded. "It seemed like the right thing to do."

"Well," Benny agreed, hooking an arm around Jack's neck as they turned back to where they had left Wheeler, "it probably is better to kill the enemy commander rather than your own. I see that now."

"Perhaps," Jack said, laughing out loud now. "But we both made an impact. The good news is, my dear Benny, that despite our victory, Commander Tytrus still really hates us both."

"That is shocking," Benny replied. "I mean, I know *you* don't deserve his respect, but I really thought I earned it out there."

They heard a voice from behind. "Hey, Vandal!"

They spun to see the elf girl from the aqueduct job. Jack waved. "So-addan?"

"Yes," she replied. "I just wanted to congratulate you." They shook hands.

"Thanks very much," Jack said. "It was dumb luck."

So-addan shook her head. "No, it was neither dumb nor luck. It was a refined instinct, physical mastery, and light-ning-fast intelligence. I'm not sure your tactic has ever been tried before in the long history of Pavilion Siege. I am a student of Pav. I'm writing a treatise for Master Du on the subject. I'd like to interview you for it sometime, if I may?"

Jack shrugged. "Okay?"

Benny smirked playfully. "If you want anything from old Benny here, I'm free as well. I also took out a commander on the battlefield today."

So-addan smiled. "Your own, correct?"

"Details that can be glossed over, for the record," Benny replied with a mischievous grin.

"Well," she replied, "you did accomplish an incredible feat today, Benny. You made Tytrus even more angry than he already was."

"What's his deal?" Benny asked.

So-addan's smile disappeared. "He does have reason for his anger. He's my cousin, so I know more of his story than anyone else here. It's an unhappy tale."

"What happened?" Jack asked.

"When he was very small, he was at the Thandalian festival in the Valley of Stars and the eighth day had come. He was excited because this was his first chance to hold a candle. He was proud to be old enough to be trusted with the flame. We were all excited to witness the coming of the Thaons over the Valley of Stars. But Rancast's army came instead, and a shardhark murdered his family in the attack. Little Tytrus tried to fight the monster, but it swatted him away, tearing out his eye in the encounter. He was left on the ground, bleeding and alone, clutching his blackened candle to his chest. That was the last festival. He made his way, after many years, to the Wayland. He's excelled here, partly because of the fuel of his rage against Rancast and all Vandals. He's a wounded soul, and he wounds others from his great pain. I'm sorry his anger has landed on you."

Jack shook his head. "Thank you for telling us, So-addan."

"Jack lost his dad," Benny said, "and his mom is pretty sick."

"I'm sorry," So-addan said. "There is pain everywhere, I suppose. Well, I must go and join the others. Are you coming?"

"We have to meet up with Wheeler," Jack said. "We may come, if there's time. Thanks for the invitation."

She nodded and waved as she walked away.

Benny let out a sigh as they walked on. "Welp, that was a downer."

Jack nodded. "How could you not be angry if that's what happened to you?"

Encounter at the Old Stone Bridge

They reached the spot where Mr. Wheeler had left them. The sky was darkening as one sun set and the other, more distant, was dipping low. Jack looked around, a sudden worry springing up inside. "Where is he?"

A Thandalian in black walked up and handed Benny his backpack and Jack a note. Without a word, he hurried away. Jack read the note aloud. "J and B—I am called away on urgent business. Get to the gate as soon as you can—before sunsset. You must not be in the park after dark."

Benny's forehead wrinkled. "We'd better go, Jack. It's late. And Mordok is waiting."

"Right." Jack stripped off his vest and headguard and, taking Benny's, ran to the provisioner and set them on the table. Turning back, he met up with Benny, and they ran along the green for some time until they reached the road to Wayfarers' Inn. They ran on, dodging scooters and nodding to a mouterslaab band that stopped to glare at them. Passing the old tavern, they hurried to the gate.

They jogged the last foggy yards. Jack reached the gate and turned back to Benny, who was trailing him. "B, we don't have the key."

Wheeler stepped from the fog. "Quickly, now," he said, producing the key. Extending it, he said, *Clavis Ignum*," and the gate swished open. Myrtle at dusk appeared, the Ancient Glade eerie and quiet. Jack stood between two worlds, glancing between both.

"Will you go with us, Wheeler?' Benny asked.

"I cannot," Wheeler replied, glancing back into the fog. A huge figure stood shrouded in the misty gap between them and the distant gate to forbidden Kaalgrad.

A deep, menacing voice came from the fog. "Let us go into the land of Kaalgrad, Wheeler. Rancast's destiny depends upon our haste."

Wheeler pointed through into Myrtle. "Beware of crows. Be careful. Be quick. I shall see you tomorrow."

"Let's go, Jack," Benny said, stepping through the gate. Jack nodded and, with a last glance at the towering form in the fog, he followed Benny through.

Twilight loomed in Myrtle, and the two boys sprinted until they shot out of the Ancient Glade. They mounted their bikes outside the shed, eyes darting in all directions as the sky purpled over with thick, threatening clouds. Frightening shadows formed as the single sun dipped lower. Lower. They launched into a driving ride, pedaling like mad till they descended the last hill and finally, gasping with exhaustion and relief, rolled past the twin parapets on the park side and then the parapets on the town side of the old stone bridge.

Sliding to a stop, they inhaled deeply and said nothing for a while, just breathing in and out.

Jack smiled over at Benny. "We made it."

Benny nodded, a weary smile appearing on his face. But it disappeared quickly when the brush by the edge of the bridge shook. Benny, nearest the tangle of brush, fell off his bike and dug into the gravel as he scrambled away. Jack leapt forward as a scraggly woman rushed from the shadows and, rasping out high-pitched soothing sounds, loomed over the boy as he clawed away. "Ben! Benny baby, it's all right, now. Oo-oo, dear mine. Allegra's here, my doll."

"Allegra?" Benny held his hands up, shielding his face from the dirty woman with wild hair and tattered black clothes.

"Get off him!" Jack snapped, fist cocked.

"Fie!" Allegra cried, baring her brown teeth at Jack. "I'll claw out your eyes, golden child!"

"Leave him alone!" Jack shouted, grabbing Benny and pulling him back.

Allegra hissed at Jack. She stepped forward, her stringy hair parting to show a series of face tattoos. "Benny, my baby, my doll. Let me help you."

"Get away!" Jack said and cocked his fist again.

"No, Jack," Benny said, reaching for Jack's poised arm. "Don't hit her. She's sick."

Allegra hissed. "Not sick, Benny baby. Not sick. Why would you say that? I'm well. Better than well. I know the way. I have found the way, my Benny baby."

"Allegra," Benny said, hands open and voice calm. "Won't you let us help you? We can get you somewhere safe. Father Lorenzo will gladly—"

"Hypocrites!" Allegra screeched. "I don't need charity. I am powerful and full of earth's energy. I am a goddess of vibrant grove and green valley. I am the force of vine and path. I am the magick of ways."

"You're nuts," Jack whispered.

Benny scowled at Jack, then turned tenderly back to the frenzied woman with wild eyes. She pointed a bony finger at Jack just as the sky cracked with a booming thunder and a jagged stab of lightning arced behind her in the park. Revealed by the lightning, on the other side of the bridge and mounted on one of the parapets, was Mordok. The shardhark bellowed a shriek and raised his wings.

Allegra's eyes grew wider as a second stab of lightning

illuminated her tattooed face. "No man commands me, Dead-man's Son," she cried over the rising noise of the sudden storm. "I am mistress of the nightwalkers and coven mother of the Order of the Fading Sun."

"Go!" Jack cried, shoving Benny toward his bike. Benny mounted with a quick backward glance of pity at Allegra, and the boys pedaled like mad for the Marino house. Rattling thunder and stabbing strikes of lightning punctuated their escape. They raced past a smoldering tree that hissed in its charred-out middle. Allegra's warning wail followed them down the road as the rain cascaded down.

Chapter Eighteen

The Lost
Dance

J ack woke early, before the sun rose over Myrtle. He said his prayers, did his fifty pushups and crunches, then ate a bowl of Cap'n Crunch. While he ate, he read the rest of the tenth chapter of *Great Blades and Their Masters*, picking up where he'd left off when he fell asleep the previous night. He was home. Despite his fear and the invitation from the Marino family to stay with them, he had insisted on going home. *If I start letting fear control what I do, I'm finished.*

He packed his lunch in a brown bag, including two bologna sandwiches and a Star Crunch cookie, and headed out the door. At school, Michelle's book club met at lunch to talk about *Treasure Island*, and Jack, chomping his sandwiches, tried not to embarrass himself. He nearly succeeded, but for an unfortunate sudden coughing laugh that sent chewed bologna chunks flying into Michelle's hair. "I'm so sorry," he said as he fought off the choking cough that went on and on till he stumbled into the dim hallway and found relief at the water fountain.

After school, he and Benny visited the hospital. His mom's weakness was impossible to hide, and her prognosis was unchanged. They prayed and laughed together until she kicked the boys out to go enjoy a beautiful day.

With Jack's heart aching, they left to meet Wheeler at Wayland's gate. They told him about the previous night's encounter with Allegra and that they saw Mordok on the park side of the bridge. "Did you see any crows?" Wheeler asked. They shook their heads.

In the Wayland, they toured several class sessions of acolytes and only ran afoul of Tytrus once. Throughout the day, Wheeler continually expressed alarm at what Allegra had said and done. He muttered, "Thin places, forsooth," and shook his head. "Anything might come through, and then the gate radius is no sure thing." They practiced swords with Wheeler in front of the foggy gate before sunset and made it across the old stone bridge with plenty of time to spare. No sign of Mordok. No sign of Allegra.

A good day.

They fell into a routine of school, hospital, and Wayland for a succession of weeks. At Myrtle Middle School, Jack coasted. He skipped the baseball cookout and never played at the park when pickup games were on. He enjoyed Michelle's book club but did nothing else extracurricular, resisting the football and the newly formed soccer teams' coaches' urgent pleading to join their teams. Soccer was tempting, however, because he did love the game and it had been his dad's favorite sport. But Jack was laser-focused on getting out of Myrtle, and his main strategy was to escape by way of the Wayland. Baseball had become his backup plan.

Benny stayed afloat in school but lost out to a rival broadcaster in his hopes of being the official announcer of the football team's home games. He did, however, get to do in-school P.A. announcements and split his weekend hours between the Wayland and working at the family restaurant. On Sundays, he went to Saint Andrew's Catholic Church, and Jack went to Ebenezer Baptist.

Jack's mom continued to worsen, losing weight and sleeping more and more. Dr. Singh applied to have her join an experimental treatment, but she hadn't been admitted yet. Jack's urgency to get her into the Wayland grew intense. He learned that if he passed his novitiate exams, he would be allowed to move into the Wayland and bring his mother. She could then receive care there. Wheeler warned him it wasn't certain they could treat her, but he did say it was the only way to admit her into the Wayland. Jack was resolute.

Jack's fame, which began in the battle melee, grew in the Wayland, alongside a resentful contempt fanned by Tytrus and his allies. Many could see nothing good about a Vandal, and they wouldn't give the new boys a chance. But Jack quietly gathered admirers as he thrived in classes and in every scholastic activity—even as a novice acolyte who wasn't officially in the academy yet. Tytrus booted him from his Pavilion Siege army, so Jack accepted an invitation to join a rival. In the Wayland, Benny struggled on in Jack's vast shadow, the same as he did in Myrtle. He bought a secondhand—possibly once-stolen—electroglider at Mademoiselle Sylvia's, and Jack often hopped on the back as they darted from class to class across the odd city bound by fog. This did not improve their popularity, but it was handy. Benny excelled at the culinary arts and outshined Jack by miles in that course. Jack endured it, even enjoyed it, because of how happy it made Benny.

Vayner was in that class, and she became one of a small group of friends that resisted the pull of Tytrus and his allies to reject Jack and Benny.

Wheeler led them in and out every day at the tree gate, but many days that was all they saw of him. He was busy with the sages' council and their persistent problem of what to do with Rancast. Rumors grew that Rancast would escape and reclaim his power, and his devoted armies across many worlds were said to be inspired by the certainty of his return—especially the rebels in Thandalia. Talk of Rancast's escape became so pervasive that it seeded nearly every conversation. Things were tense inside and out of the Wayland, but Jack always preferred to be in the Wayland. His loathing grew for Myrtle and its sad hospital rooms and boring school. He worked hard to secure his escape.

In Myrtle, after the trees changed to a brilliant canvas of color, their leaves began to fall off and fade. Halloween arrived. The Marinos always made the most of the day, and the community often piled into Appalachianos after the school dance and trick-or-treating.

Heading to the dance, Jack sported his recycled Lando Calrissian costume from the previous year. Benny emerged from his dad's car dressed as Daniel LaRusso. Jack waved at Uncle Freddie, and the two friends engaged in their long, complicated handshake and high-five routine. Benny added an explosion sound effect at the end, but Jack shook his head. Benny smirked. "I think it adds something."

"It does. It adds lameness."

"That's a negative attitude, Jack," Benny said. "I don't think that's what Lando would say."

Jack's eyebrows shot up. "I am Lando, and I just said it."

"Come on, you ol' smoothie," Benny said, "let's get inside before someone else asks Michelle to dance before you."

"Oh, I'm not dancing," Jack replied as they walked. "I'm just here to see the costumes and build up my appetite to feast on candy and pizza tonight."

"Are we too old to go door to door and get candy?" Benny asked.

"Not even close, B. We've got years of sugar ahead of us before people start looking at us weird."

"What was that?" Benny said, grabbing Jack and pointing up at the treetops beside the school. Skeletal limbs stretched out across a peach evening sky.

"It's all that combat instruction you're getting, B. You're in a state of over-vigilance. According to Scribe Tentheron of Galden, it's from too much intense training. It's been a long few weeks, man; we're just supposed to have fun tonight. Sage's orders."

Benny shot one last glance at the treetops, then smiled and punched Jack's arm. They went inside and headed for the gym.

"Why aren't you DJing this dance?" Jack asked.

"We've been a little busy," Benny replied, "as you know. So I missed my chance and lost out to golden-throated Christopher Beltron."

"I'm sorry," Jack said. "Maybe you'll get another chance to spin some tunes soon."

Benny nodded. "Music speaks, when you can't figure out what to say."

"Dag, Benny, that's pretty deep."

Benny smiled. "I hope nobody pulls the fire alarm again. They never really got the party going again after that last year."

Entering the gym, they saw a few kids dancing, but most were plastered in knots around the edges of the gym while "Somebody's Watching Me" blared from a crackling sound system.

"Not a bad choice," Benny said, bobbing his head.

"Where is Chris DJing from?" Jack asked.

"You know," Benny replied, "it's up in the A.V. room on the fourth floor by the janitor's closet. Prime real estate."

"So he has to do the whole dance from up there, and he can't even see what's going on down here?"

"He's suffering for his art," Benny said. "I'd take the gig in a heartbeat."

"Jack!" Michelle called, as she and a few other friends crossed the gym floor. She wore a long blue dress that looked like something from Charles Dickens. "Hey, Benny. Jack, I thought we all agreed to go as book characters."

Jack held up his hands. "Lando is in the *Empire Strikes Back* novel by Donald F. Glut, so I have complied with the book club's rules."

She smirked. "I'll allow it, I suppose. Benny, I love the Ralph Macchio costume. The girls are all nuts for him."

"I'm not Ralph Macchio, Michelle," Benny replied. "I'm Daniel LaRusso. Huge difference. Huge."

"Well, if anything happens," she said, stepping into a karate pose, "it's good to know you can protect us with a crane technique."

"Does that work?" Benny asked. "Ever use it in a tournament?"

Michelle smiled. "If never done incorrectly, it can never be not proven to have never not worked."

Benny puzzled over that while Jack asked, "Who are you

pretending to be, a lady?" He winced as it came out, hand going to his mouth.

Michelle stepped back. "Is it so hard to imagine?" she said, feigning a wound. "I'm Eleanor Dashwood, from Jane Austen's *Sense and Sensibility*. My favorite novel, as I mentioned to you last week."

"Right," he replied, "sorry, Michelle. I didn't mean that."

"At least," she said, "you didn't blow chunks of bologna into my hair."

Benny bowed. "And may I say it looks even lovelier without the bologna chunks, if you can believe it."

"Thanks, B!" she said, cracking up. "Who wants to dance?" Everyone looked at Jack, and he smiled and looked away. Michelle smirked. "Come on, guys. Let's all just go out there together. We don't have to pair up. We're young. Let's just have fun and relax."

They followed her out, even Jack tagging along at the edge of the group. Bonnie Tyler's "Holding Out for a Hero" played, and they jumped around, singing along and dancing terribly. Even Michelle, who was a trained dancer, made it fun and goofy with her exaggerated leaps and twists. They were all laughing when the song ended, and they clapped and then headed for the refreshments table.

"That was fun," Jack said, handing Michelle and the other girls some punch. "I was determined not to dance, but that was fun."

Michelle received the cup of punch. "Thanks, Jack, but I'm not sure that what you were doing could be classified as dancing." They all laughed, Jack most of all, and the chatter continued till the group broke up in various waves and Michelle,

Benny, and Jack were alone.

"How's your mom?" Michelle asked.

"Thanks for asking," Jack replied. "She's struggling to stay awake much. She's lost a lot of weight. It's hard to watch."

"I'm sorry, Jack," she said. "I'm going to see her tomorrow, with Mom."

"Thanks. Your mom's visits have been a huge help. Mom loves her, and she always feels encouraged by her notes and the notes from the ladies at church."

They fell silent a while. Benny left to get a snack and then returned with a disturbed look.

"What's wrong, B?" Michelle asked.

"Probably nothing," he answered. "Just keep thinking I see something out of the corner of my eye."

Jack sat up. "Yeah?"

"Yeah."

Michelle frowned. "I wouldn't say this to most people, but do you guys ever feel like something's a little off in our town?"

Jack nodded. "Always."

"No, Jack," she said, frowning, "I don't mean the way you look down on Myrtle. I mean like something is happening here. Something weird. Like, from a movie." Jack and Benny looked at one another, then quickly away. Michelle pointed. "Like that, that right there; that was weird. What is going on? You two have been acting strange for a while. Even stranger than you always did."

Benny coughed and feigned offense. "I am just exactly as weird as I've ever been, thank you very mucho."

"Have you seen anything unusual?" Jack asked, with rising unease.

Michelle frowned. "It's hard to put a finger on it, but I did get this crazy feeling just before coming over here. I had this sense of sadness and worry come over me. I thought it was just anxiety about the dance maybe, though I've never felt that before. When I get anxious, my back itches. I know that sounds weird, but my back has been itching—hurting too—a lot lately. Then, I went outside to get some clothes off the line, and I saw a huge bird flying overhead. There was something odd about it, beyond just how big it was."

Jack rose. "I just remembered I need to talk to Mr. Wheeler."

"Me too," Benny said.

"Mr. Wheeler? The bookstore guy? Wait a second, guys," Michelle said, holding up her hands. "What's going on? You can tell me. Maybe I can help."

Benny looked nervously at Jack, and Jack tried to stay cool. "I've got to go to the bathroom," Jack said. He slipped past Michelle. Benny followed. A backward glance showed Michelle hanging her head.

Once in the hallway, Jack motioned for Benny to follow. "Should we contact Wheeler?"

"I don't know, Jack. I'm scared."

"Me too," Jack replied, "but it's not that bad. She saw a crow, probably, and you've been seeing something tonight, right? Is it a crow?"

"I don't know, Jack, man. It was like a shadow. A big one."

"Not great," Jack said, looking both ways. He pushed a door open into a classroom. "Let's think," he continued, jogging to the window and opening the blinds to peer outside. High in the topmost branches of the old oak tree beside the school and standing out stark against a reddening sky, a giant bird perched.

181

With a rasping shriek, it leapt heavily from the branch and, beating its wide wings, swooped down toward the school.

Chapter Nineteen

The Monster Mash

J ack spun around and dashed into the hallway, Benny on his heels.

"What're you gonna do?" Benny said, voice high with worry.

"We have to get everybody out of here," Jack said, ignoring the students he passed as he ran. "Find a phone, and call Wheeler's bookshop. Meet me at the bikes."

"How are you gonna get everyone out?" Benny asked.

"Go, Benny! Call Wheeler!"

Benny darted off toward the office, while Jack scanned the hallway walls. He jogged ahead, dodging a suspicious, scowling teacher emerging from the bathroom.

Finally, he found what he was looking for. A scream sounded from the far end of the school, followed by a loud pop. The lights flickered and died, leaving the hallways totally dark. The emergency lights began their throbbing pulse, and kids pushed past, hurrying down the hallway. Some were laughing, while others looked concerned. "It's real!" he shouted. "Get out, everyone!" They picked up the pace and he turned back to the wall. Jack pulled the fire alarm.

The ringing began at once, peeling in long bursts every ten seconds. He ran along the hallways, fearful a giant crow would swoop around the corner any moment. He snagged a fire extinguisher from the wall and hauled it along as he ran, shouting for students to get out of the building. Finally, after checking the empty office, he stowed the fire extinguisher by the door and ran outside. He saw Benny facing his direction amid a crowd of students headed away from the school. The principal was telling the kids to go on home or on to their trick-or-treating, because the dance was officially over, and the gym wouldn't reopen. A transformer had blown, and they wouldn't have power tonight. School, he said, would probably even be canceled tomorrow. That drew a cheer from the scattering students.

Benny saw Jack and hurried over. Jack glanced up at the school and saw some strange shadows cross over through the fourth floor windows. He reached Benny.

"See anything?" Benny asked.

"No birds," Jack replied. "Any luck reaching Wheeler?"

"None," Benny said. "Hey," he called, seeing the group of friends they had danced with earlier, "are you guys okay?"

"We're fine," Mary, a tall girl with braces, said as they drew closer, "but I'm worried about Michelle. She's supposed to be trick-or-treating with me and then sleeping over tonight. But she hasn't come out."

Jack didn't answer, just sprinted toward the door. He skidded to a stop by a group of costumed students, one dressed as baseball legend Pete Rose in a full Cincinnati Reds uniform. "Sorry," Jack shouted as he snatched the bat before running into the building. Benny trailed him, letting out a low whine of anxiety.

The halls were eerily quiet as the two boys slowed to walk beneath the dim, uneven glow of the slowly flashing emergency lights. Jack gripped the bat, a wooden Louisville Slugger, and glared into the gloomy hallway. Reaching the gym, he eased open the heavy door and peeked inside. There was nothing inside but streamers trailing from a lonely mirror ball in the gym center. The snack table was deserted, and the music was off.

Benny tapped Jack's shoulder and whispered, "They probably just didn't see her leave. She's probably fine."

"You're probably right," Jack replied, peering down the long corridor. "But probably's not good enough." He glanced at Benny's terrified face. "Hey, B. Go on out and tell Mary and the others that she's going trick-or-treating with us. Tell them everything is okay. I'll be back out in a bit. I'll just do a quick check." Jack pushed his friend in the right direction. "Go ahead, B. It's fine. I'll be out in a few—right behind you."

Benny turned to go, hesitated, then left in a slumping jog.

Jack turned back to the hallway and walked forward. He found the stairway door and quietly eased it open. He raced up the four flights and emerged into the hallway. As he moved along and his eyes adjusted to the odd pulsing light, the shadows cleared, revealing an overturned table, with papers and books scattered over the linoleum floor.

Jack reached the corner and, rounding the bend, found the overhead emergency lights wrecked so that only two of the ten were working. Many of the usual long fluorescents mounted on chains were busted, some half-dangling and swaying weirdly in the half-light. The darkness at the end of this hallway was near total, and he strained to see what was hidden in its murky depths. A putrid smell filled Jack's nostrils, potent like a skunk but suggesting burnt feathers and hair. He nearly retched, turning it to a cough. When he looked up again, an enormous crow leapt from the gloomy end of the hallway and beat its wings in giant pumping motions toward him. Its beak split wide to reveal shark-like teeth, and the crow loosed a shriek that stunned Jack.

Jack staggered and bent, then rose in time to dive to the side. The biting beak just missed him, but a knife-like talon darted out, shredding the edge of his costume's cape. He lurched from the wall and pivoted back as the great bird turned and came at him again, its red eyes tracking his motions. Jack ducked as the collision came, and the beast tore at his side.

It was on him.

Jack shot out an elbow to defend his ribs. Bringing the bat up, he tried to protect his head. Jack grew desperate as the crow screamed in his ear, biting and clawing at him. He squatted low and then burst up, throwing the bird back. Then he turned in a circle and swung out with his bat, connecting with the creature's wing. A crack sounded, and the wing bent sickly down as the crow pitched sideways. It landed on its talons and squawked in rage, then ran at him. Jack choked up on the bat and stepped forward, prepared to deliver a deathblow, but at that moment a second crow shrieked from behind and glided at him, snapping its beak and baring its sharp talons. Jack ducked back, limbo-style, as the bird shot overhead, grazing his belly with its claws. Up in a moment, he ran further into the darker shadows the crows had come from. He heard them, flapping and scrabbling in pursuit.

Jack could vaguely make out the end of the hallway and the double doors leading to the stairway where he might escape. A hasty backward glance told him he would not make it. One crow was nearly on him. He breathed deeply and tried to think of his training. He stopped.

Jack Zulu turned to face the swooping crow. It cried out in grim delight as he did, murder in its eager eyes. He feinted as if he would dodge sideways, dropping the bat down low, then dug in his stance and brought the Louisville Slugger around in a driving cut that caught the shocked bird between its red eyes. There was a sickly crunch, and the crow fell in a ruin. Jack gasped as the fallen crow turned to ash, drifting away in a thousand brittle pieces that disappeared as they rose.

The second crow came, screeching as it ran looping up in half flight as its talons shot toward Jack. He swung his bat again, striking it full in the body so that it slid backwards ten feet. And there was Benny, flashing in. He blasted the fire extinguisher to further stun the creature. As its howl was drowned in the gagging spray, Benny gripped the fire extinguisher firmly in two hands and drove its solid end against the crow's head. It fell with a thud and, in a moment, was fading to ash and floating away, until it entirely disappeared, leaving only the residue of its acrid smell.

The two boys nodded to each other but had only a moment to be pleased. They heard a loud scuffling echo in the hallway. They knew what it meant. *More crows.* They raced through several hallways to reach the place and found a crow bearing down on Michelle, who stood alone in a classroom doorway beside a cart of janitorial supplies. Jack sprinted like mad, knowing he would be too late. He watched as the crow reached her. "No!"

Michelle ducked gracefully as the crow snapped its beak; then she stepped aside quickly, kicking out and connecting with the bird so that its momentum took it into the classroom. She slammed the door shut as another crow emerged from an open classroom across the hall.

Michelle reached for the janitor's cart and, in desperation, snagged a long mop. She struck out at the beast with the wet mop end, driving it back a moment. Then she drew the long mop handle back and snapped it over her knee. The crow beat its wings and darted at her. As its wings shot out, she drove the sharp end of the shattered mop handle into the open middle of the monster. With a hideous shriek, it fell and faded to ash. Jack reached Michelle's side, and they hugged, Benny joining in as he caught up, gasping.

"Are you okay?" Jack said in a hasty stammer.

"I'm okay, Jack. I've gotten past a few of them. You guys?"

"Yeah, we're okay," Jack replied. "We gotta get outta here."

Michelle frowned angrily, gazing through the window at the crow trapped in the classroom. "I don't like these things in my school."

Jack felt his blood rise, and he locked eyes with Michelle. He patted the bat in his hand as she reached for the broken mop handle. They nodded to one another. He reached for the door.

"Whoa, whoa, whoa!" Benny called and slapped Jack's hand. "Are you two crazy? We're not fighting these things. They're monsters from another world! We need to get out of here."

"You want to leave this for some janitor to find?" Michelle asked.

"Or some teacher?" Jack added.

Benny looked at them with a horrified disbelief. "Yes!" he said, his voice high. "Of course I do! We're children. Let's leave the monsters to someone else!"

Jack and Michelle exchanged a look. "Stand behind us, if you want, B," Michelle said. "We're not waiting for the janitor. We're going to clean this place up ourselves."

Jack nodded. "I'm with her, Benny. We need to deal with this. It's our fight. We're the reason they're here."

"And after that," Michelle said, "you can tell me what on earth is happening around here—the whole truth."

"What on earth indeed," Benny said, sighing. He glanced through the classroom window and saw the crow flying at the door. A loud slam followed, and the door rattled. Benny grunted. "Michelle, you're in a dress!"

She pulled up the hem of her elegant dress to show her dance leggings underneath. "I can move fine. Worry about yourself."

Benny exhaled heavily. "Okay, if we're going to do this, we need to hit them with everything we can. Confusion. Distraction. And, you know," he went on, gesturing at their weapons, "the hard and/or sharp stuff, too."

Another rattling smash, and the door hinges bent. "One more and he's through," Michelle said. Jack nodded, and they stood side by side in front of the door, Jack with his bat poised and Michelle ready with her makeshift mop-handle spear.

Benny checked the classroom and brandished his fire extinguisher. As the crow flew for the door again, Benny yanked it open and blasted the smoky foam in the crow's eyes. Jack swung clean and knocked the creature sideways, and Michelle followed with a killing stab.

The emergency lights pulsed as the three friends turned and, side by side by side, walked down the hall in the wake of the black ash fading.

Chapter Twenty

Caught at
the Crossroads

J ack battered the last crow with his home run swing, sending it wailing across the gym so far and high that it crumbled to dust before it landed. They had cleared the school, floor by floor, and each had a few new scars. Benny's bite wound was the worst. A crow had sunk its teeth into his left bicep before Michelle could kick it free and then impale it with her mop-handle spear. Jack was amazed at Michelle, but not surprised. She had more than held her own in the fight and seemed to come alive while they hunted down every last crow.

"Nice one, Jack," Michelle said, high-fiving him as the crow's ashy end punctuated their victory. "Benny, you okay?"

"It's sore," he replied from the gym floor, "but I'm not worried about it."

"What were those things?" Michelle asked.

"It's a long story," Jack answered, hurrying to Benny. He peeled back Benny's karate gi sleeve and looked at the wound. The wide bite marks were red and oozing green at their edges. "I think we need to get him some help."

"The hospital's not far," Michelle said, helping him up.

"I think we need to take him somewhere else," Jack said. Benny nodded. Jack, still gripping his borrowed Louisville Slugger, led Benny out of the gym and out the front doors. The cool air felt good, and he inhaled deeply. The foul-smelling crows had stunk up the whole school, and all three were grateful to be out in the fresh air again. The half-moon shone as kids in costumes received candy from porches all around the neighborhood. The school courtyard was empty except for the principal and a few others on the far corner near the power company truck. Workers gathered around the pole that held the burned-out transformer.

"Are you going to tell me what's going on?" Michelle asked as they all hopped on their bikes.

Jack nodded. "Yes, but it's going to sound weird and unbelievable."

"After what we just did," Michelle replied, "I'm ready to believe in weird."

Jack explained as much as he could as they pedaled past a busy Appalachianos and an abandoned Wheeler's Good Books. Michelle nodded, taking it far better than he expected. "So, anyway," Jack concluded as they passed Gander's gas station, "we're novice acolytes now—hoping to be full acolytes—and Wheeler told us if we ever had major trouble to go to the tree gate and tap on the keyhole knot three times. I'm not sure what else we could do."

"What if we meet up with Mothman?" she asked.

"That's why we kept our weapons," he replied, reaching back to be sure his borrowed baseball bat was still stuffed in his backpack. Michelle still carried the broken mop handle as she rode.

"Feeling a little woozy, guys," Benny said, swerving in the road.

Michelle steered her bike closer to steady Benny. "Maybe we should take him to the hospital."

"The gate to Wayland is closer now," Jack replied, "and anyway, if the crows are through some thin place, then maybe Mordok isn't bound by the old gate radius himself. We don't know what this could mean. The hospital might be just as dangerous as the park. And my mother's there. I don't want to lead some beast to her. We've got to find Wheeler."

"And Mr. Wheeler is some kind of senator there, in Wayland?" Michelle asked.

"Yeah, he's a sage," Jack answered. "Benny, can you pedal fast? We're going to take this hill and try to ride straight for the tree."

"Yeah," Benny said. "I can make it." He was sweating, but Jack didn't know if that was from the exertion of the fight and ride or the crow bite. He looked pale, but Benny kind of always looked pale. It was hard to tell in the moonlight.

"Let's go," Jack said, rising to pump the pedals, "as fast as we can."

Michelle nodded, and they flew down the last hill, shooting onto and over the bridge. Jack winced a little but tried to look brave for Michelle's—and Benny's—sake. They pedaled hard to reach the top of the little hill that led to the baseball diamond, with no sign of trouble. They passed the maintenance shed and picked up speed again, darting into the woods. Into the forbidding gloom of the Ancient Glade, they raced on.

"This is the creepiest night of my life," Michelle said as the three friends rode close to each other.

193

Jack nodded. "Let's hope it doesn't get any creepier."

"There it is," Benny said, nodding his head groggily toward the huge old tree. "See the keyhole knot?"

"I see it," Michelle said.

A sudden loud sound of beating wings came from behind them.

Jack acted fast, swerving his bike into Benny, who then collided with Michelle. They all fell in a sliding tangle as Mordok descended, lashing out with his single claw as he swept over them. Jack was first to pop up. He drew the bat from his backpack and prepared to strike.

Mordok banked, his huge form visible against the half circle of the moon, and then swept back toward the kids.

"The door!" Jack called. Michelle popped up and raced for the tree.

Mordok was intent on Jack, who was standing nervously in front of Benny. Benny had not risen from their bike wreck. Jack wanted to run, but he didn't dare leave Benny.

Mordok dove, his glistening wings nimbly bringing him close enough to strike out with his good right arm, claw arcing just over Jack's head as he ducked. Jack rose then, bringing the bat down on Mordok's arm. A grunt followed, and the monster's stubby left arm shot forward and struck Jack's face. Jack dropped the bat as he spun down.

Jack blinked on the forest floor, sure he had blacked out a moment. When he rose, Mordok held Benny in his powerful grip. Benny was unconscious, and Michelle lay motionless by the gate tree, still breathing, thankfully.

"Acolyte Jack," Mordok hissed, "where is the gate key?"

"I don't have it," Jack said, rising slowly to his knees, his voice quavering. "I think you know that."

"'Tis true," Mordok replied, "but you might get it for me." The shardhark extended a bony finger, tipped with a long sharp nail, to Benny's neck.

"Not him!" Jack cried. "Not him. He's no threat to you. Don't hurt him, please."

Mordok grinned, his slimy tongue licking his long teeth. "You are unacquainted, I fear, with the laws of battle—laws even shared across realms. I have conquered him in battle, and he is mine, by rights. So is the female. I may kill them at my leisure. They are trophies of combat."

"Take me, instead," Jack pleaded. "I'm no great warrior, but please take me instead of them. I'll be your trophy of war. Take me!"

Mordok looked at Benny's pale neck and swallowed. Leering back at Jack, he nodded and tossed Benny to the ground. Benny groaned, rolled over, and lay still. Mordok laughed at Jack's pained expression. "You weak fool. He is not worthy of your company. He is what we call in the Dominion a kaalfoon. But I agree to your terms. You are now owed to me, a debt I doubly own because you took my hand. But my master will restore all I have lost and more. He has heard of you, and he desires you to know the truth and so grants you and your kaalfoon a limited parole. I will come again for my debt, and you will do for me anything I ask."

Jack's heart raced, and he shook his head. "I can't just..." he began, but trailed off. Mordok took a step toward Michelle. Jack stepped forward quickly. "Yes," he said, "I agree to your terms. Send for me and I'll meet you. I'll do as you ask."

"It is well, Jack Acolyte," he said, smiling. "I will send a crow and call you to this place. Neither kill my crow nor refuse my summons. If you do, your life is forfeit. I will destroy you, your kaalfoon, and the girl as recompense."

Jack's stomach churned and his head swam. He didn't know how the laws of these other worlds worked. He didn't know how binding an agreement like this was. But he had no weapon—the bat, useless anyway, lay too far away to reach—and no way to defeat a monster like this. Maybe if he had the Prism Blade, or any blade, he could try. But he couldn't let Benny and Michelle die. He knew that. Jack nodded. "Yes, yes. I agree," he said, as his heart wrenched. Guilt spiraled into his gut, and he doubled over as the shardhark cackled and leapt into the sky, flying deeper into the Ancient Glade.

It felt like forever before Wheeler responded to the triple knock. Jack had tended to his friends and was about to try to drag them to the hospital in Myrtle when Wheeler finally arrived. "I am so sorry, Jack!" Wheeler cried, stepping through the foggy gate. "The council was voting to set a date for Rancast's removal from the Wayland. The thing hung there in the balance—the work of years and years! I dared not leave."

"It's okay," Jack replied. "We survived. But Benny got bitten by a crow, and we had a fight. Michelle joined in."

Wheeler's face went from deep concern to alarm. "Michelle fought with you? Tell me, Jack, was she hurt at all?" Jack pointed. "She's right there ... resting? I don't know how badly she's hurt. I think we all were hurt some. Maybe she just hit her head. I don't know." His throat was tight. "I didn't know what to do, sir. I don't know what to do."

Wheeler knelt and embraced the boy. "It's all right now, Jack. I am sorry, son. I should have simply come sooner. I perhaps could have and failed with the council—I do not know. I am here now, son, and we will get them help. A crow's bite is not fatal if it is treated quickly. Let us get Benny inside Wayland right away."

"And Michelle," Jack said. "We can't leave her here. Mordok's out there."

"Mordok?" Wheeler asked. "Did he find you?"

Jack nodded.

Wheeler frowned, kneeling to lift Benny. "All right now, Jack. You pick up Michelle and bring her along. We must find Benny some help. These bites are treated with a serum. I usually have some at the ready, but I failed to bring my pack when I hurried from the council. Come along, Jack."

Jack lifted Michelle, gazing at her beautiful face as he did, her curls catching moonlight. Jack's heart grew heavier still. He felt as if he had sold his soul and brought Michelle into an unpredictable world where dangers lurked around every corner. He remembered, then, how she had handled herself when danger *was* around every corner, back at the school, and he shook his head. Feeling more than he understood, he stepped through the gate into Wayland.

Chapter Twenty-One

A Book on
a High Shelf

I n a room on the second floor of the Wayfarers' Inn, Jack watched the apothecary spread balm on Benny's bite. Michelle remained unconscious on one of the beds in the corner.

Mrs. Hoff, a plump woman with an untidy tangle of hair in a disheveled bun, wiped her hands, touched Benny's cheek, and turned to Jack and Wheeler. "He'll be fine. Just needs sleep. Same as her—rare, beautiful child," she said, nodding to Michelle in the corner.

"Thank you ever so much, Mrs. Hoff," Wheeler said, bowing. Jack bowed as well.

"This for his wounds again in a few days," she replied, smiling and handing over the tin of balm, "and he'll be good as geff."

"Bless you," Wheeler said. "Should you like an escort back to your shop?"

She shook her head. "You know they'll not bother me. I'm just next door and am no threat to one nor the other. They'll call me when they've hurt who they've hurt, either side." Mrs.

Hoff straightened her apron, crossed to gaze at Michelle a moment, shook her head, then opened the door to leave. As she did, loud voices drifted up from the common room below. The door closed again.

Jack walked to the door. "What's going on? Have they heard about what happened with Mordok? Are they angry with me? I didn't know what to do. I had no sword or anything. I didn't have what I needed to make a good fight!" This last part was said bitterly, and Wheeler seemed to receive it as an accusation.

"I understand you, Jack," he replied, looking down. "You may be easy in your mind regarding the arguments downstairs. They are nothing to do with you. I regret what happened to you tonight, extremely. In no way would I diminish it, but allow some context. There is much more going on than you know or can fully understand yet."

Jack nodded. "Oh."

"I let you down, Jack, and I am sorry," Wheeler said.

"You were only doing your duty," Jack replied, "fulfilling your role as sage. I understand, sir. But can you help me understand what's happening?"

"You are a wise man, Jack Zulu. I shall tell you all. It is now the time of festival for the Thandalians. They are always sad, as are we all, during this time. The true festival cannot happen, not in Thandalia, for the war is raging, nor can it be properly done here in the Wayland, and the eighth day will not be what everyone knows it should be. So, it is a bad stage for these events with Rancast's fate. And, because we could get nowhere on the council regarding this matter till now, the timing of what has happened is much worse. At the sages' council tonight, we voted to banish Rancast, something I never thought possible. We cannot execute him, though in truth he deserves it. Because of those who vote to help him—like Raftereen and his ilk—the council cannot agree to such a punishment. We have always opposed banishment because there is nowhere he can be banished to that he cannot return from. Until now. I have secured an impenetrable prison on Kaalgrad, the realm he entirely ruined by his misrule. In the prison there, he will be unable—we hope and believe—to rejoin his army and extend his perverse dominion."

"Why are they arguing down there?" Jack asked, nodding toward the common room below.

"They have heard the word 'banishment' and believe it means he is going to be freed and exiled, only to return in power to murder and destroy once more. The council—because of Raftereen and his allies—could not issue a statement that clearly stated he was going to be imprisoned in Kaalgrad—but he is. Raftereen has made sure our joint statement could only say 'banishment,' and that has the good people of many races in the Wayland in a fury tonight. The Thandalian refugee camp is up in arms, of course, though some of their wiser elders—and their sage herself—are trying to help them understand. But the timing is awful, I readily admit. For the ordinary Thandalian refugee to hear that we are merely banishing Rancast during their sacred festival will seem a deep, heartbreaking betrayal, to be sure. It is a mess, Jack. And events like what happened tonight in Myrtle with Mordok and the crows are happening all over the twelve realms."

"It's what he wants," Jack said. "Rancast. He wants everyone fighting and hating each other so he can be free to prey on our divided parts."

Wheeler's eyebrows rose. "Very astute, young sir."

"Divide and conquer, right?"

"Indeed." Wheeler paced the floor. "In fact, Jack, I must return to my duties here. I must show my face among those debating, starting down below and then into the refugee camp itself."

"Isn't that dangerous?" Jack asked.

"It is all dangerous," Wheeler replied, smiling. "I am alive, son. And when you are alive, you can be killed. But it is not only that it's dangerous for me out there. I am also dangerous when I go out. I go out armed with the light, and I am dangerous to the darkness."

Jack smiled. "I wish I'd had your Prism Blade when I fought Mordok. I didn't have anything."

Wheeler paused his pacing. "Tell me what you had."

"Nothing at all. I had nothing."

"Forgive me now, Jack, but I do not believe you," Wheeler said. It was kindly said, but Jack was hurt. "Tell me every detail of what happened."

Jack did. He explained every angle and every move of the encounter with the shardhark. Mr. Wheeler asked him several pointed questions about the relative positions of people and objects, and Jack—a little irritated—answered each one. "So, I was standing there," Jack concluded after ten minutes of explanation, "empty-handed and with no options, so I had to make the deal."

"The deal is weighty, yes, but you needn't feel overly obliged. You must do what is right, regardless of what agreements you made. If you had agreed, wrongly, to drown a baby, you would be doubly wrong to follow through." Wheeler stroked his beard and two wrinkle lines formed between his intent eyebrows. "I have taught you many maxims of battle, have I not?"

Jack nodded. "Yes. Fight the man, not the blade. Attack by considered defense and defend by considered attack. Men defend by vigilance. The eyes, not the hands…"

"Yes, yes," Wheeler said, holding up his hand. "Tonight, you shall hear another, harder lesson. Can you hear it, Jack? Are you prepared to receive it now?"

"Yes, sir," he answered, swallowing hard.

Wheeler sat down beside Jack on the bed and looked him in the eyes. "You already have what you need."

Jack looked down, and a thousand objections rushed to his mind. He started to speak but fought back the urge to spout off his first, emotional reaction. He breathed in and out and considered. After a minute, he spoke. "Respectfully, sir, I did not have what I needed. I needed a good weapon. I was a pawn, and I needed to be a knight. I needed what I didn't have. I needed more."

Wheeler nodded. "It is a kind of true, what you say. But it is a kind of falsehood. Have you read Sage Pernith?"

"No, sir."

"He was a Thandalian scholar of the last age. He said, 'We see that our hands are empty and cry out for our lack, when we should see that we have hands and kneel in gratitude.'"

"I was supposed to fight him with my bare hands?" Jack asked.

"It is not to be taken literally, although you had some options there. But I will not pile on, dear Jack, with verbal blows to bring you lower. I am your friend, to be certain. I will only say that I have found, in your own account, twenty-seven ways you could have fought back against Mordok. That you did not see them is no indictment of you, understand? You will learn, given time. I am a warrior of centuries."

"If you had the Prism Blade, sure—" Jack began.

"No, Jack. Without the blade, or any blade, there were still many options," Wheeler said. "If you cannot be a noble warrior without an enchanted blade, then you should never wield one at all."

Jack shook his head. "I'm trying to understand, sir. You think I could have fought Mordok with what I had—which was *nothing*?"

"No, son," Wheeler replied, "I am saying you surrendered when you believed the lie that you had nothing—when you believed the lie that you did not have what you needed. You lost when you looked at your empty hand and did not see a hand. You lost when you believed a pawn cannot take a rook."

"It doesn't feel fair," Jack replied, his voice cracking.

"It is a book on a high shelf, Jack," Wheeler said. "And it holds a wisdom that goes far beyond battles. I hope you see how much I respect you by asking you to stretch for it."

Chapter Twenty-Two

Red on
the Green

Jack stood in the shadows of the balcony walkway overlooking the common room of the Wayfarers' Inn. Below, Wheeler reasoned with the angry crowd and slowly won most of them over. Jack marveled at how Wheeler approached these discussions in much the same way as he had advised the boys to fight with their swords. He went for the man, not the weapon. Wheeler didn't attack his opponents, but he seemed to try to win them over. He did not seek to destroy their arguments but rather to speak to the person. Jack mused from the shadows about that last maxim Wheeler had given him.

You already have what you need.

Frowning, he returned to the door of their room and quietly turned the knob. Inside he found Michelle sitting up. "Hi, Jack," she said.

Jack waved. "How are you feeling?"

She yawned. "Honestly, I feel incredible. Did someone give me some medicine?"

Jack nodded. "There was an apothecary, Mrs. Hoff. She

gave you a healing draft. Just a drink. You seemed to be sleeping peacefully, so we let you sleep."

"How's Benny?" she asked.

"She said he'd be fine. She's dealt with lots of bites like these recently, I think."

"What happened?" she asked. "The last thing I remember is some huge monster crashing into us. There was a scuffle, and I ran for the tree. Something hit me. Then I woke up here."

Jack explained what had happened, without going into too much detail about the bargain he'd struck with Mordok. He still wasn't sure what he could have done differently. "So we brought you here. Do your parents think you're sleeping over at Mary's?"

"Yes. They don't expect me till after school tomorrow."

"And we told Mary you'd be with us," Jack said. "Since school's canceled tomorrow anyway, we might not be in as much trouble as I thought."

"At least we're alive," she said. "Thanks, Jack."

"I didn't do much, really," he said. "I'm just glad you guys are okay."

Benny stirred. Michelle looked from him back to Jack. "Where's Mr. Wheeler now?" she asked.

"He's out arguing with some of the locals. I've been listening from the balcony, and I've learned a lot about this place I didn't know. It's more unsettled than I expected. When you walk around the town, it's just so old. You think nothing can disrupt what they have. But Rancast—the villain I told you about on our bike ride—has really upset things. He's ruined worlds, and his wars have impacted every single realm in some serious ways. Some realms are fighting against his army right now."

"That's awful," she said. "You say they resent all earth people because of him—because of Rancast?"

"Yeah," Jack replied, "he's human, like us. Apparently he's kind of superhuman. He took powers from all the realms and is like a god, or like Hercules or something."

"Terrific," she said. "You said they call him a vandal?"

"Well, they call all humans Vandalians, or Vandals. Because of him, most are suspicious of all of us. Really, though, most of the races here are pretty similar to us. At least in appearance."

Michelle smiled. "No bug people?"

"Not that I've seen."

"Good. I'm not a fan of the normal-sized bugs back home." She stretched. "Speaking of home, shouldn't we get back?"

"Yeah, I think so. But we have to wait till dawn, if that's okay with you. Mordok will be in the park at night. And I'm not sure what's happening in the streets here, either. I think Mr. Wheeler wants us to lie low."

Benny rolled over and leaned up on his elbow. "Did you say breakfast?"

Jack laughed and walked over to check on his friend. "No, I didn't. Are you hungry?"

"Starving," Benny answered.

"I'm shocked," Michelle said, crossing to join them as Benny sat up on the bed.

"Michelle?" Benny asked, surprised. He looked around the odd room. "Where are we? When are we? Oh," he said, blinking as he nodded, "it's coming back to me. Are we at the Waycool Inn?"

"Yep," Jack answered, ignoring his nickname for the Wayfarers'.

"Then maybe they'll send up some geffbred for a wounded warrior?"

Jack smiled. "I'll see what I can do." He moved toward the door, but it opened, and Wheeler came in, looking drawn. "Have a seat, sir," Jack said. "Can I get you anything?"

Wheeler shook his head, looking past Jack to the other kids. "Feeling better, Benito?" Benny shot the old man a thumbs-up. "And Michelle?" he asked, his face pinched at the edge with a hint of worry, "are you well, my dear?"

"I'm fine, Mr. Wheeler," she replied, pulling at her curls. "Never better."

"We shall get you home, friends," Wheeler said. "I only need to check in with the Matron Elder Swane, and I shall escort you to our gate and over the bridge safely. If explanations are needed for your parents, I shall make them."

"We might be okay, there," Michelle said. "Me and Jack have it worked out. But thanks."

The window brightened behind its curtain, and Wheeler walked over and opened it wide. The first sun was rising over the rim of fog, and he invited Michelle to come and see. Jack watched over her shoulder as the suns rose, one near and one beyond, like an echo. She smiled wide, and a tear slid down her cheek.

Wheeler spoke softly. "Special, is it not?"

She nodded, gazing on at the remarkable sunrise breaking over the Wayland. Jack stood reverently.

Benny coughed. "Goes great with geffbred."

There was a knock, and the door opened. Wheeler spun, and his hand went to his blade. Edwin—the tall proprietor—hurried in and raised his hands. His face showed grave concern.

"It's just myself, Wheeler."

"What's happened?" Wheeler asked, his hand not leaving his sword's grip.

"Thandalia," Edwin replied. "There was a surprise attack in the night as they tried to perform some of the rites of the festival, and now the gate is flooded with fresh refugees. They're pouring in now, and many are hurt. It's them, of course," he said, spitting to the side.

"Rancast," Wheeler growled.

Benny frowned. "How can he do so much when he's in prison? He is still in prison, right?"

Wheeler nodded. "His agents act at his command, and they are sewn into every seam of the twelve realms. But now's no time to talk. We need to help."

"Aye," Edwin said. "My staff is preparing more food as we speak. We're ready to help howsoever it's needed. You know where to find me."

"Thank you, Edwin," Wheeler said. "We shall be down in a moment and ready to carry food and whatever supplies you have ready. Get a cart for us, if you please?"

"Aye," Edwin said, disappearing out the door.

Wheeler reached into a closet and emerged with the boys' swords. "Take your blades, men."

They nodded, buckling them on. "However we can help, sir," Jack said. "We are ready."

"Come with me as I assess the situation," Wheeler said. "Then we shall get Michelle home."

Michelle frowned but followed Wheeler and the boys out onto the inner balcony and down the wooden stairway.

In fifteen minutes, they were pulling a cart to the edge of

the green, the boys carrying trays of geffbred, and Michelle, stacks of bandages. As they came over the hill, the devastating scene unfolded. Far worse than before, the refugee camp was overrun with a long train of wounded, displaced Thandalians.

Jack's heart sank, and he glanced over to see Michelle's eyes were filling with tears.

"Meet me here in an hour," Wheeler said. "Just unload the cart and stay close. Bring supplies here and do as the elders say. I must go. This is a dark day, indeed—one long-feared."

They stood staring as he hurried to a distant crowd of leaders, who were pointing and shouting in exasperation.

"It's too much," Benny said, eyes scanning the horizon with horror. "There are too many."

Michelle looked from the awful scene back to her friends. "We can't help them all. But we can help one. Just one, B. Then, maybe, another. Come on."

She set down her stack of bandages at the designated drop area, then took handfuls of geffbred and waded into the crowd, handing all she had to the first weary Thandalian woman resting on the grass. She returned for more and hurried back into the sea of refugees, finding frightened children and serving them food. She picked up a squalling toddler and soothed her with a hummed melody while the child's mother rested and the family ate. Jack followed her, at first with the idea of protecting her against unseen dangers, but soon he became her assistant, carrying water from the aqueduct line and bringing more food and blankets from the drop area. Benny was soon invited to join a band of cooks from his class who fired up a grill on the edge of the green and began distributing fresh, hot meals on the spot. Every return trip to the drop point where new supplies were being donated, Jack saw Benny hard at work, mixing or cooking or serving, tucking a stray curl back beneath his Myrtle Cardinals hat, the suns' light glinting off his brace-faced smile. His glasses slipped, and he pushed them back up, concentrating intensely on his task.

"Quick now, Jack," Michelle said, "blankets and bandages this time. And if you see any of that salve they used on Benny, I think it would come in handy."

"You got it," he said, jogging back to the supply drop and searching through the disorganized sections. He grabbed blankets and found a few bandages, then rushed back to Michelle. She was poised over a small band of Thandalian men, all wounded and several shivering. Their wives and mothers were gathered around, doing all they could for these warriors wounded in the battle. Michelle poured water on a long leg wound, dabbing it with a towel. Jack hurried off again to retrieve a tin of balm. Soon he was back by Michelle's side as she treated minor wounds for Thandalians the doctors weren't able to reach yet.

After an hour of hard work, a system of triage emerged where the worst injuries were treated by the best doctors, and other basic needs were tended to by volunteers like Michelle and Jack. Jack had returned from another trip to the staging area and was looking for Michelle when he saw a grave patron in a blood-spattered robe calling for attention from atop a cart. His long silver hair was braided and bound in the back, and his short beard was of the same color. He held up his hands and began to speak in Thandalian. *"Cree-us fil hanno blester foon talla, nel-Thandal."* An interpreter appeared at his side and translated into Common English. "'Tis another grave day for Thandal home. A day of graves. More and more, and upon festival. We thank you all for your kind acts. We believe we now have things in hand. We ask, in accordance with our ways, that all Otherlanders withdraw so that we might serve our own."

Jack frowned. Reluctantly, he moved back to where Benny's crew of cooks had begun packing up their station.

Benny waved to him, then held up a single finger. While waiting, Jack scanned the crowd in search of Michelle. There was no sign of her. He looked from the Kaalgrad gate down past the aqueduct to the edge of the crowd. Most of the non-Thandalians—the Otherlanders, as the elf patron had said—had withdrawn a respectful distance from the now swollen refugee camp. But Michelle wasn't among them.

Benny appeared, wiping his hands on the dirty apron he still wore around his waist. "Where's Michelle?"

"I don't know," Jack replied, frowning.

"She got right into the thick of it, real fast," Benny said.

"You did pretty well out there too, B." Jack patted his friend's back. "Uncle Freddie would be proud of how you served these hungry, hurting people. Great job, man."

Benny smiled and bowed slightly, a very Waylandesque gesture. "There's Wheeler." Benny pointed across the divide between Otherlanders and Thandalians to where their mentor stood in conversation with several Thandalian elders. Wheeler nodded, shook his head, and gestured with his hands, as though trying to make a point. The elders frowned, looked down, and said nothing. Wheeler inhaled deeply and nodded, then turned to cross the distance to join the rest of the Otherlanders. Halfway across the divide, he turned and faced the Thandalian elders and all the camp. With the suns rising high beyond him, he bent to his knees and placed his head on each knee in turn. Jack, Benny, and the whole host of helpers imitated him.

Wheeler then rose and crossed the rest of the way. He was immediately met by leaders of various Otherlander groups. Jack and Benny drew close enough to hear that they were questioning him about all kinds of things. Some asked about the counterproductive pride of the Thandalians, others about the war that was restarted in other realms. Some demanded to know why the sages were releasing Rancast into Kaalgrad, and wasn't that where he'd started all his escapades? Wheeler made his way through the crowd and found the boys. He turned back to the crowd and raised his hands for silence. "Go and see your representatives, I beg. See the administrators for the sage of your own realm. I can't tell you more than I already have. My statement is available at the blue tower."

As he turned back to the boys, someone shouted out, "You have time for these novices, but not for us?"

Wheeler turned and snapped back, "These novice acolytes are my constituents. They are from Vandalia, and I will see them now. Away with you, now! Go and prattle away at your own sage!"

The crowd broke up around Wheeler, and he sighed, squatting on the grass. The boys joined him. "I'm sorry, Wheeler," Jack said. "This has been a hard few days. Have you slept much?"

"Not at all, Jack. You?"

"I'm young," Jack replied with a smile.

"I, to be certain," Wheeler said, rubbing at his eyes, "am not."

Jack scanned the crowd of Otherlanders again as it began breaking up and heading off the green. "Sir, we can't find

Michelle. I'm starting to get worried."

"Fear not, Jack," Wheeler sighed. "She is just there." He closed one eye and pointed to the refugee camp. Seven elf-eared toddlers sat around her in a circle while Michelle, rocking a Thandalian baby, told them a story or sang to them. Jack couldn't hear, but he saw her lips moving and all the little eyes locked on her.

"Sneaky," Benny said. "I guess if I was gonna bend the rules for one of us, it'd be to keep her over there."

"She has done good work," Wheeler said, "and you lads did very well, too. I am proud of you. This is a hard day, and the first of what might be many more to follow. I am pleased by your behavior. You brought what you had to the battle in front of you, and you did much good."

Chapter Twenty-Three

A Dose
of Rurality

Jack slept in. It was Thursday, and he was home alone. School was canceled again and was likely to be canceled for the rest of the week. The principal said it was because of the electricity being out, but Jack suspected the cleanup from their epic battle with the crows had something to do with it. He dressed, ate, and soon rode his bike down the winding hill from his house toward town. He passed the old stone bridge, feeling a deep tug to turn his handlebars toward the Ancient Glade and the gate that could take him away from Myrtle. There were troubles in the Wayland, sure. But they were fantastic adventures in a fantasy land he'd always dreamed of, and he wanted to be there. Jack pedaled on, passing Gander's Gas, then the neat row of shops on Sequoyah Street, including Mabe's General Store, Wheeler's Good Books, Myrtle's Diner, and the new arcade and ice cream shop called Invasion of Fun. Jack smiled at the corny name and rode on, finally reaching Lively Memorial Hospital.

In room 213, his mother lay dying.

She was asleep, as she had been the last many times he

had come. Sometimes, she wouldn't wake up the entire time he was there. He would sit with her for hours and kiss her gently as he left.

Today, she woke for only a few minutes, prayed for him, and urged him out into the beautiful fall sunshine. Jack obeyed, leaving the room with his heart heavy. All his hopes hung on passing his novitiate and getting them both into the Wayland. He planned to ask to use Mr. Wheeler's room at the Wayfarers' Inn for a short time, till he could find better lodgings. And that spot was close to Mrs. Hoff, and she would be the first he would consult about his frail mother.

As Jack walked out the hospital doors, he found Benny and Michelle standing out front, their bikes stashed near his. "Hey, guys," he said.

"Hey, Jack," Michelle said, a sympathetic smile below her compassionate eyes.

Benny wrapped Jack in a hug. Michelle joined in. "Thanks," Jack said, voice choked.

As they walked to the bikes, Benny turned to Jack. "Michelle was just telling me about how her day went with the Thandalians. I think she's hooked on the Wayland, like us."

Michelle nodded. "I really want to go back."

"It's an amazing place, right?" Jack said. "I want to move there. I think it could be a great place for me and Mom to live."

Michelle looked down. "How is your mom?"

"The same," he said. After a pause, he added, "Worse."

"I'm sorry," Michelle said.

"Yeah, buddy," Benny added.

"So many of the Thandalian refugees have lost parents," Michelle said. "Especially their fathers, who have been fighting

Rancast's army. They're doing terrible things to those people. It was hard to see."

"You were a huge help to them, Michelle," Jack said. "Wheeler was telling us a little of what you did. Did you have any trouble from your parents?"

"No," Michelle replied. "Dad's been busy on a case that's taken him out of town and hasn't been home that much, and Mom has her hands full with the boys. So I was able to kind of dodge any confrontation—without lying. How about you, Benny? Do your parents get suspicious?"

"No," Benny said. "They know everything. I'm not one hundred percent sure they entirely believe me, but I told them everything."

"Weird, right?" Jack asked.

"Kinda cool," Michelle said. "Honesty with parents. You're a revolutionary, Benny."

"You guys hungry?" Benny asked. "Being this cool sure works up an appetite."

Jack smiled. "Is the 'free food' deal still valid?"

"Sure is," Benny said, "and we'll even extend a 'cops' kids eat free' coupon to the third member of our intrepid world-hopping squad. Come on!"

They jumped on their bikes and pedaled down to Appalachianos, where they ate pizza, pepperoni rolls, and hot dogs, listened to Benny complain about the jukebox, and played Galaga in the small arcade. When Benny's final belch signaled it was time to leave the pizzeria, they wandered out into the alley. Evidence of Allegra's graffiti still showed on the dumpster, so the boys explained about Benny's old babysitter and her apparent slide into madness.

"I hope she's okay," Benny said, tossing a smashed Mountain Dew can he'd picked up from the parking lot into the huge bin. "I've been extra worried about her ever since that night by the bridge. Has anyone seen her since?"

"I haven't," Michelle said. "She's on the prayer list at our church, so I knew about her. And I've seen her around town, either sleeping on a sidewalk or shouting at some store owner who kicked her out. I hope Mordok didn't—"

"Me either," Jack said. "I felt bad for abandoning her there, but she seemed like she might really hurt someone. She's lost touch with reality."

"I think she's been tricked into that phony witchcraft stuff by those weirdos who meet under the bridge," Benny said.

Michelle frowned. "There really are people who do weird stuff under the bridge? I thought that was just a hoax—like the alligator in the sewer, or the kid who exploded from eating Pop Rocks with Coke."

"Wait," Benny said, raising his hands, "so you're saying nobody exploded from mixing Pop Rocks and Coke?"

"I think the alligator in the sewer exploded that way," Jack smirked. "That's where Old Man Gilbert got those boots."

Benny whistled. "I'm not sure what to believe now. Next thing you'll tell me there's a portal to another world behind our baseball field."

"Anyway, I hope Allegra's okay," Michelle said. "It's horrible what's happened to her."

A noise in the dumpster caused the three kids to jerk back, reaching for each other. Jack recovered the fastest and stepped forward, fists cocked.

A pair of raccoons poked their heads over the dumpster's

lip. They seemed to smile, then darted along the rim before diving back in, one flipping an acrobatic somersault.

Benny held his hand over his heart. "That almost scared me."

Michelle giggled, and soon the boys joined in. "Jack, why don't you show us around Wheeler's bookstore?"

"I know what you're doing," Jack said. "You're hoping we can get back into the Wayland today, even though Wheeler said we should spend the day here."

Michelle shrugged. "I like books."

"Okay," he said, "let's go."

They grabbed their bikes and made their way toward the bookstore. Michelle pulled over before they reached the main strip. She pointed to the farmland nestled in the valley behind the shops. "Something's going on down at the McClures' farm. I think Vicky's out there. Let's go check it out." She led the confused boys back the way they had come, then turned off onto a gravel side road that quickly gave way to dirt. As they neared the farm with its large barn and several scattered out-buildings around a modest farmhouse, they saw a few children gathered in the field. They recognized Vicky McClure, their classmate, and some of her younger siblings. "Something's wrong," Michelle said, leaping from her bike and rushing to vault over the barbed wire fence.

"Wait, Michelle," Jack said, hurrying after her. Benny followed, taking the fence-crossing more slowly.

The kids were gathered around a cow lying on the grass, and when Vicky turned toward them, there were tears in her eyes. "Oh, Michelle!"

"What is it, Vicky?" Michelle asked, folding her into a hug.

"It's Fat Sallie," Vicky said, "our cow there. She's having some kind of trouble delivering her baby calf, and my mom is out of town and Dad's at Papaw's."

"Okay, let's call your papaw's house," Jack said.

Vicky shook her head. "Phone's out. I don't know what to do."

Michelle nodded, then turned to Benny. "B, go get some help. Hurry!"

Benny, who had just made it past the fence, saluted and turned to cross it again. Michelle turned to the youngest two siblings. "I've got a big job for you two. Are you old enough for a job?" They nodded, wiping at their teary eyes. "Can you two sweeties go wait by the phone? It's gonna come back on soon, and we might get a call from someone who can help. If it rings, answer it and tell them what's happening, okay?" They nodded and ran toward the farmhouse. Michelle turned to the next oldest kid to Vicky, a boy named Jeff. "Jeff, go get a big pot and boil some water in it and bring it out here. And brings some rags too. Can you handle that?" He swallowed hard, then looked over at Jack.

Jack nodded. "I've seen Jeff lift some heavy stuff, and man, he flattens kids bigger than him during football season. He can do it." Jeff looked from Jack to Michelle, then to his sister. He nodded, then darted off toward the house.

"Okay, Vicky," Michelle said, "have you ever done this before?"

"No!" she said, her voice high-pitched and panicked. "You?"

"Not yet."

Jack stepped toward the distressed cow. "You seemed like you knew what to do, Michelle. Why'd you send for the boiled water?"

Michelle smirked, moving in closer to inspect the cow. "They always do that in movies, and anyway, those kids needed jobs. Jack, you ever deliver a baby cow?"

Jack shook his head. "Not yet, but I was hoping I'd get a chance to today. Thanks, Vicky." He smiled at his classmate. "We'll get through this. We'll do our best. That's all your parents would want."

"That's right," Michelle said. "Now, me and Jack will play midwives. And I think Fat Sallie will do most of the hard work. Just talk us through what you've seen your parents do in the past."

Vicky nodded, slowly regaining her composure. "I can do that. Thanks, guys."

In an hour, the new calf was stumbling around in the grass, and Vicky hugged Michelle as both girls wiped happy tears away.

"You did it," Vicky said. "I don't know what I would have done without you. Thank you so much, Michelle. And you, Jack. You guys are the best."

Michelle smiled, washing her hands in the hot water. She laughed and pointed as the clumsy calf collapsed again, then stood once more, testing out his thin legs. "I'm not sure what they're supposed to do, but he looks okay to me."

"Looks like he's had something other than milk to drink to me," Jack said, laughing at the staggering newborn. "Should I get some more hay from the barn to spread around? Is Fat Sallie going to be okay?"

"I believe we have enough hay. Thanks, Jack. I think they both look fine," Vicky answered, smiling as the clumsy calf leaned against his mother. "This is pretty much how it usually goes, I think. I wish I'd paid closer attention. It was kind of beautiful, even with the messiness."

"It was magical," Michelle said. "I am so grateful we were able to be here to see it."

Dust stirred on the road, and soon Mr. McClure was racing from his truck toward them. After an exuberant recounting from Vicky, he was shaking Jack and Michelle's hands. "You two might make good vets. You midwifed a healthy calf delivery today. Way to go! I think we'll call him Mack, after you two. Thank you ever so much."

"Vicky was our guide and leader," Michelle said. "We'd have been lost without her. Maybe you can call the calf Macky?"

Mr. McClure hooked Vicky into an embrace. "Macky, it is."

Benny appeared on the road, breathing hard as he stowed his bike and made his way over the fence and into the field. Jack and Michelle said goodbye to the McClures and jogged over to meet him. "Mr. McClure said you got a hold of him," Michelle said. "Great job, B."

"I called from Wheeler's place," Benny said, gasping. "There was a note for us there." He handed the note to Jack, and they read it together.

> J, B, and M—
>
>   Meet at J's tom. morning. (Friday.) Not sure what time. Pack for all-day journey. Field work.
>
> —W

"What's field work?" Michelle asked, "and why was I included?"

"I guess you're a novice acolyte now," Benny said. "Field work is required for all NAs."

"But what is field work?" she asked again.

Jack smiled, rubbing his hands together. "It's a journey out of the Wayland and into one of the twelve realms."

Chapter Twenty-Four

The Talisman
of Lacus Morsus

A fter the birth of Macky on the McClure Farm, Jack, Benny, and Michelle spent the rest of the day having fun around town. They ate ice cream and played arcade games at Invasion of Fun, raced up and down the stomach-dropping hills of Fletcher Lane, skipped stones on Sleepy Creek, visited the Mystery Nest Museum of Oddities, and finished the day off with a second trip to Appalachianos. They debated the best toppings for hot dogs. Michelle was insistent that a true West Virginia Dog—mustard, slaw, and chili—was best. Jack's head hurt from laughing so hard, but maybe it was just the Vertigo Room at the Mystery Nest playing games with his mind. They walked Michelle home, pushing their bikes along the empty streets. The boys promised to call first thing in the morning so that Michelle could meet them at the old stone bridge for their adventure into, and beyond, the Wayland.

Jack woke up smiling from a dream of walking with Michelle along the banks of Sleepy Creek, kicking leaves and laughing. Benny had been there too. Jack rubbed his eyes.

Benny *was* there. He was curled up in a sleeping bag across the living room from Jack. And the dream was more of a memory. They *had* kicked leaves along the bank of Sleepy Creek—and skipped stones too. What a day. He grinned. But his smile disappeared when a thump came from the kitchen.

Jack grabbed his second bat, this one aluminum, and tiptoed over to Benny. He put his hand over Benny's mouth and whispered. "Wake up. I think someone broke in."

Benny's eyes shot open wide, and he pulled Jack's hand off his mouth. "Gross, Jack."

"I didn't want you to scream," Jack whispered.

"I wouldn't have screamed," Benny whispered back.

Jack crept toward the kitchen, and Benny, having grabbed a lamp, trailed his friend.

Bat cocked and ready, Jack stepped into the kitchen with a shout. "What're you doing?!"

"Eating," Wheeler replied casually, hunched over a bowl of Apple Jacks.

"Mr. Wheeler," Jack said, heaving a long sigh, "you scared me to death."

"Perhaps you did not receive my note," he said, wiping the milk dribbling into his beard, "or the answering machine message I left?"

"No, sir," Jack replied, "we got both. I guess we expected you to knock."

Benny was still wide-eyed, and he tiptoed closer and whispered, "How did you get inside, Wheeler? Did you use magic?"

Wheeler side-eyed the crowbar leaning against the kitchen door, then nodded to Benny. "Yes. Magic."

"We're super excited about field work," Jack said, reaching

for the Cap'n Crunch. "Where are we headed?"

"I shall explain on the way," Wheeler said, rising.

"Do we have time to eat?" Benny asked eagerly.

Wheeler consulted his watch, then nodded. "Yes. Where is Michelle?"

"I'll call her." Jack crossed to the wall phone and made the call. Michelle answered on the first ring and said she'd head over. "She's on her way," Jack said.

"You have ten minutes, lads," Wheeler said. "Eat up."

Benny reached for the box of Apple Jacks, frowned, shook it, and cast a suspicious glance at Wheeler. "This was full last night."

Wheeler shrugged. "Probably Jack."

Benny frowned. "Jack's a Cap'n Crunch man. Did you eat the entire box?"

Wheeler looked away and spoke absently. "Magic works up a big appetite, to be sure."

Benny settled for Cap'n Crunch, and soon they met Michelle on the porch.

"Good morning," Wheeler said, with a slight bow, and the boys waved.

"Good morning, fellas," Michelle replied. "Wayland ahoy, right?"

"Indeed," Mr. Wheeler said. "Let us begin."

The kids pushed their bikes along as they walked down the steep, winding hill and over to the old stone bridge. Wheeler explained as much as he could to catch Michelle up. By the time they reached the Ancient Glade, she was pelting him with questions. She was especially curious about how the new refugees were faring.

"They are sensitive on the point of honor, especially about receiving Otherlander aid," Wheeler said. "Yesterday was a difficult day, once again, but the Thandalians already established in the Wayland were a great help. The crisis, while not over, has eased. Rancast's allies are active, however, and that is what today is about."

"Forgive me," Michelle said, " but won't the three of us be getting in your way?"

"You might," he replied, "but not all three of you. Benito is doing field work with Master Hundell of the culinary arts. He was impressed by what you did during the crisis and wants to bring you along for an ingredients buy in Galden Prime. Your friend Evayner is going along, as well as a few other Garthian students. Jack and Michelle will accompany me."

"Are you sure I should come?" Michelle asked. "I'm not trained or experienced in this stuff."

Wheeler stopped and turned to face her in front of the gate to Wayland. "Do you want to come?"

"I do."

Wheeler smiled. "You showed how ready you are, Michelle, when you stepped in to help desperate and frightened folks at their most vulnerable time, right after you had gone through one of the most terrifying nights of your life. If you choose it, I should welcome you as my third acolyte." He bowed low to her.

"I accept," she said, bowing in return.

They crossed into the Wayland.

Soon, with the boys wearing their swords, they made their way to the street corner outside the tower. Jack and Michelle said goodbye to Benny, leaving him with Master Hundell and his band of eager acolytes. Benny looked happy, chatting with

Vayner as the master hailed a carriage.

Jack and Michelle joined Wheeler on a carriage of their own that took them through town and on to the far side of the Wayland. All along the trip, Wheeler explained various places and their history, going into far more detail than he ever had before. He took particular care with the history of the Thandalian folk in the Wayland, finally pointing to the seven arches over a domed building with a cupola ringed with stars. "That," Wheeler said, pointing, "is the House of Thandal. Inside, they speak their native tongue and practice their ways. It will not surprise you that it is forbidden to outsiders. Many are there during this festival week."

Michelle nodded. "I have heard some of them talk about the festival, but they all seemed too sad to give much detail."

"It is supposed to be an eight-day celebration," Wheeler said, "but now they mourn and try to recover from the latest blow."

"What are those?" Michelle asked, pointing to a series of statues lining the courtyard behind the gate. The statues were of huge flying beings arcing across a sky of burning lights, with elven children bowing below.

Wheeler nodded to Jack, who took up the tale. "Those are the Thaons, godlike beings among the Thandalians. They lived far away in a holy city, Andos. Those statues are showing the eighth day of their festival in the Valley of Stars—coming up in only a few days' time. The Thaons would fly overhead as the fire lanterns rose, and the hearts of Thandalia would rise, reminding them of their heroic past and hopeful future." I've read about it and have dreamed of seeing it," Jack said, blinking as he gazed at the statues.

Wheeler sighed. "I have seen it, and it is truly glorious. But Rancast," he said, blinking hard, "but for Rancast."

Michelle seemed to understand the tragedy without asking for specifics. "So they have endured more than the recent wars and uprooting. They are wounded really deeply. It's no wonder they resist efforts to help, especially from Vandalians like us."

Wheeler nodded.

Soon the carriage stopped on the corner of a street in a colorful quarter of town. It seemed almost the opposite of the Myrtle gate side, with its Wayfarers' Inn and quaint, plain buildings. These cottages and shops were all painted various colors, each only one solid color. The effect was a wild variety, and it reminded Jack of a beach community, somewhere like California. They stepped out.

Wheeler paid the driver, then turned and pointed to the distant gate beyond another stone bridge that could have been the twin of the one on the other side of the island. "This is the way to the gate of Rodredom, another elfin realm whose folk are of some distant relation to the Thandalians. I love the Rodrai, a nomadic people, mostly unconcerned with great matters of inter-realm conflict, but I am sorry to say that their sage is growing old and unreliable in his mind. All their sages since the beginning of the Wayland, elected for terms of their natural life, are called Rodd as they assume office. I have agreed to help Sage Rodd by resetting a kind of battery inside his realm. Someone—and I have my suspicions who—has fiddled with the balance of an important source of energy in their ecosystem. Sage Rodd lent me his key, and I shall return it when we return, job done. I need Rodd to continue voting with our alliance, and little favors like this go a long way. We cannot afford another defector to Rancast's allies. Raftereen is eager to steal Sage Rodd to his infernal cause."

They walked toward the bridge. "Is this battery ecosystem thing hard to reset?" Jack asked.

Wheeler inclined his head back and forth. "Not if the keeper is sleeping."

Jack and Michelle exchanged a nervous glance. "And if the keeper's awake?" Jack asked.

"Then," Wheeler said, producing a small gray object that, at a glance, seemed to have an arrow-shaped head featuring a box-faced little carving. "I shall be glad to have brought the talisman of Lacus Morsus."

"That's, uh, comforting," Michelle muttered as they crossed the Wayland-side bridge and headed for the tree gate. The tree, big and beautiful and surrounded by the high stone wall, just like the Myrtle gate, had a hollow middle and a keyhole knot.

"If you only knew," Wheeler said, kissing the talisman and replacing it in his coveralls pocket.

Wheeler produced the key and uttered some phrase that sounded like gibberish. The door swished open. Jack and Michelle followed him through, into a breathtaking world of lush greens and blues, stretching out across a landscape of moss-covered rock and long gray vines hanging from trees whose tops pierced the low clouds. Mr. Wheeler had briefly introduced them to the strange science behind this realm. Light from ten small suns fell in a series of beams that broke in uneven patterns through the bank of clouds above.

"Wow," Michelle whispered.

"There lies our way," Wheeler said, drawing Caladbolg— the Prism Blade—and pointing to a long arching bridge.

This was made of huge dark boulders cut roughly and bound together by a golden mortar. It looked like real gold to Jack, and he whistled softly as they walked ahead. Fog rose in roiling waves from the vast cavern beneath the bridge, which had no railings. The road over the bridge was open, and as the archway rose, the rocky road looked slippery and narrow. The bridge was long, maybe half a mile, and Wheeler, with a smile back at his companions, stepped onto it.

As Wheeler's foot touched the bridge, a low grumbling growl thundered from the foggy depths of the cavern.

Wheeler stepped back off the bridge and took off his glasses, wiping them, before putting them back on. "I regret to say that the keeper is awake."

Chapter Twenty-Five

The Cave of
the Crystal Eye

Jack pulled Michelle back as the ground beneath them hummed. Wheeler turned to them, his gold-rimmed glasses reflecting the emerald light of this strange world. "The keeper will rise and defend the bridge," he said quickly as the rumbling swelled. "When he does, you two must descend into the cavern and find the crystal cave. Take the high vines down. The strangling vines at the bottom will reach for you, but you have what you need. The caves are part stone and part crystal, and you must run into the one pulsing with an orange glow. Set this," he said, pulling out a fist-sized stone of transparent glass with what looked like a green-blue eye in its center, a network of vein-like lines spidering out from its center to its edge, "in place of the one pulsing orange. Bring the orange one back to me. In fact, it could be red by then. If it is dark red, then hurry. Well, just hurry anyway."

"How do we get back up?" Jack asked. "And what if we fail?"

"There's a stairway that rises from the edge of the caves to the far side of the bridge," Wheeler said. "And do not fear, Jack. You can accomplish this. Here," he said, fishing into his pocket and bringing out the dull gray talisman. "*Lacus Morsus*," he whispered and stuffed it into Jack's sweatshirt pocket. It was surprisingly light. Wheeler handed Michelle his satchel. She eased the eye-stone inside and doubled the strap so it clung tightly to her.

"What will you do?" Michelle asked.

"I will deal with the keeper," he replied, just as a giant arm—three clawed fingers on its end—broke the lower fog bank and shot up beside the bridge. "Go!" Wheeler shouted, racing onto the bridge as the creature—a huge, rock-like beast—bellowed as he gripped the bridge and pulled himself up out of the fog.

"Let's go, Jack!" Michelle cried, reaching for a long vine. She tugged on it, making sure it would hold her weight, then leapt off the landing and began climbing down. Jack followed, matching her pace as they descended into the foggy cavern. His last glance at Wheeler showed the agile old man dashing just past the outstretched arm of the cavern beast and making for the far side of the bridge.

Down they climbed, into the layer of fog. The vines looked like they would be slick, but a sticky goo oozed from within them, making their climb far less difficult than they expected. They eased through the thick layer of fog and looked down on a vast valley honeycombed with caves. Away to their left, a mountain stood with three huge caves in an upside-down triangle positioned above a row of huge block plates of stone. The blocks had perhaps once been painted or plated gold but now were gray, broken, and covered in moss. They landed on the hard floor of the cavern and began at once to move toward the triangle of caves. Jack cocked his head and closely examined the cave wall. The top left cave was pulsing red.

"We've got to hurry," Michelle said. "That skull is about to blow."

Skull? Jack looked again. The caves weren't shaped like a triangle. They were two eyes and a nose, with those blocks for teeth beneath. The skull's right eye was pulsing red. "Awesome," he said, frowning, as he dashed after Michelle.

Michelle tripped. Jack bent to help her up and saw that a thinner, rope-like vine was tangled around her leg. A second vine shot out and wrapped around her arm. He drew his sword, preparing to slice the vine trapping her arm. But his own arm was caught by a springing gray-green rope. He struggled against its hold, but the more he moved, the tighter the vine twined. He staggered as vines gripped his leg. Just before he was completely swarmed over by vines, he tossed the sword to his left hand and chopped hard the moment he caught it. The vine snapped with a springy crunch, and his right arm was free. He switched back to his right hand and sliced away the bindings on his legs, then freed Michelle with several deft strokes. Free for the moment, they rushed ahead, more vines darting at them as they went. They leapt over many, and Jack hacked away at any that caught them. Soon they reached the base of the mountain and dodged past the ancient plates, finding a stairway that led up to the caves. They rushed up and darted inside the right eye, its throbbing red light making them squint as they entered. The clear cave walls refracted the light, but its source was deep inside, and they ran to reach it.

"There!" Michelle shouted, pointing at the stone at the cave's end. It was nestled in a kind of cradle, with crystal fingers holding it in place. Michelle drew out the clear stone, and Jack, hesitating only a moment, grabbed the red pulsing eye. He expected it to burn him, but it was cool to the touch. He stuffed it inside the satchel while Michelle gently set the new stone within the finger cradle. A loud click followed, like a seal being set in place. The pulsing light was replaced by a gentle blue-green glow. Jack wanted to laugh. Then he noticed a trickle of smoke and frowned. Michelle, searching for the source, opened her bag. The old red stone, now pulsing faster than ever, was smoking. Their eyes widened and, without a word, they raced for the cave's entrance.

Reaching the entrance, Jack and Michelle found the stairway again and took the stone steps two or three at a time, gasping as they climbed the steep valley wall. Some of the stone steps were transparent, and many were beginning to crumble or were broken off entirely. As they climbed higher and higher, the stairway's incline rose, and soon it seemed they really were climbing nearly straight up. Jack was determined to look down as little as possible as he led the way. Quick backward glances assured him Michelle was with him, but he had to concentrate on each step—and now grip as the climb steepened—as they ascended.

"This is not good, Jack," Michelle said, taking her eyes off the stairs and gazing into the smoking, pulsing satchel. "It's going to blow up, I know it!"

Distracted by the urgent pulsing, her grip slipped and she began to fall. Jack shot out a hand and snagged Michelle's desperately reaching hand. "Gotcha!" he called. "Easy, now. Come on up." Leaning against the wall and bending his knees, he reached for Michelle's other hand and pulled her up past him. When she was on solid footing again, he carefully unwrapped the satchel and hooked it over his own shoulder. As he did, the small gray talisman Wheeler had given him fell out of his pocket and dropped to the cavern far below. "Ah!" he cried, and his shout echoed in the cavern.

"It's sacred," Michelle said, with a nervous glance at the satchel. "Maybe we should go back and get it."

"Let's get up to Wheeler," Jack said. "I'll come back and get it once he deals with this bomb rock."

She nodded and they climbed on, rising into the thick layer of fog. The monster's roar echoed above them along with occasional smashing sounds. Jack prayed Wheeler was still up there. The stones grew incredibly slippery as they entered the misty layer, but the incline leveled out somewhat, and they made good time. Soon, they emerged from the fog. Wheeler stood on the bridge across from the keeper, crouched to launch. Jack dug in and, despite intense weariness, pushed ahead. He was far from Wheeler, but he would not let his mentor fight alone—not if he could help it. Vines hung from one bank of fog high above the bridge, down into the second layer just below them. The creature swatted several strands of the gray-green creeper, then leapt at Wheeler, who dodged back and retreated toward the end of the bridge.

The keeper broke off a massive piece of his rocky arm and threw it with a roar over Wheeler's head. It smashed into the rock wall above Jack and Michelle and shattered into giant shards. Those boulders shook and twisted, forming into dozens of smaller keepers that, with a commanding roar from their source, charged at Wheeler from behind.

Jack and Michelle climbed on, watching fearfully as Wheeler turned to face these newly spawned flintmonsters.

The first met Wheeler on the edge of the bridge, and he ducked, then raced at the second. Its fist shot out in what would have been a killing punch, but Wheeler sidestepped and brought Caladbolg down to sever its arm. The multicolored edge of the Prism Blade blurred as it raced back and sliced the creature so that the two parts fell on either side of the bridge. The next creature was still preparing to strike when Wheeler's blade cut it three times so that it fell in a sliding divide. He met them all, darting in for a stroke, then leaping aside to avoid a crushing blow. He danced around the many enemies, slicing them to pieces as the angry keeper roared.

When Wheeler had cleared away most of the flintmonsters, he shouted down to Jack and Michelle. "Success?"

"We have the stone," Jack called up, "but I lost the talisman."

"Throw the stone to me!" Wheeler cried.

Jack nodded, whirled the satchel, then launched it high. Wheeler snagged it and hooked it over his shoulder. "Come on!" he cried, urging them up.

They hurried on, higher and higher, but still had a winding climb to reach the bridge. And what they were supposed to do once they reached the bridge, Jack had no idea. The keeper wailed near the center of the bridge, and his flintmonsters moved to block Wheeler's only way of escape.

The keeper roared and his minions attacked all at once, filling the thin bridge in a stampede of stone. Wheeler bent, slicing the first few and managing to unbalance others so that they pitched over the edge. He spun around, dodging and slicing as he took them apart. But just as the last monster fell, it landed a glancing blow that sent Wheeler's sword flying back and over the edge. The Prism Blade landed just ahead of

Jack and Michelle, and they stared with horror at Wheeler, sprawled on the high bridge as the keeper moved toward him, his clawed hand outstretched and his eyes glowing green.

Sweating and his lungs burning, Jack raced toward Caladbolg. The Prism Blade glimmered in the path ahead. A scream from Michelle made him spin around. The keeper hunched just above Wheeler, its claw poised to kill.

But Wheeler was reaching inside the satchel. He ripped free the smoking stone, now pulsing darkest red, and drove it into the crevice in the monster's chest. It let out a confused, angry howl as Wheeler darted under its legs and leapt off the bridge just as the red stone erupted, shattering the keeper, and bridge, apart.

"No!" Jack cried, as Wheeler fell into the foggy abyss, and an orange ball of fire filled with huge chunks of smoking stone expanded to fill the sky above him.

Chapter Twenty-Six

The Conqueror
of Worlds

Jack froze for a moment, his heart shattered and numb. Then he pressed down the rush of intense grief. He must get Michelle back home safe. He lifted the Prism Blade. *Who does this belong to? Oh, please let Wheeler be alive!* "There's only one way out now," he said, face twisted with grief. "Back down and hope there's a way up on the far side."

Michelle reached for his hand. "Let's go!"

Down they climbed, dumbfounded and afraid, eventually descending below the lower line of fog. Wincing, Jack squinted down at the crystalline caverns. He did not want to see Wheeler's body on the bottom.

He didn't.

"Where's Mr. Wheeler's body?" Michelle asked tearfully.

"Down here," a voice called. Wheeler! They looked directly down, Jack's heart beating fast, to the only place they hadn't looked. And there was Wheeler, leaning against the cave entrance to the restored eye. "I snagged a vine on the way down. Sorry to alarm you. That was a bit more eventful than I planned, but I am happy to say you both passed the field work portion of your novitiate."

Scrambling down, they finally reached him. "That was nuts," Jack said, returning Caladbolg to its rightful owner. "I thought you were—"

Wheeler embraced Jack. "It is not my first time nearly dying," he said. "I have been doing it for centuries. In fact, I have done it here, with one keeper or another, about a dozen times."

"You've done this before?" Michelle asked.

"Yes," he replied. "That accounts for some of my confidence. The valley always regrows a keeper, and he always rebuilds the bridge. It is a good thing, too. It discourages meddling with these caves. But my own experience here does inform one's approach. And, on this occasion, I had help. Things did get a little hairy at times, but I think you both did quite well."

"I lost your talisman," Jack said, head dipping. "I'm so sorry, sir. I'm afraid to ask where you got it—from some glorious prince of a long-lost realm, I guess."

Wheeler smiled and raised his eyebrows. "Apple Jacks," he said.

"What?" Jack asked, shaking his head.

"I got it in your box of Apple Jacks this morning. I believe it is called a Starbot—an excellent name, by the way. Kudos to Kellogg's. It is a cereal toy."

"You've got to be kidding me," Jack said.

Michelle started laughing. "Oh, my."

"I thought you could use a bit of a confidence boost, Jack," Wheeler said.

"From now on, how about just the truth?" Jack replied.

"Agreed, my friend," Wheeler said, and they shook hands.

They found the 'talisman,' a small plastic toy that changed from a space shuttle to a robot, and Jack pocketed it as they crossed to the other side.

"I believe that belongs to me," Wheeler said, extending an open hand.

"Be grateful you have a hand," Jack replied. "There's no way you're getting this back. It was my cereal, which you ate. I at least get the toy."

Wheeler frowned. "I'm collecting them."

"Not this one," Jack replied. "You already have what you need."

Wheeler smiled. "I suppose that is fair."

Michelle blinked. "We're in this super-nutty fantasy land and you two are the weirdest things here."

They fought, once more, through the strangling vines till Wheeler led them at last up a winding way to the gate. It took a long time, but they finally arrived at the gate. Wheeler produced the key and said the words. The doorway opened, and they were back in Wayland. Reaching the street after a short walk, they hailed another carriage, then made their slow, trotting way back to town.

When they were passing the tower, an elf in a black uniform ran out into the road to meet them. "Sage Wheeler," he said, bowing. "I've been looking for you. Sage Rodd is in with him."

Wheeler's face went pale. "With Rancast?"

"Aye," the elf replied, "the report came a few hours ago that he was eager to return the favor you were doing him. So he purposed to negotiate with Rancast for a cessation of hostilities in Thandalia."

"Curses!" Wheeler leapt from the carriage. He hurried

toward the tower's gilded door with twelve stars stretching across its top. The elf paid the driver. Jack and Michelle looked at each other; then they followed Wheeler alongside the elf in black.

They slid in behind Wheeler as he passed through door after door and descended staircases in turn, till they reached an anteroom filled with armed guards of various races.

The officers stepped forward and bowed to Sage Wheeler, then parted as he and his novices came through. The guards walked behind and signaled for the huge gates to be opened. These were turned by keys in sequence and were never all opened at once. After more and more guards, and more and more gates, they came at last to a small holding cell half-shrouded in darkness. Outside that cell of impossibly thick bars of iron, an aged elven patron in a plain robe with an ornate headband leaned on a whittled staff and whispered into the cell.

"Sage Rodd," Wheeler called, ignoring the jail cell's shadowed inhabitant. Wheeler ran across and wrapped his arm around the old sage. "Will you walk with me, my dear friend? I have news of the keeper and your world I must share at once." The black-clad elf hurried to open another door, and Wheeler led Sage Rodd inside another room off to the side. Both spoke in low tones as the door closed behind them all.

Jack and Michelle were left behind. Jack wasn't sure Wheeler even knew they had followed him down here. He was about to turn to Michelle and suggest they follow Wheeler when a deep, resonate voice came from the shadows of the jail cell. "Ah, a pair of acolytes from our world. Where are you from on earth, young ones?"

Jack and Michelle exchanged a glance. Jack wasn't sure

what to do. He was convinced Wheeler had forgotten about them in his fears over Sage Rodd being exposed, with weakened mind, to Rancast's influence. Was it better to ignore Rancast or to confidently answer? Jack decided he was not afraid to speak the truth. "We're from Myrtle."

"A quaint place," Rancast replied. "It has been long since I was there. I'm from the Emerald Isle, myself. A small village once called Carter's Mill. In truth, I was glad to leave when I did. There is so much more out there." His voice was steady, but passionate. And it was as sweet in the ears as honey. He went on. "My ambitions could not be limited by the gates of a quaint village. Small places for small men. Great men break away."

Jack said nothing. Michelle seemed about to speak, but she bit her lip. Rancast stepped into the half-light a bit closer to them, revealing the huge outline of his frame. He was tall, something like seven feet, and muscular beyond anything Jack had ever seen. He went on. "I haven't always been like this, Jack Zulu," he said, and Jack was alarmed that Rancast knew his name. "I was small once, a mere man. Now, I am more. Much more. I will never die."

"You can be killed," Jack said. "We don't believe your lies."

"I am no liar, Jack," he replied. "You can hear a lie, and so, search my words. There's no lie in them. I believe every word. I did not say I cannot die. I said I will never die. And I never shall. These cowards do not have the will to kill me, nor the strength to hold me forever. So I will be free again."

"You'll rot in Kaalgrad," Jack said.

"Will I?" Rancast asked, laughing softly. "Deep down, you know that is not true. Even Sad Wheeler knows it. He knows it better than anyone else. You must ask yourself, young Jack, what you would like your fate to be when things change here. What future do you want to see for yourself, and for those you love most, when the new order comes and I rule the Wayland and every realm?"

"I want you as far from everything good as possible," Jack replied, and Michelle—her face confused—took his hand. "I want you defeated and imprisoned and all your followers wrecked."

"And your mother dead?" Rancast asked softly.

"You don't talk about her!" he snapped.

"If I don't, who will? Who will give her the vial of life I have set aside for her?"

Jack was quiet, but Michelle spoke. "That's not true. My parents are alive and well, and I will see them soon. My brothers are—Is this what you do?" Michelle asked, her voice rising. Jack didn't know what she was responding to. Rancast hadn't mentioned her family. She went on. "Do you tempt vulnerable people with promising lies till they bend to your will? It's wicked!"

Rancast laughed, a deep, jovial chuckle that was—despite the wall Jack tried to build in his heart against this man—endearing. "You are a fighter, young thing. Not what you seem, either. Jack is a champion, like me, waiting to decide which side he is on. You are something else. I can almost grasp it. But you, Jack, I know as I know myself. It is the same story. You are too magnificent for this low station and these small lands. You must escape, and I can help you. I can heal your mother and give you scope for your greatness. Listen to my voice, Jack. I am not lying, and you know it. I can. I will, Jack. I will. Only go to Mordok and ask for the vial of life. He will give it to you, and your mother will live. And you, my boy. You. Will. Ascend!" He threw all his conviction in that last message, and Jack felt his flimsy wall of defense falling.

Michelle, darting a worried glance from the hulking man in the shadows of the cell to Jack, pulled her friend toward the door. She jerked the door handle, but it didn't budge. "Don't listen to him, Jack! He's doing something to us." She pulled and pulled, then hammered the door with her fist. "Help us!"

Rancast laughed behind them, his joyful voice filling the dim room, until at last the black-clad elf—eyes terrified to find them there—let them in. Jack looked back as Michelle pulled him through the door, glimpsing Rancast's face as light streamed in.

He was handsome, with flowing blond hair and a long brown beard. He looked like a warrior out of an ancient legend. He was strong and stood straight, with an honest smile on his tanned face. Jack's heart filled with undiluted admiration for Rancast, conqueror of worlds.

Chapter Twenty-Seven

A Great
Breaking Is at Hand

Jack's head spun as Wheeler's pale face appeared before him, blurring at its edges.

"Jack, my dear." Wheeler leaned over the place where Jack sat. "I am sorry, lad. I'm a fool. I did not attend. I was so concerned for Rodd. Oh, lad."

"I'm okay," Jack replied, "just a little dizzy."

Wheeler shook his head and turned his worried gaze to Michelle. "And you, dear? How do you feel?"

Michelle stood, arms crossed. "I'm fine. That villain's words did nothing for me but make me angry."

"A wonder," Wheeler said, "but I am not terribly surprised. You are made of sturdy stuff, Michelle Robinson."

"I come from a long line of strong people," Michelle replied.

"You do, indeed," Wheeler said. "Did you hear what Jack heard?"

"Huh?"

Wheeler guided her to a seat beside Jack in this small, plain room. "Rancast is triple-tongued. He can speak to three people in his presence at the same time, while each hears different things. At times they overlap. But his mind is capable of dividing and carrying on these conversations."

Jack felt a surge of admiration for the man—more than a man.

Michelle's mouth dropped open. "So he takes the old 'white man speak with forked tongue' to the next level."

"I am afraid so," Wheeler said. "I think Jack needs rest, from our adventure but also from this encounter. There is little I can do to root out the seed Rancast has planted in his mind and heart, but I will do what I can. You," he said, dropping low and gazing into her gold-flecked eyes, "will be okay."

Jack's vision faded to black, then returned in flashes of moving through the prison, back up to the tower's main floor. Hazy images of concerned adults, including Mrs. Hoff. Drinking a foul-tasting tonic. Wheeler's room at the Wayfarers' Inn. Black. Blinking, eyes open, and a hazy scene of men with their hands on his head. Odd white collars and warm oil on his head. Hands. Blinking, his gaze finding a seam between the encircling men. Wheeler, kneeling by the door, with Michelle and Benny stooped beside him. Jack closed his eyes, and his mind wandered to a memory of Benny's church and its odd smells and flickering candles. Then deep, deathlike, dreamless sleep.

Jack woke with the echo of a headache that disappeared entirely as he drank the delicious draft set on the bedside table in Wheeler's room.

"Jack!" Benny said, leaping up to grab his friend by the arms. "You're awake. Man, I'm glad to see it. I thought you'd never come out of it."

"What happened?" Jack asked, as he cycled through the last moments he could remember.

"Rancast, man. That evil dude got in your bean, big time," Benny said, tapping his forehead. "They treated you with a major 'sleep-it-off tonic.' It was scary."

"Is Michelle okay?" Jack asked, sitting up.

"Right as rain," Benny answered. "Not a scratch on her, man. Solid as a rock. Her back's been bothering her, but Wheeler thinks she'll be just fine."

"I'm really relieved to hear that," Jack said.

"She's down at the refugee camp," Benny said, "as usual. She's been helping there every day. They're prepping for their festival's eighth day, a huge bummer since all seven days so far have been one disaster after another. Their hopes have never been lower, and it's super depressing going around the camp or any Thandalians."

"Eighth day, already?"

"Yeah, man," Benny said. "It is all happening tomorrow. It's the eighth day of the festival, and Rancast is being taken to Kaalgrad the same day. Wheeler's been busy seeing to those details. I can tell he's not going to feel settled till that villain is sealed in his prison and the key to Kaalgrad is locked in the deepest vault. I'm glad you're awake, man. We'll be witnessing history tomorrow."

"How long have I been out?"

"Like, thirty-some hours. How's the ol' noggin? Is Rancast burrowing into your soul, or what? Is it like *The Wrath of Khan*, with those little bugs in your ears and you can't say no to his evil commands? Seriously, is it bad?"

Jack stood and, discovering his clean clothes draped over a chair, started getting dressed. "It was weird. I guess he has some powers in his words, and he's really, really convincing, man. But I'm over it." His eyebrows came together. *Am I? He can cure Mom. I know he can. He can get us out of Myrtle, and she will be okay.* He shook his head. "How's Mom?"

"I've been checking on her, man," Benny said, his face sad. "Brother, I won't lie. It's worse and worse. She is beginning her treatment tonight. The one Dr. Singh had to get approval for. She's been sleeping so much. She doesn't know what day it is. She hasn't been worried about you. My mom's been with her almost all the time. When she asks, Mom just says that you're with good ol' Benny, having an adventure. She always smiles at that and goes back to sleep. I'm sorry, Jack."

"I've got to go see her," he said, pulling on his shirt.

"Okay, yes," Benny said, "but I'm supposed to let Wheeler know the moment you wake up. I'm already a little behind on that. So just sit tight, and I'll be right back." Benny held up a finger and then turned and left the room.

Jack tied his shoes and headed for the door. *I'm not waiting around for permission to see my mom.* He opened the door and headed downstairs to the Wayfarers' common room. He crossed the long room, and stares from nearly every guest—mouterslaabs, elves, Garthians, and others—followed him. Edwin, the proprietor of the inn, met him near the door. "Where ya headed, lad?"

"What's that to you?" Jack snapped back, then thought better of it. "I'm sorry. I am just going to see my mother in Myrtle. I'm worried about her."

"Yes, of course. Why don't you wait for Wheeler?" Edwin asked.

"Good idea," Jack replied, nodding slowly and sinking into a seat by an empty table. "Could I have some geffbred and beans?" he asked.

"Aye, lad," Edwin said. "You're a good one, ya know? Lots of Vandals I have seen in my years here, and you're a good one. I know it."

"Thank you," Jack replied, smiling.

Edwin walked back to the bar and, with one glance back at Jack, disappeared into the kitchen.

Jack quickly rose and left.

Once outside, he began jogging. Soon he was sprinting over the bridge, the misty edge of Wayland rolling over and into the ancient gateway. Reaching the Myrtle gate itself, he stopped, finally realizing he had no way through without Wheeler's key. His mind raged at the injustice, and he closed his eyes as vivid images appeared of new paths opening—other, better ways through thin places into other worlds. Somehow, he knew it was possible—was absolutely certain—and his mind strayed into explorations of ways that went far beyond what he had ever known, but somehow had always been at the edge of his understanding. An image of Allegra appeared in his mind, and she looked far less crazy than she had before. Almost beautiful, she was poised and powerful. Allegra was opening a door for Jack, an ordinary door—room 213 in Lively Memorial Hospital—and he went through, thanking her as he did. In his mind, he walked in and saw his mother sleeping peacefully. She was awakened by a doctor, impossibly tall and strong with a captivating voice, and he gave her a vial of golden wine. She drank it down and was young and beautiful again.

"Jack!" Benny cried, breaking him out of his vision. "Jack, stop," Benny said, pulling him away from the gate.

Jack realized, with some embarrassment, that he had been banging on the ancient tree gate, screaming at it to open. Staggering back from the tree, he collapsed on the grass, rubbing at his eyes.

Benny, breathing hard, sat beside him. "Are you okay, man?"

"I don't know, Benny."

Soon Michelle and Wheeler came running, and the old man knelt by Jack while Michelle sat beside her friend.

"It is to be expected, Jack," Wheeler said. "And it is my fault. I cannot believe I let this happen. I am so sorry. The treatment helped, but it cannot cure all the harm done."

"Rancast is putting stuff in Jack's mind," Benny said, and his voice sounded frightened and angry. "He's making Jack into something he never was."

Jack shook his head, suddenly more frightened than ever before. "No. It's really me. It was always there."

Wheeler nodded. "Jack is right. Rancast tells a kind of truth in order to amplify lies. He finds what is already there—and with you, Jack, I am afraid to say it was easy for him—and he dials it up. He amplifies what is disordered inside us, and it grows. He is like his master, never a creator, only a perverter of the good things already made." Wheeler grew more emotional and began to sound—in passionate tone, not in substance—a little bit like his old enemy. "Rancast bends what God intends and makes a weapon to strike at heaven. His tricks of the mind and his out-sized strength and speed are all powers he has conjured from dark magic hidden deep in various realms.

His enchantments are wrung from the most vulnerable. His elixirs of life come at the cost of a million deaths. His cures are murder. He will not be humble and receive but must grasp and steal—forever restless. He is a dragon-hearted fiend intent on breaking every good thing down so he can stand atop the rubble and say he is a god who made the ruin. My heart gags at his schemes. From my weary old soul, I defy and denounce him!"

Michelle touched Jack's arm gently, then turned to Wheeler. "Can Jack go see his mom?"

"Of course, child," Wheeler said, wiping sweat from his brow. "Forgive my passion. I struggle with guilt over my lapse. It has meant, for our Jack, an encounter with this vile enemy long before I hoped. But the truth is, it was always likely to happen, and it was always likely to be too soon. We will all face him, I know. If our roots are not strong, he will pluck us up. We must stay in the soil we were created for and reach down deep. Or Rancast will tear us out, as he has with legions across the twelve realms. Tomorrow is an important day, and I am concerned about Rancast. He has a long history of escapes. Yes, Jack. Go to your mother and pray. Pray for her and us and for the whole world—for every world. A great breaking is at hand, and we must stand together against it."

Chapter Twenty-Eight

The Valley
of the Shadow

J ack nodded gravely as Wheeler explained how the next day he would be totally engaged with the transport of Rancast to the Kaalgrad gate and beyond. They would have to keep the Wayland-Myrtle key, guarding it carefully, and use it to enter and leave the Wayland on their own. "I cannot meet you, my dears. But you meet together at dawn and come. Come and stand alongside the white-robed Thandalians as they gather to witness—not what they should see, the glorious Thaons gliding overhead as the fire lanterns rise, but the shameful walk of Rancast to his forever prison."

As Wheeler drew out the key, Michelle and Benny looked at Jack. But Wheeler didn't give the key to Jack. He gave it to Benny. There was an angry, wounded twist in Jack's gut.

"Guard it well, Benito," Wheeler said softly. "I will take it again tomorrow, once Rancast is locked away. It would be dangerous for me to have more than the one key I will need while escorting him—the key to Kaalgrad. And I trust you to keep it till then. I shall see you three tomorrow." With a tender squeeze of Jack's arm, he turned and left.

The three friends stood before the gate. Benny extended the key and said, "*Clavis Ignum,*" and they crossed into Myrtle.

Soon after, Jack walked into the grim hospital room, heart heavy and mind disturbed. His mother was asleep, and she looked terribly weak lying there. Jack eased into his customary chair and gently took her hand. A desperate determination swelled inside him. *Only I can save her. I must save her. I will do anything and everything to save her. I have to get out of this awful place and change my fate.* He thought of Wheeler just now, leaving the key to the Myrtle-Wayland gate with Benny, because now, all of a sudden, even though he'd never once let them down—now, now Jack couldn't be trusted?

Benny had said he would keep it safe, and they could all three meet at the gate after dawn and go into the Wayland together. Benny—bumbling, unremarkable Benny—would be the one to hold the key. Jack's heart flared in a rush of hot anger.

Rancast's words came plain to his mind. He saw them and heard them and knew them by heart.

"*Only go to Mordok and ask for the vial of life. He will give it to you, and your mother will live. And you, my boy. You. Will. Ascend!*"

Jack's mind saw Rancast's face, a smiling, bright intelligence with masculine warmth and true greatness plain in every detail. Jack's hope stirred at the possibility of saving his mother. He would be a hero. A legend. He would change his future forever.

"Jack? Jack, son? Can't you hear me?"

Jack blinked and shook his head, then saw his mother sitting up with a concerned look on her haggard face. "Mom?"

"There you are," she said, squeezing his hand weakly as her face now broke into a frail smile. "There is my Jack. You must have been having some nightmare. Your face looked pretty scary just then."

"I'm sorry, Mom," he replied, kissing her cheek, "it's just been a long few days."

"Did you and Benny get into some kind of trouble?" she asked.

"No," he replied, "I'm just tired."

She frowned. "It's okay not to tell me, but don't tell me lies." When he didn't answer, she continued. "Well, son, I saw Dr. Singh earlier, and they will continue the new treatment tonight. He said we should know if it's working—one way or another—pretty fast. We'll either see a radical improvement on my levels or . . . well . . . it'll continue to go the other way."

"What are the odds?" Jack asked, wincing.

"Pretty awful, to be honest," she replied. "But I'm not sure if you've read one of my favorite philosophers, a certain H. Solo. He says, 'Never tell me the odds.' We might do well to heed this great intellectual."

Jack nodded, kissing her hand. "Okay, Mom."

"I'm hopeful, son. Whatever comes, I will win. 'Yea, though I walk through the valley of the shadow of death, I will fear no evil.'" Jack looked out the window. She went on. "I'm not afraid, son. I'm just worried a little about you."

"I'll be okay," Jack said. "I'm going to get out of here. I'm going to be a . . . a star."

She smiled. "You're already a star, son. You already have it all. Speaking of stars, I have something for you." She fished in the drawer beside her bed and pulled out a police badge enclosed in glass. She opened the display case and took out the badge, then handed it to Jack. "Your birthday's in a few days, and I wanted to make sure I gave this to you—just in case..."

"Thank you so much," Jack said, tears sliding from his eyes as he gazed at the blood-stained badge. "It's the best gift I've ever been given."

"Your father was a gift to me—to us both. How he loved holding you, singing his Zulu songs to you, and praying over you. He was a strong man, quiet in many ways, but he would speak over you, son. He loved you so much."

"I wish I could remember," Jack said, wiping at his eyes.

"You can remember him through me," she replied. "I've told you so much about him, but I don't know if I ever told you about his last case. Well, what little I know."

"Tell me," Jack said, sitting up.

"He and Steve—Officer Robinson—were on a case together that was unsettling and strange. All I knew was that Ruben consulted more than just forensics and law; he was talking to pastors and history professors and even calling back home to South Africa to speak to some 'traditional medicine' people he knew, though he didn't care for their kind of magic—witch doctors, that kind of thing. They're real, even if it seems strange to us. Ruben grew up with them causing problems for his dad. These witch doctors sometimes have a thing called Muti, where they take a bone or some part of someone, and they believe it steals their power. He said there was a connection between this 'traditional medicine' in Africa and some of the old folk magic of Appalachia. Ruben didn't discuss the specific details of his cases with me because he didn't want me to worry, I guess, and, well, it was one of his ways of taking care of me. That case went on and on and led to several trips the two of them went on together. That last trip, well, he never came home, and the blood on that badge there was the last part of him I ever saw. We buried an empty box. But Steve saw him die. He wouldn't say much else—and that wounded me for many years—but he did say that Ruben chose the right thing over the easy thing and that he died fighting for the right. He told me Ruben said the twenty-third psalm as he lay dying. One psalm and a million unanswered questions. But I have said that single psalm—prayed it, Jack—thousands of times over the years. Sometimes angry and sometimes content, but I keep saying it. And, I can say without any little bit of wavering that right now I believe it more than I ever have in the past."

"I don't get it! Why didn't Officer Robinson just tell you everything?" Jack asked, his sense of injury intensifying.

"I don't know, Jack. Maybe you should ask him. At some point I gave up trying to control everything, or even just understanding. I realized that, while terrible evils occur and justice is often delayed in this life, I lack nothing."

Jack's nose wrinkled in disgusted grief. "How can you say that? You lack so much! Your husband. Your health. A future! How can you say that?"

"I've said it thousands of times, and I believe it, son. The Lord is my shepherd; I shall not want. I lack nothing. It doesn't mean things are always rosy; it means I have to trust, even when I'm sad and sorry and I don't understand."

"Well, I don't understand!" Jack cried. His mother folded him in her frail embrace.

"Me either, Jack," she said. "I'm just learning that humbly receiving is usually better than fully understanding. Even as I lie here, dying, I lack nothing."

Later, after his mother drifted off to sleep for the night, Jack left, bewildered and fearful he would never again see his mother alive. When he reached his bike, leaning against a lamppost outside the hospital, he saw a paper rolled up and stuffed in the front wheel spokes.

He looked around and spotted Allegra hurrying away at the edge of the parking lot. She glanced back, eyes wide and knowing, then disappeared into the forest. He unfolded the note.

Mordok has what you need. Witching hour.
Bring the key.

Chapter Twenty-Nine

The Crisis
and the Key

Jack paced as Benny slept on the couch at the Marino's. Jack knew exactly where the key was. He knew Benny better than anyone, and there was only one place the key could be. It was the same place he kept the mask from Sylvia's. It wasn't a question of where the key was but whether or not he should take it. He wrestled for hours, his long rest at the Wayfarers' Inn having thrown off his sleeping pattern.

This witching hour appointment with Mordok was an impossible quandary. He couldn't possibly ignore it; nor could he really go. He felt compelled to go, for love of his mother and because of his agreement with Mordok. He wasn't sure if he even had the option to ignore the summons. What awful consequences would that bring? Benny and Michelle would try to talk him out of it and prevent him from going, so he had to steal the key and go, to protect them and to save his mother. Maybe he should take the key, go into the Wayland, try to find Wheeler, and ask for his advice. But, no, Wheeler was occupied with Rancast. Jack was on his own. He could tell Mordok he would never negotiate with him. He could refuse to help him in any way. But, on the other hand, he didn't even know what Mordok would ask. He must at least listen. But he couldn't consider a deal with a known accomplice of the greatest enemy he knew.

A quandary.

"Jack," Benny said from the couch, bleary eyed, "you hungry?"

Jack laughed. "I'm okay."

"You're not gonna believe this," Benny said, sitting up on the couch with a yawn, "but we have some leftover pizza upstairs. I could heat some up for us."

"Go back to bed, B," Jack replied. "We can eat in the morning."

Benny squinted at the clock. "Looks like it's nearly morning. The witching hour nears."

Jack frowned. "Why'd you say that?"

Benny held up his hands. "Easy, dude. It's 2 a.m. Nearly the witching hour, right? Remember our last midnight trip to the park? Good thing we had Slingy."

"I guess so," Jack said, frustrated. "Go back to sleep."

Benny stood up. "No thanks, man. I think I'm up now. Looks like Jack needs his best friend."

I don't need anybody! Jack almost said it aloud. "I'm okay."

Benny walked over and stood in front of Jack. "I gave the key to Michelle. It's not in my secret spot you think I don't know that you know about."

"What?" Jack snapped back, pointing an accusing finger. "But Wheeler gave it to you. Why'd you give it to her?"

"Because of this, Jack. Because of what you're going through." Benny patted Jack's arm, then walked toward the stairs. He stopped at the bottom. "I'm not the smartest, Jack, or the bravest, or the best athlete—I'm not all the things you are, man. But I am your best friend, and I love you. You're my brother—the only one I have now. And I'm not gonna let them turn you into something you're not. You're not Rancast, and you never will be. You're like Wheeler—mixed with Dr. J and the ghost of Shaka Zulu. I'm not letting them mess you up, man. No way. I've got your back, Jack."

Jack wiped at his eyes, trying to fight back a flood of pent-up tears. Benny hugged him. "Let it out, bro. The quicker you're done crying, the quicker we can go upstairs and get some pizza in our bellies. It's going to be a long day. We might need it."

As dawn approached, the two boys met up with Michelle at the top of the last hill looking down on the old stone bridge. They said little, but, laying down their bikes, each gave the others a short hug.

"Did Jack freak out last night and try to find the key?" Michelle asked.

"Yep," Benny replied. "But leftover pizza is a great cure for the troubled soul."

Jack laughed, then smirked at Benny.

Michelle looked into Jack's eyes. "You okay, Zulu? We've been worried about you."

"I think I'm going to be okay," Jack answered. "Thanks for being my friend."

"It's been an adventure, for sure," Michelle said. She reached back to rub her shoulder.

"Back still bothering you?" Benny asked.

"Yeah," she said. "It hurts pretty bad. When we get back later, I'm going to maybe go see the doctor."

Jack frowned. "Are you sure you shouldn't go now?"

"And miss this event?" she asked. "No way. I've heard too much about this festival from you and from my friends in the refugee camp. I wouldn't miss this for the world. We're going to see history, with that disgraced villain going where he belongs."

"I hope nothing goes wrong," Jack said. "I have a bad feeling."

"That's probably cuckoo Rancast in your head, making you think crazy stuff," Benny said.

"Maybe," Jack replied, "or it could be the midnight pizza talking."

"You guys ready?" Michelle asked.

The boys nodded, and they all remounted their bikes. "Remember," Benny said, "ride hard all the way to the tree, no stopping. We don't know if Mordok can get loose now or not. Wheeler seemed a little hazy on that, so let's keep our heads."

Benny tightened his backpack straps and made sure his sword was secure in its sheath. Jack pulled his blade out an inch, then jammed it back in hard. He nodded to Benny. Michelle said, "Let's go!" and they pushed off, pedaling hard downhill, building up momentum that they used to shoot across the bridge and up the small hill leading to the baseball diamond. They pedaled hard, picking up momentum again as they rode into the woods, soon coming to the great trees of the Ancient Glade.

Jack cast nervous glances to the side, certain Mordok would swoop in once again and, this time, kill them all. But he pressed on, riding fast and breathing hard. They reached the tree and leapt from their bikes, now sprinting to the gate. All three extended a hand toward the tree. In Michelle's hand, the actual key. In Jack's, a shiny badge. Benny's hand held a remote control. But Benny didn't look like Benny. Jack glanced over and smiled at Wheeler's face. With Benny masked to appear as Wheeler, they hoped Mordok would think twice about attacking.

They were wrong.

Michelle reached out for the keyhole knot and stuck in the key, shouting "*Clavis Ignum!*" just as Mordok swooped down. Jack spun, pocketing the badge and drawing his blade. He hacked at Mordok, but the monster knocked him aside. He hit the tree and slid down. Michelle danced away from the gate, while Benny drew his own blade and shouted at Mordok. The shardhark flapped his wings out wide, bellowed an angry curse, and made for Michelle. He kicked out, sending her sprawling back to collide with a nearby tree. She crumpled to the ground. The two boys ran at him with swords poised to strike, and he turned and rushed them. They held their nerve and, shouting, prepared for the head-on clash. At the last moment, Mordok broke away, beating his wings furiously, and flew through the open gate.

Rancast's shardhark was in the Wayland.

"No!" Michelle screamed, jumping to her feet. Jack ran to check on her, but she impatiently pushed the boys forward. "We have to stop him!"

Jack's mind was all chaotic, so he clung to Michelle's words. They hurried through the gate, and Jack reached back through for the key.

Chapter Thirty

The Battle of Kaalgrad Gate

J ack shot through the gate and dashed ahead, shoving the key into his left pocket. In his right pocket, the blood-flecked badge pressed into his leg. He ran over the bridge, eyes darting everywhere for Mordok.

There was no sign of the monster.

Jack dashed past the Wayfarers' Inn and down the empty street till he reached the greenway gate and darted through. His mind was clearing. On his right the refugee camp lay empty, but for some children. Before him, a massive gathering trailed down on either side of the way to the mist-shrouded Kaalgrad gate. An enormous host was lined up to witness Rancast's last journey. There were two crowds and a lane between them through which the prisoner was being marched. On Jack's right, the white-clad Thandalians stood in dignified silence. On his left were people from every other race in the Wayland. The Thandalians, defiant and proud in their pain, wore their finest jewelry, so that their white clothing shone with golden edges. They carried candles, a sign of hope that all was not yet lost. Tytrus, tears filling his good eye, clenched his candle and glared at Rancast. Jack, eyes darting all over for any sign of Mordok, raced down the Otherlander side of the crowd, till he could see the procession clearly.

A flag bearer led the procession, hoisting high the twin-tree banner far out in front. Wheeler appeared as grave as death as he marched at the head of a column of strong soldiers, escorting the shackled Rancast. Wheeler looked tired, but alert. In one hand he held the key to Kaalgrad, and his other hand never strayed far from the hilt of Caladbolg. Rancast was gagged—Jack was relieved to see—and chains bound him fast, but still beauty and power emanated from him. He dwarfed Wheeler and his guards. The two men could not have been more dissimilar in so many aspects, but—seeing them side by side for the first time—Jack noticed that they favored one another in subtle ways. Jack stopped, eyes locked on the two men ahead of him: Rancast and Wheeler. Two versions of what he might become.

He rushed ahead, heart pounding as he dodged through the Otherlander crowd. A last backward glance showed Benny helping Michelle, who seemed to have fallen close to the edge of the refugee camp. Elf-eared children, left behind in the camp, gathered around her. But the best way for Jack to help Michelle, and everyone else, was to keep moving. He had to find Mordok and stop him. He neared the procession just as the train of warrior escorts and the giant prisoner were preparing to cross over the bridge to the foggy Kaalgrad gate.

Jack hesitated, unsure what to do. He scanned the crowd, the skies, and the ground in all directions. *Where is that mothman villain?* He was afraid to disrupt this—to the Thandalians, sacred—procession and was keenly aware of what he risked if he cried out now. But, convinced it was right, he ran into the gap and shouted, "Wheeler, Mordok is in the Wayland!"

A woeful moan emerged from the crowds as Wheeler spun toward Jack. The Prism Blade was out in a moment, but no blade could defend against the firebomb that hit the soldiers surrounding Rancast. Wheeler and his men were blown back, fire spreading around the fallen guards. Only Rancast stood amidst the blast, uninjured, his gag gone as he laughed loud and strained against his bonds. The enchanted firebomb had come from the fog around the Kaalgrad gate, and Jack cursed himself as a fool for not expecting it. From the mist, Mordok beat his wings and raced in, a bandolier of firebombs across his chest. His good hand wielded his war hammer, which glowed weirdly at its sharp tip, and he struck free his master's bonds. Jack, eyes wide as he searched for Wheeler amid the fog and fire and the sudden scrambling of the crowds, rushed forward. Others were charging forward too, he saw, including an angry band of Thandalian acolytes and elders, who hurtled toward Mordok and his now-freed master.

The wide gap gave Rancast time, and Mordok's second firebomb, lobbed into the front lines of the advancing Thandalians, gave them more time still. Jack winced and ran on, searching for Wheeler amid the chaos. He spotted him as a brave band of Thandalians, some charred black from the blast, helped the sage up. Tytrus was among them, wounded but helping to drag Wheeler to his feet. Wheeler was calling out and looking around on the ground. *What is he looking for?* He had his enchanted blade. Jack continued rushing toward the gate, dodging around the others who bravely attacked Mordok as yet another firebomb struck nearby. Jack's ears rang as he staggered from the blast, but he kept his feet and continued toward the gate, where the clash seemed destined to come. Still, Wheeler searched the ground, till his eyes met Rancast's some thirty yards away. Rancast grinned and bent to pick up the key to the Kaalgrad gate.

"No!" Wheeler shouted, and he shot forward with Caladbolg poised.

Rancast rushed for the tree gate. Jack dashed in, drawing his sword, and stood in front of the ancient tree.

"Stand aside, apprentice," Rancast said, smiling as he blocked Jack's desperate sword stroke on his naked wrist with no more than a scratch. Rancast moved with unbelievable speed. The huge man stepped ahead and shot out a casual arm, knocking the boy aside easily. Jack landed hard and rolled over, his sword still in hand. He saw a notch in it where it had struck his enemy's wrist. *Is he a man? What kind of a creature is he now? What can I do to stop him?*

"Nothing," Rancast said, turning to Jack. "There's nothing you can do but join me. You can join me and see your mother healed and your fate changed forever. I am opening a new way for you," he said, placing the key in the gate and muttering harsh words. Wheeler was racing toward them, with a band of Thandalians just behind him.

The gate swooshed open, and a teeming army of crows flew through the opening, pouring into the Wayland, a black swarm of biting, screeching terror. The stench was as alarming as the sight, and Jack gagged as a retching threatened in his throat. But he recovered and saw Rancast laughing as the crows attacked Wheeler and his band. Wheeler killed the first dozen with his flashing rainbow-edged blade, but there were so many that he was soon driven back. Staggering, he fought hard to stay afoot as the crows continued to pour in from the gate and spread out to terrorize, attack, and confuse the people of the Wayland. A terrible tornado of crows surrounded Wheeler, and try as he did to battle against them with Caladbolg tearing through scores of them, they kept coming from Kaalgrad. Hundreds of the beasts fell, cut to pieces and crumbling to ash at the sage's hand. Heaps of ash were kicked up and sprayed all around by the desperate fight. Crows terrorized the Thandalian refugees, Benny and Michelle among them, who used whatever they had to fight back. But Jack could see that Michelle was hurt. She staggered to her feet and struck out at the crows but soon stumbled again. Benny, sword in hand, fought hard by her side.

Jack felt helpless, tasting blood in his mouth and feeling his lip swelling. The crows had to be stopped. They were still pouring in from Kaalgrad in astonishing numbers, and he didn't know if the teeming mass would ever diminish. Jack dashed to the gate—despite Rancast's hulking form—to try to close it. A powerful hand jerked him back, and he turned to find Mordok gripping his sweatshirt and dragging him back. Mordok threw him to the ground hard and stood over him.

"Never move, young Jack," Mordok barked, "or you will receive what I owe you."

Jack looked past the shardhark to the gate. Rancast stood there, whispering some foul incantation, directing the army of crows. Rancast mumbled his dark spells, never straying far from the tree gate himself as he eyed Wheeler. Despite the sheer weight of numbers and the enchanted madness that drove the crows on, Wheeler fought like a legend out of time and moved ever closer to the gate. Tytrus and other white-clad

Thandalians were by his side, battling on through wounds and exhaustion.

Jack tried to rise, but Mordok shoved him down again.

"Master?" Mordok said.

Rancast turned to see Jack. "Have you the vial, Mordok?"

Mordok, his severed stump of an arm pressing Jack down, used his good hand to pull free a vial from his bandolier. It glowed golden, and the shardhark held it up. "Here, Master."

"Jack," Rancast said, turning his attention to the boy, "there isn't much time. But you have a choice, even now. You can escape your small existence and use your power to gain ever-growing enhancements toward perfection. You can be like me! You may heal your mother, a first great sign of the power you will own, and bring her with you into a new life beyond what you've ever known or imagined. I took this vial from Andos, and it will heal anything it touches. A drop, Mordok."

Mordok's red eyes grew wide, and a greedy grin spread over his skeletal face. He removed the cap from the vial and poured a drop onto his stub of an arm. A shuddering spasm made the shardhark wince, but his arm extended, growing back from wrist to hand, until he was whole again.

Jack gasped.

"It is yours, Jack," Rancast said, smiling wide, "this vial and a thousand kingdoms, if you follow me."

Jack darted a glance at Wheeler, who pushed closer and closer, overcoming the crows even faster as Rancast's attention was diverted to Jack.

"It's hard," Jack said.

"I know," Rancast replied, his eyes wide and bright, "but now is the time. Forget that old fool and join me. I am ever young, and ever conquering, and I will rise until I reach the highest pinnacle and contend for all."

Jack nodded. "Okay," he said. "I'm coming."

Rancast squinted at him doubtfully, but Mordok smiled and let Jack up. Jack looked from Wheeler, to Rancast, then to Mordok. Drawing his sword, Jack spun and brought his blade around with a cry, slicing off Mordok's freshly grown limb. The creature cried out and Jack dodged around his lurching strike, darting for Rancast with his notched blade held high.

"I defy and denounce you!" Jack cried.

From the Kaalgrad gate, the crows poured in behind Rancast, whose smile had been replaced by a menacing rage. His eyes actually glowed red and his hands balled into fists that pulsed with power. Jack knew this meant his end, but he was determined to go down fighting. He raised his blade and rushed ahead.

Then Wheeler was at his side! The gray sage was striking down crows as he came on. Rancast's gaze flew from Jack to Wheeler, and Jack saw, for a fraction of a moment, some fear in the man's eyes. The great enemy inhaled, surveyed the scene in a sweeping look, then stepped through the tree gate to Kaalgrad. Rancast used the key to close the gate from the Kaalgrad side. But Wheeler dipped low as he ran, snagging a firebomb from Mordok's bandolier and hurling it with terrific force. The firebomb sped ahead and passed through the closing gate. A bright orange shattering explosion sent concussive waves through the gate into Wayland. The tree gate shook as a winding band of lightning-like fire rippled around its trunk and through its limbs and shook free every leaf as the ancient bower faded to gray and its open middle collapsed.

Rancast was gone. The gate was dead.

Jack spun around. The great tornado of crows, having now scattered and broken Wheeler's Thandalian companions, caught up with him at the gate. Wheeler shoved Jack away and resumed his terrible battle with the impossible number of snapping, shrieking beasts.

Jack rolled over on the ground, then rose, determined to help Wheeler. Then an arcing blow from the glowing tip of a war hammer flashed toward him.

Jack darted aside, barely avoiding the killing strike. He sliced at the shardhark, but Mordok blocked the stroke. An exchange followed, Jack deflecting or dodging aside and attacking when he saw an opening from his foe. The fight infuriated the one-armed Mordok, who raged at Jack with frenzied attacks. Jack kept cool and focused on his training as the monster raged on. Jack's strategy was simply to buy time until someone came to help. He couldn't defeat this monster alone, and his hope was in delaying the inevitable.

But no one came.

Wheeler and the finest fighters were engulfed in the tornado of crows. Loose crows, their teeth bared and biting, terrorized all around, driving the crowd back toward the refugee camp. If Jack fell now, then with Mordok at their head, this crow horde was poised to cause incalculable harm to the fleeing refugees, who had already been through so much. Jack had to make a stand. Here. Now.

Watching Mordok's wild eyes, Jack picked his moment and drove his blade in. The tip reached the monster, but turning aside, the beast brought his war hammer down and shattered Jack's sword. The monster struck Jack's face, and Jack staggered back, trying to return the strike with a punch of his own, but he was driven down as Mordok's wings beat and the beast pressed forward. The shardhark descended, his great wings wide and his slobbering, crazed face hovering over Jack. "Now, for repayment," he said, pulling free a jagged-edged dagger and pinning Jack's right arm.

Jack blinked, glancing over at Wheeler, who had finally lost Caladbolg. The enchanted blade lay on the ground between Jack and Wheeler, as the old man desperately fought on.

Jack looked Mordok in the eyes. *If I could reach the Prism Blade. If only it were closer. If I was its master. If I had anything at all!*

Wheeler's words came to him, then. *You already have what you need.* And he thought of what he had. A fist to hit with? A sheath? A bloody badge? A key? Mordok's steaming, slimy drool dropped in globs as the evil creature smiled in exultation at Jack's defeat. Jack closed his eyes, trying to see all he could without the distraction of sight.

Then Jack knew. He saw Mordok's rib-lined middle and the flimsy grip his stubby, bloody arm had on Jack's left hand. Jack strained with his right arm against the coming dagger slice, while his left hand drew out the key. Jack's left hand shot upward, and he drove the key deep into Mordok's chest, shouting, "*Clavis Ignum!*"

The key grew blazing hot and burst the astonished monster's heart.

Chapter Thirty-One

A Sunburst
in the Sky

Mordok fell and Jack rose, shoving the dead shardhark aside with a grunt. Jack examined his burned left hand and arm. Ignoring the pain, he staggered toward the crow tornado. Jack bent and gripped the hilt of Caladbolg. Wheeler still battled against the crow host, and Jack ran to him. He cut his way through the tornado of crows, receiving bites all over, and made eye contact with Wheeler. He tossed the blade, and Wheeler's hand closed around its grip. Jack fell back, throwing exhausted punches at the air as the crows swept over him, driving him down, their teeth sinking into him again and again as his flailing arms missed them over and over. He fell, not even protecting himself as he smashed onto the turf, his head rebounding against the ground.

Then Benny was there, sword flashing out. Standing over his friend, the boy battled. Benny was bleeding, his glasses were gone, and he was favoring his left leg. Jack was so tired, he felt an almost irresistable urge to never rise again. He'd received innumerable bites, so maybe that was exactly what would happen. He would lie down and never rise. His mother's words came to mind: *There are worse things than death.* He smiled and half-closed his eyes.

"Jack!" Benny shouted, hand reaching down for his friend. Jack saw no crows, but he heard them in the distance. *Why is it so dark?* He let Benny haul him up and followed his pointing finger. The crows were overhead flying in a huge body, like a hurtling cloud of doom. The mass of crows was so vast that it blocked out the suns in an eerie twilight, and mist stretched out like fingers from the edge of the city. The crows loomed over the refugees, who scrambled to protect children as the great mass began to descend.

"What's happening?" Jack asked, taking faltering steps toward the camp.

"I don't know, man," Benny replied, reaching to steady Jack. "They just started massing overhead, and now they're attacking the Thandalian camp."

Jack blinked, and, with a sudden stab of worry, he came more fully awake. "Where's Michelle?"

"She sent me to help you," Benny replied, turning to point, "from the hill right over th—"

Both boys stood in stunned silence as Benny pointed toward the hill. The circle of Thandalian children surrounding Michelle was widening as they slowly backed away. Michelle was on her knees, her shoulders hunched over and twitching. A golden light seemed to glow behind her in the strange eventide darkness. One leg rose, and she knelt with only one knee on the ground now. The light behind her grew, and the gathered Thandalians gasped and fell back.

Michelle stood then, her head coming up and hair flying back to reveal elven ears and eyes aflame with light, while golden wings slowly unfolded behind her. She leapt up, her wings beating as she ascended high above the staggered Thandalians, who bent to the ground in wonder.

The girl with golden wings rose.

Higher and higher she climbed, and Jack's heart swelled. The Thandalians were singing now, and she seemed to glow brighter as the song's volume climbed, reverent and defiant and, most astonishing of all, full of hope.

Michelle's arms shot out, fists opening as her wings stretched wide and she glided ahead. Then, aiming straight for the great horde of crows, she burst forward, and fire seemed to trail in her wake. She flew on. The crows met her fiery flight in the skies above the refugee camp and burst into flames as they neared her, careening down in a thousand arcing drops of black smoke and ash. Cutting a fiery gash like a line of gold in the huge army of beasts, she at last reached their very middle. Gliding in an upward arc as her momentum eased, she threw out her arms again, and her golden wings glowed with a white-hot brightness as flames burst from her, destroying waves of the surrounding monsters in turn as the flashing circle of flame widened in a tremendous sunburst. A satisfying crackling sound accompanied the cascading deaths of ranks of crows as they evaporated in black, ashy blasts while the sunburst continued to race outward. A cry started in the Thandalian camp and swelled into a raucous cheer as the last of the crows died by the light of the girl with golden wings.

Jack felt like his heart would burst with joy. He and Benny, gape-mouthed and smiling, hugged. Benny was hopping, and soon all the battered soldiers were on their feet raising fists and cheering. The Thandalian fighters near the Kaalgrad gate hurried to the camp to celebrate. The Otherworlders lingered near the edge, hugging and cheering and wiping away tears. Matron Elder Swane walked into the gap between the Thandalians and the other races of the Wayland and, after a glance back to gauge her own community's favor, waved for the others to join them. Wheeler came first across the divide, bowing to Matron Swane and extending a candle he had picked up from the grass. She took it, and they turned toward the suns. Soon, other elders were stepping forward, inviting the guests to celebrate with them. The Wayland's people of every other race merged with the Thandalian crowd in an outpouring of love and joy.

Jack watched Michelle, who banked after the giant blast and flew toward the suns. He watched until she grew small, far out over the ocean of fog that ringed the Wayland. Then she banked and headed back. Buzzing excitement and hurried conversation followed among the Thandalians and their guests.

"They will have their ceremony," Jack said wiping at his eyes, "after all these years."

Jack heard a grunt behind him, and he turned to see one-eyed Tytrus, half-burned and bleeding, lean up on his elbow. He had fought valiantly by Wheeler's side. Jack and Benny hurried to him.

"Maybe you should lie still, friend," Benny said. His injuries were bad.

"Please," Tytrus said, "help me up." Slowly and tenderly, they lifted the wounded elf to his feet.

"Easy, now," Jack said, helping support Tytrus's weight,

though he was fading and knew he could fall himself at any moment.

"I was wrong about you Vandals," Tytrus said. "Please forgive me."

"Of course, Tytrus," Jack said. "We fought together today. And I hope we always will, from now on."

"Always," Tytrus replied, bowing as best he could. "I saw what you did, by the gate, with Rancast. You could have gone with him, and … and saved your mother. You didn't. And you killed the shardhark. I saw it all."

Benny, supporting Tytrus on his other side, smiled. Jack nodded to Benny, and he dipped low to pick up a candle. He handed it to Tytrus.

Tytrus reached for it, smiled with tears in his eyes, then sagged. Jack grunted, rose, and shifted his weight to help him stay upright. "Hang in there, Tytrus. She's almost here. Listen, Benny, follow my lead."

As Michelle, the Thaon girl with golden wings, approached, the gathered Thandalians faced her. They stretched their arms wide, left hand open and fingers extended while the right held a candle. Their guests imitated them. Jack and Benny helped Tytrus assume the posture. As Michelle flew overhead, glorious in golden beauty and bright power, their arms rose high, and flames burst on their candle ends. They turned as she flew past, bringing their arms low, then crouching, and finally kneeling, touching their heads to each knee in turn. Tytrus wept as the boys helped him reach his knees; then they laid him down gently again.

Jack, feeling dizzy and exhausted, crumpled beside the elf. Benny knelt beside Jack, his own hard-won wounds from the battle showing. Jack gazed up, over the celebrating crowd in the Thandalian camp, into the blue distance, where golden wings shimmered on the brown-skinned girl in the sky. His friend. The last Thaon.

Chapter Thirty-Two

Earth
to Jack

Where am I?" Jack asked, sitting up in bed. His head ached, and so did most of the rest of his body. *Oh, back here again?* He squinted, looking around the familiar room Wheeler kept at the Wayfarers' Inn. Jack examined his arms, abounding in cuts and bruises, with one long bandage wrapped around his left forearm. *I guess that's where Mordok's heart blew up on me.* Sitting up slowly, he reached for the glass on the bedside table. He gulped it down in one long, grateful drink. Wiping his mouth, he got up and began dressing. Nice new clothes were draped over a chair: a full acolyte's uniform. He dressed in the barley-colored pants, the crisp white shirt, and the neat blue jacket. He put on the high boots, though they felt strange to wear. He wished he had some sneakers. There was a white cape, but he left that on its chair. As he donned the blue jacket, the door creaked open and Wheeler's face appeared. "Ah, Jack!" he said, hurrying inside, "you are up at last! I knew Mrs. Hoff was to be trusted with your restorative rest timing."

Wheeler was clean, though he also bore many bruises and wounds, and was dressed in a kind of suit with an open robe over top. Despite the black tape wrapped around one hinge of his broken glasses, he looked more like a wizard than ever. But Jack couldn't help but still see the groundskeeper and bookstore proprietor alongside the warrior sage. He was all of those things, and Jack smiled wide at him.

"Are you well, sir?" Jack asked, extending a hand to his mentor.

The old man paused, smiled, and pulled Jack into a hug. "I am very well, son. Very well, indeed. And I am so proud of you, Jack. Such an astonishing thing you've done. You are the talk of the Wayland and the twelve realms. Which reminds me," he said, glancing at his watch. "We shall be late, if we do not hurry."

"Late for what?" Jack asked, as Wheeler snapped up the cape and laid it on Jack's shoulders.

"Come and see," Wheeler said, opening the door and motioning him over. "Do you trust me?"

Jack smiled and strode through the door. Wheeler passed him on the stairway, and Jack saw, as he descended, a packed common room. The room erupted in wild applause as Jack was spotted on the steps. People of every race, including a huge contingent of delighted Thandalians, rose and cheered. Jack turned to Wheeler, confused.

"Just follow along, Jack," Wheeler said. Then, as he nodded to a corner, four others dressed like Wheeler, with long robes of office, stepped into the open space at the center of the large room. The room quieted. Jack recognized Sage Rodd but also a short sage who was dark-skinned with human-like features—a Garthian, he believed. A third was a tall Thandalian, and the last was an ancient gray mouterslaab. They walked forward, and Wheeler crossed to join them.

The Thandalian sage cleared her throat. "Jonathan Zulu Rubenson, please come forward."

Jack nodded, nervously glancing around, then walked toward the five sages. He stopped and bowed. "Light and hope," he said, his fist over his heart.

"Light and hope," the sages replied.

The Thandalian sage went on. "Master Zulu, it is known to this council what you have done for the Wayland at large, the twelve realms in general, and my own kind in particular. We have a deep sense of gratitude at the results of your great heroism and of our debt to you. You are not only a valiant foe slayer, but you are the bringer of hope. You brought the Thaon maiden to us, and she has lighted our hearts like nothing has for many long years. So, Jack Zulu, we thank you. And we beg you will accept of us this small token of our esteem and gratitude."

The Garthian sage turned and received something from an aide, then pivoted back toward Jack. "Come and kneel, Jack Zulu," she said.

Jack obeyed, stepping forward and dropping to one knee. He gritted his teeth at the pain this caused but kept silent. The smiling sage set a medal around Jack's neck, a huge medallion strung on a bright ribbon that now rested against his chest.

"Rise, sir," Wheeler said. "You are given the freedom of the Wayland, and by this token I welcome you into the Order of Valor. A Waylander! A hero for us!" He shouted, and the sages took up the cry. "A hero for us! A Waylander!"

The common room erupted in applause, and the unified call of "A hero for us!" echoed around the room. Jack smiled and bowed, overwhelmed by the attention and honor.

Each sage shook his hand, and, last of all, Wheeler drew close. "I know it's a lot," he spoke into Jack's ear, "but it matters. For us. For them. It matters. That medallion is enchanted, a wonder wrought by the mouterslaabs of Gesh-hev. It's from the same rare metal as the spear of Dortez. You read about that, right?"

"I did," Jack replied, struggling to know what to do. "Thank you, sir."

Wheeler frowned sympathetically. "What can I do for the Wayland's favorite hero, Jack? Name anything, and we will do it."

Jack drew close to Wheeler's ear, and his voice choked when he said, "I want to go home."

Wheeler nodded, smiling with such love that Jack had to fight back tears. "I thought so. Follow me, son."

Jack followed him through the common room, where cheers continued as he neared the door. They left the inn and found a far larger crowd outside, and a fresh cheer met Jack as the suns loomed overhead. The cheering crowd lined the road leading down to the Myrtle gate, and they sang and clapped and threw flowers into the path as Jack walked on, waving as he went. Children darted out and dared to reach for his outstretched hands and then leapt with the thrill of success. Many adults tried to stop him and share their gratitude, but Wheeler propelled him on. Soon they crossed the inside bridge, where the last of the gathered grateful gave him seven long cheers and saluted him with a final wave of "A hero for us! A Waylander!"

Jack turned and bowed; then he and Wheeler walked the last stretch to the gate. Without another backward glance, Jack left the Wayland.

Back in Myrtle, Jack removed the cape and folded it, tucking it under his arm. He took off the medal, wrapped it carefully, and slipped it into his back pocket.

Wheeler closed the gate and turned to Jack. "It is not another magical medal, but I have a gift for you, son." Jack looked up, and Wheeler smiled at him. "Here," he said, placing a black pawn chess piece in Jack's open hand. Jack smiled in return and shook his head as he examined the piece, and they resumed their walk.

Jack was silent as they passed through the Ancient Glade, and Wheeler let him be. Finally, as they reached the baseball field, Jack stopped. "Thank you for the gift, sir. I'm so full of questions, but I'm afraid to ask."

"Then do not, son," Wheeler replied. "Not yet. I want to take you somewhere."

"You know where I want to go," Jack said, thinking of the sad hospital.

"I do."

They walked on, crossing the old stone bridge to find Uncle Freddie's car waiting. They climbed inside and, after Uncle Freddie reached back to pinch Jack's cheek and pat it affectionately, they drove ahead. When the car pulled up at Appalachianos, he almost objected. But he got out and followed them to the door. Uncle Freddie opened it, and, heart beating hard, Jack walked inside.

Near the door, sitting in a wheelchair and looking better than she had in months, was his mother. Michelle stood on her one side and Benny on the other. Jack staggered forward, then fell to his knees in front of her chair, then surged up to hug her tenderly. Her embrace was surprisingly strong, and

Jack buried his head on her neck and wept.

After a long time, he looked up and saw her beaming face. "How?" he asked in a hoarse whisper.

"Dr. Singh's treatment is working, son," she said, tears streaming down as she clung to Jack's face. "I'm on the road to being well again."

Jack's heart leapt, and he hugged her again. Finally, he rose and looked around. Benny moved in for a hug, and Michelle followed quickly after. "You guys," Jack said, "I am so confused."

"It's your birthday, Jack," Benny said. "Of course we had to throw you a party at the best restaurant in Myrtle, West Virginia."

"Michelle," Jack said, head stretching to look at her back, "I'm surprised to see you here—like this."

She smiled. "It's complicated, Jack," she said, "but I'll tell you all about it, soon."

"I'm so glad to see you," he said, and the friends hugged again.

"Who's hungry?" Benny shouted, and they all clapped as pizzas were brought out to the tables and the jukebox came to life.

Jack ate and laughed, relieved and delighted like he never had been before. They brought out the cake, decorated with a Cincinnati Reds theme, and sang to him. He blew out his candles and made a wish, whispering to his mom that his greatest wish had already come true. The party went on, and everyone laughed and ate and sang and enjoyed the night. Michelle and Jack found Benny by the jukebox, and the three friends linked arms.

"Some night," Benny said.

"The best," Jack replied. "I'm smiling so much my face is hurting."

Michelle shook her head. "Be careful you don't grow wings from your cheeks."

Jack laughed, then asked, "What happened to yours—your wings?"

"It's a long story, Jack," she replied, "one that I'm still trying to figure out. Wheeler's helping, but he says I may need to go to Andos to understand the full story. But that's not going to be easy."

"I'm just glad to see you here," Jack said, then turned to Benny, "both of you."

Mrs. Robinson wheeled Mom over in her chair. "I've got to get this lovely young woman back to her hospital room. Dr. Singh would be so mad if he found out we busted her out for this."

"Mom!" Jack said, bending by her chair. "What in the world?"

She smiled and came close. "You're not the only one who's on an adventure."

"I'll drive her back," Mrs. Robinson said. "You kids are welcome to come."

They piled into the Robinsons' van, and Jack sat down, feeling the medallion as he sat. "Oh, Mom," he said, stretching up toward the front seat, "can I show you something magical?"

She glanced back, and both Michelle and Benny stared skeptically over at Jack. "Of course, son."

In a few minutes, they were getting out of the van on a dirt road, and Jack was rolling his mom over to the fence. "See that calf over there by its mother?" He pointed to the young calf playing close to Fat Sallie beneath a wide peach sky broken with lines of deep purple. "Me and Michelle delivered him. His name is Macky. He's probably the best calf ever. I'm sure he'll grow up to be a top, top cow."

"Well done, Jack," Mom said. "You really have been busy. But this is so close. I always assumed you'd be having adventures far away."

Jack smiled and looked up at the spectacular evening sky as the first snowflakes fell in soft arcs all around them. "I love it here."

The End.

THE WAYLAND

THANDALIA GATE

PAVILION SIEGE GROUNDS

KAALGRAD GATE

THE GREEN

THE GOCK

THE SAGES TOWER

EARTH GATE

THE WAYFARERS' INN

THE GREAT TREE

About S. D. Smith

Sam Smith is named after the prophet Samuel, but no one could foresee how he would one day go bald. Back in the 1980s, when Sam was young and had a full head of dirty-blonde hair, he would ride his bike and make up fantastic worlds in his mind. (Many involved fighting the commies.) He grew up, but never grew out of his love for make believe. Now he makes believe professionally from his home in Grandview, West Virginia, alongside his wife, Gina, and their four kids.

SDSmith.com

About J. C. Smith

Josiah Smith is named after his uncle and the famous boy king, but his paternal ancestors were more likely to be subsistence farmers than royalty. Like the young king, Josiah got started early. He's been helping his father with stories for many years, and writing his own tv shows and movies as a teenager. Jack Zulu began as a tv show Josiah developed, but became a collaboration when the novel idea was born. Josiah lives in Grandview, West Virginia, with his co-author father, mother, and his three siblings.

JosiahCSmith.com

From the Authors

Readers know there are books that make you, and writers know there are books that are made up of you. Our job is to make up stories, but the stories are always made up of us and everyone we love. This time, we made a story together, father and son, and that's what you just read. We wrote Jack Zulu together and it's as homemade as Papaw's birdhouses or Granny's chicken casserole. We were keen to lean in on the setting, a small town in West Virginia, a made-up place named after our beloved mamaw, Myrtle Elizabeth Smith. Our little town was always going to be affectionate for us, but it's more than that. Myrtle is at the heart of the story. This book is about Jack—after going through many adventures in amazing places—discovering a fantasy world that evokes wonder and gratitude. He discovers West Virginia.

West Virginia is our home and the home of our fathers and father's fathers going back and back. We love this place deeply, but not in a grasping, mean way. We love it the way we want everyone to love their places.

The longing many of us have to leave our places is based on an inability to see them for what they usually are, places of wonder and beauty. What will help us see them more clearly? The best fantasy stories and fairy tales can.

> "These tales say that apples were golden
> only to refresh the forgotten moment
> when we found that they were green. They
> make rivers run with wine only to make us

298

remember, for one wild moment, that they run with water."

G. K. Chesterton, Orthodoxy

We already live in a fantasy world. The fact that we aren't continually astonished and humbled is evidence that we are captured by an evil enchantment that must be broken. The best, most faithful stories help do that. They let us see Reality, by looking at something made-up for a few hours. Author Heidi Johnston says that stories that tell the truth about the world God made are "not an escape from reality, but an escape into reality." She's right. The Lord of the Rings books are an escape into Reality. Narnia is an escape into Reality. We hope this book, with its rural accent, is too.

This isn't to say that once we see the world more accurately that all will be safe and okay. We really do live in a fantasy world, but fantasy worlds are scary. Ours is too. We have villains and vice, darkness and dragons. Evil and ugliness contend and win in countless battles across the land. So there's a good fight to be had in our world. You are a character in the Story, not the main character and not the author, but you have an important part to play. What you decide and do matters.

Our hope is that this story inspires and delights you, fuels gratitude and wonder, and makes you more dangerous to the darkness.

S. D. Smith and J. C. Smith

NEW STORIES WITH AN OLD SOUL

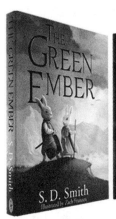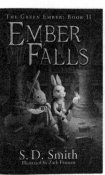

Join Heather and Picket on the adventure
that has captured readers all over the world.

SDSmith.com/GreenEmber

DO YOU LOVE HEATHER AND PICKET?
FOLLOW THE STORY OF JO SHANKS!

The Green Ember Archer Series

SDSmith.com/Archer

ARE YOU AN ASPIRING WRITER?

With motivation, inspiration,
and instruction, author S. D. Smith
invites writers to launch
into their writing adventure
with confidence and competence.

Learn more at
SDSmith.com/Writers

JACK ZULU WILL RETURN

Be the first to learn about book two,
plus get new stories from
the world of the Green Ember,
news about events, contests, giveaways,
and more...

**Sign up for S. D. Smith's email updates at
JackZulu.com/Updates**